"Are you okay?"

Cassie nodded, then shook her head as the tears came. She swiped at them and glanced up at the rooftop, where the wiry young carpenter who'd handled the hotwire was standing, braced at the edge, staring down at the two of them. She turned her face away from the house so the men couldn't see, and Jake pulled her around in front of him, shielding her from view with his huge shoulders....

"Look, I don't want to add to your stress today," he offered gently. "We can finish our business another time."

"Okay," Cassie said. But she was so upset that she couldn't even recall what business, exactly, they'd been discussing. *Dynamite.* Oh, damn. She'd blurted that word out like a threat. And she hadn't remained civil as she'd planned, not at all. And now she'd started to shake and cry like a fool because one of her men had got hurt. Jake Coffey had certainly seen her at her worst, and now she'd have to face this man— this *handsome*, *intimidating* man—in civil court the day after tomorrow.

Seeing him again felt like the last thing she needed. And yet, as she watched him walk away, it felt like the only thing she wanted.

Dear Reader,

This book is set in an area that is suspiciously similar to my hometown. Locals will recognize a few landmarks, but none of the people. The characters come straight from my imagination.

I want to emphasize that because, though my father taught me much about the home-building business, he is *nothing* like the character Boss McClean in this book. My father is the most honorable and loving father any daughter could ever ask for.

Though I create my characters from scratch, they do experience the same joys and struggles we all share.

Jake Coffey and Cassie McClean must each find a way to forgive the past in order to embrace the bright future that beckons them. I loved writing this story because forgiveness, I sometimes think, is the most beautiful word in the English language. Well, maybe forgiveness is the second most beautiful word. The most beautiful word in any language is, of course, love.

Keep your cards, letters and e-mails coming. They feed my spirit and inspire me to be a better writer.

P.O. Box 720224, Norman, OK 73070

www.superauthors.com/Graham

My best to you,

Darlene Graham

Dreamless
Darlene Graham

TORONTO • NEW YORK • LONDON
AMSTERDAM • PARIS • SYDNEY • HAMBURG
STOCKHOLM • ATHENS • TOKYO • MILAN • MADRID
PRAGUE • WARSAW • BUDAPEST • AUCKLAND

ISBN 0-373-71091-7

DREAMLESS

Copyright © 2002 by Darlene Gardenhire.

This edition published by arrangement with Harlequin Books S.A.

® and TM are trademarks of the publisher. Trademarks indicated with ® are registered in the United States Patent and Trademark Office, the Canadian Trade Marks Office and in other countries.

Visit us at www.eHarlequin.com

Printed in U.S.A.

This story is dedicated to Jennifer Leigh Gardenhire
My dear daughter
And my precious "first fan"

CHAPTER ONE

CASSIE MCCLEAN had just about had her craw full of Mr. Jake Coffey.

She removed her soiled leather work gloves finger by finger with vicious precision, squinting out over the Ten Mile Flats and watching that hated man's pickup jolt up the narrow gravel road that shot straight toward her like a mile-long arrow.

That road, that ridiculous…*cow path* of a road, was the most recent spear Jake Coffey had chucked into their escalating series of skirmishes. In the spring, it had been the watershed. In the dry weeks of August, the grading dust. With him, it was always something.

Her plans would be unfolding perfectly by now were it not for Jake Coffey.

Ten Mile Flats lay below her in a gentle sea of green winter wheat, a marked contrast to the high, darkly wooded ridge that she had christened The Heights. With its brick and wrought-iron gates, its curving concrete streets and newly installed underground utilities, The Heights was as sophisticated as the Flats were rustic. And that's exactly what Cassie had envisioned.

She had counted on the fact that Ten Mile Flats would never change. Out there, horse-farming operations with miles of white fencing and pristine barns

had been producing their champions since the turn of
the century. And as long as the horse farms were
there, those bottomlands would spread forth like a
hazy patchwork quilt, meeting the curve of the South
Canadian River, creating an unobstructed, timeless
view, complete with breathtaking Oklahoma sunsets.
The future homeowners of The Heights were willing
to pay a fortune for that view. Yes, everything was
perfect. Everything except Jake Coffey.

She bit her lip and whacked her gloves against her
palm. *That man.*

She had jumped through hoop after hoop to appease the landowners out on the Flats. Many of them
had come to consider Cassie's exclusive, luxury housing addition as a welcome cushion between their
peaceful farms and the urban sprawl creeping westward from the city of Jordan. All of them had come
to accept, grudgingly, that The Heights was a quality
development of classic homes.

All but Jake Coffey. Owner of the nearest, the largest, the most productive of those horse farms.

What was that man going to complain about *now?*

At the base of the hill, where the pricey lots were
pocked with massive red rock formations that veered
into a narrow creek, the noise of rock crushers
cracked the morning calm, answering Cassie's question.

Of course. Undoubtedly he'd gripe about the rock
crushers and the track hoe hammer and the bulldozers
making so much noise as they cleared the lower lots.

Well, wait till the dynamite started!

The noise was certainly going to be the next thorny issue with her nearest neighbor, Cassie was sure. She wondered if he was going to overreact, as he had over the road access. A temporary restraining order, for heaven's sakes! Forcing Cassie's grading equipment, her delivery vehicles, and now her concrete trucks, to drive all the way around on Troctor Avenue. Five long miles out of the way, each way, when *his* road through *his* dadblame antiquated horse farm was an easy shortcut from Highway 86.

The elderly sisters who'd previously owned Cassie's land had held an easement to use the road through Cottonwood Ranch—mostly to haul feed to their wild goats in their rattletrap Toyota pickup. When Cassie bought the land, she made sure she got the easement in the deal. She thought everything was fine and that she could pass through Cottonwood Ranch until the interstate loop under construction to the north was completed.

But Jake Coffey had claimed that the easement allowed for light traffic only and that Cassie had "so changed the use of the easement that it had become an excessive burden on the road." Or, rather, his lawyer had claimed that. And now, the man was seeking a permanent injunction. *Permanent.*

Well, with that nasty maneuver, Louis Jackson Coffey had turned their peevish little telephone feud into all-out legal war. Cassie had contacted a lawyer and filed a counteraction of her own.

And right now it looked like the whole thing was about to get up close and personal.

Fine. C. J. McClean was more than ready to take on Louis Jackson Coffey.

When the crushers ceased their pounding for a moment, she slapped the gloves against the leg of her overalls and turned to holler up at the foreman from Precision Stone. "Darrell! This limestone looks perfect. Let's get that chimney rocked up today."

Darrell Brown, husky, middle-aged, hardworking and brutally honest, gave her a salute from high up on the twelve-pitch roof. "Yes, ma'am!"

Darrell's crew and a couple of the framing carpenters were hammering away, nailing toe boards and protective wood planks over shingles still slick with morning frost. "Just so long as you're happy with the quality, Ms. McClean," he called over the noise. "I don't want to be knocking no low-grade limestone off of this monster."

He jerked a thumb at the chimney towering behind him. The thing peaked a full seventy feet in the air— tall enough to clear all three stories of the eleven-thousand-square-foot house and the tops of the massive black oaks sheltering it.

Down the hill, the rock crushers started up again, cutting off further conversation.

Darrell shrugged and Cassie smiled, waving him off. She surveyed the woods rising up behind the house, remembering the design challenges those huge trees had presented. The timber on this hill had cost her in more ways than one, but on the outskirts of Jordan, Oklahoma, a forested crest like this was dear.

Every home builder from here to Oklahoma City had tried to get his hands on this land, and Cassie, using extreme patience and her aunt Rosemarie's social goodwill, had finally secured it for a fair price from the eccentric Sullivan sisters. In the deal, she'd promised that any tree over thirty feet tall would be preserved—a promise that had put her architectural skills to a real test. But C. J. McClean was always true to her word. Always.

In the end, she would make a killing off this exclusive housing development, but it was the quality and integrity of the homes, not the profit, that mattered to Cassie. The lasting beauty. Ever since she was a little girl, the one thing that had always made her spirits soar was the sight of a well-built, well-designed home positioned on a beautifully landscaped lot.

Pride rose in her chest as she backed up, giving the frame of the most recent house she'd designed a quick once-over. Board by board, stone by stone, her dream houses were becoming a reality. All custom-designed, all over ten thousand square feet, these majestic homes would grace this crest for generations to come. And her name, her *good* name, C. J. McClean, would stand solidly behind them. It was a hell of a dream— one she'd carried in her heart ever since the day her father had gone to prison. And now it was a thrill to see that dream materialize right before her eyes.

Darrell Brown would start the stonework on the Detloff family's chimney today. The Becker place was already partially framed. At the highest and most westward cul-de-sac, country-and-western singer Brett Taylor's enormous concrete slab would be poured by week's end.

Barring rain, of course. Cassie frowned at the sky where soggy clouds threatened to band together and make trouble. It was already November and soon chilling rains would delay work on everything from concrete to brick masonry. At least she had this first house weathered in, which meant she could keep the indoor subcontractors busy through the winter.

She sighed. There was never any shortage of things to worry about in the building business. She sure didn't need the likes of Jake Coffey adding to her stress.

She cut an angry gaze back to the red double-cab pickup as it raised a plume of dust, fishtailing round the development marquee.

While Jake Coffey's truck pell-melled up the hill, Cassie marched to her own white one, the one with the Dream Builders logo stenciled on the door—a tasteful aubergine logo that she had designed herself.

Cassie McClean lived a life entirely of her own design. She enjoyed riding around town with the radio blasting so loudly on her favorite oldies station that even with the truck windows rolled up, the guys on the second-story roof could hear the pulse of the music. Everybody in the building business knew who she was. Big blond ponytail. Bouncy energetic stride. Too young. Too successful. Boss McClean's only daughter.

She liked it that way…except for the Boss McClean part, that is. She shook off that thought.

She ripped open the truck's door and snatched up her cell phone. When the noise at the bottom of the hill ceased again, she punched the speed dial for her lawyer's office. She was determined to face this Coffey bully well armed.

"How's our little countersuit shaping up?" She paced back to the curb and spied glints of red winking in and out of the bare trees as Coffey was forced to slow down on the steep, winding streets. Even the streets in The Heights were designed to contribute to the atmosphere of privacy, serenity, peace.

She nodded as she listened. When Mr. Jake Coffey parked that truck, he was, by George, in for quite a roaring earful.

"Excellent," she said, after her lawyer had told her everything she wanted to hear. "Fax the letter." She punched off and stepped up onto the curb.

The red pickup braked with a screech right in the middle of the cul-de-sac. A large, long-legged man in a cowboy hat and sunglasses muscled his frame out, slammed the door and strode toward her.

From the top of his dusty black Stetson to the tip of his scuffed brown boots, the man exuded virile masculinity. His bearing, his movements and what she could see of his face, his jaw, his mouth—all of it—looked handsome, sexy.

Cassie just hated that.

She deteriorated into a complete klutz around good-looking, sexy men. As C. J. McClean, she could hold her own with the rough-cut good old boys in the construction business any day. But around any eligible, attractive male she reverted to little Cassie, the awkward tomboy raised by her strange maiden aunt.

Jake Coffey was single, or so she'd been told. But why did he have to be so danged appealing?

He stopped on the pavement a yard short of her person, regarding her from behind reflective sunglasses. "Ms. McClean?" He did not remove his shades.

She kept her place up on the curb, which gave her only a slight boost against his massive build.

"Yes?" She was determined to keep this carefully civil. Deliberately cool. But she did not remove *her* sunglasses, either. Civil was one thing, but she refused to make this confrontation easy for him.

"I'm Jake Coffey. Owner of Cottonwood Ranch." He jerked a thumb over his shoulder toward the spread at the bottom of the hill. "We've talked on the phone."

She glanced at the logo on the pocket of his jacket—the same one was on his pickup—an unimaginative black silhouette of a horse's head with Cottonwood Ranch in a semicircle of script wrapped below it. "I know who you are, Mr. Coffey." She did not extend her hand.

They hadn't "talked" on the phone the last time. They'd shouted. Well, *she* had shouted. He always kept his voice infuriatingly low while refusing to budge about anything. Lately, it had been this restraining order. "What brings you up to *my* turf?"

Cassie was glad she was wearing sunglasses because she almost rolled her eyes at her own baiting tone. Here we go, she thought, the klutzy tomboy is already acting defensive. Why couldn't she ever just act normal?

He didn't respond to her taunt. "Seems you and I have another problem this morning, ma'am."

"*We* have a problem? *I* don't have a problem." Cassie spread a palm on the bib of her overalls. "My work is proceeding on schedule."

He hooked his fingers in his back pockets and planted his booted feet wide, with his torso settled low on his hips and his pelvis thrust forward, like a man who sat atop a horse a lot, which she supposed he did. Under his worn denim jacket, tucked into a dusty pair of Levi's, he wore a faded black T-shirt that stretched over a well-developed chest.

"Ma'am," he repeated, looking over his shoulder in the direction from which the noise had started late yesterday, "*we* have a problem." His soft voice belied his firm stance. He looked back at her.

His skin was weathered, tan, and he had a black five o'clock shadow though it was only eight in the morning. His full lips were chapped-looking and slightly pouty, turned down, as if he might spit out something vile at any moment.

A most unpleasant man. Most threatening.

Cassie cocked a knee and took a dainty swipe at her thigh as if his dustiness had somehow contaminated her overalls. "Okay. Exactly what is it *now*, Mr. Coffey?"

His head had ticked in the direction of her gesture, as if it distracted him. He clamped his lips tight and looked back up at her face. "I've been up most of the night with my horses." His voice was tired, unemotional. "That rock crusher down there sent my broodmares crawling up the stable walls yesterday. Kept 'em skittish all night. Another day of this and I might lose a couple of my winter foals. If I do, I am holding you legally responsible.''

She'd listened to him on the phone often enough. His voice was always low, controlled like this. But in person, it carried a resonance that rolled from deep in his chest. She hadn't felt *that* during their terse phone conversations. And underneath it all, she clearly sensed his rising ire.

She let one eyebrow arch high enough that it cleared the frame of her sunglasses. ''I doubt you can do tha—'' Unfortunately, the crusher drowned out her last word, underscoring the man's argument.

I don't, he mouthed as he made an emphatic jab at his chest.

''How can you—'' Cassie shouted as the crusher took another vibrating bite out of the hill—*boom, boom, ka-boom!* Unfortunately, the noise halted before she finished on a high note ''—possibly hold *me* responsible?'' The men up on the roof turned their heads toward her shouting. More quietly she continued, ''I am in no way liable for what happens to your horses.''

''You don't have to make all that noise. You could have that rock chipped out by hand.''

Was this man *insane?* She yanked off her sunglasses so she could give him the benefit of her most incredulous stare.

''Mr. Coffey—'' now it was she who kept her voice lethally low ''—removing a ledge of imbedded red rock that size with *little pickaxes*—'' she pinched a thumb and finger together in front of his face ''—would take *weeks,* perhaps *months,* and we've got to have those lots cleared soon so we can pour concrete before the first fall freeze. If the noise disturbs you, I suggest you move your horses to a quieter location.''

She started to turn away, but he stepped around her, jerking off his sunglasses and matching her flabbergasted expression with an incredulous one of his own.

''Move twenty-two mares? Do you have any idea what that would cost? And where would I take them? *Texas?* That noise ricochets over the whole of the Flats. You can hear it all the way to the river! Cottonwood Ranch was down there a long time before you started building these fancy houses. You can just *shut down* those machines until after my mares foal—''

''Absolutely not. Do you know what that machinery cost? I can only rent it for a limited time, and while I'm paying for it, I'm using it every minute of the day.'' Cassie had not reached her level of success by wasting money.

He planted his fists at his belt. They were into it now. ''Not where there's a noise ordinance.''

''For your information—'' The accursed booming started up again, seeming to support Jake Coffey's grievances all the more, and Cassie hated the fact that she had to raise her voice again. ''I have obtained a noise variance.''

''Well, there you have it—'' Coffey said sarcastically.

When she cupped a hand to her ear, he leaned closer, bringing the aroma of horses, smoky wood and fine leather forward with him. He smirked while keeping that maddening voice level.

"I reckon when my horses read that variance, they'll calm right down."

Cassie felt her blood pressure spike. Nothing irked her more than being mocked by a man. The Scottish temper that she had inherited from Boss McClean boiled right to the surface. "They can *eat* the variance, for all I care." She narrowed her eyes as she stared into his infuriatingly calm ones. "Those crushers *stay*."

Heads jerked around on the roof above.

She clamped her lips and gritted her teeth, hating herself for flaring up in the same way her father always had.

Jake Coffey's color heightened and the line of his mouth tightened, but his voice remained calm, in spite of the deafening noise booming from the base of the ridge. "I thought maybe I could come up here and deal with you, man to ma—neighbor to neighbor. But I can see plain dealings won't work with you. Never mind, then. I'll be back with the sheriff in one hour." He turned toward his truck.

She slapped the gloves against her thigh, wishing she could whack his hat off with them.

"The sheriff can keep me off your road, but that is all!" she shouted, even though, now, the crushers were silent. "And that'll end soon enough when we put a stop to your blamed injunction. By the way, I've added the crushers to the countersuit I'm bringing to court—" her voice went spiraling up to a shriek "—*and* the dynamite!"

Coffey froze with his hand on the door of his

pickup. His head swiveled toward her. For the first time he shouted back at her. *"Dynamite?"*

"My attorney's faxing your attorney a letter right now." Cassie waltzed toward him. "We're going to get this damn road business squared away, once and for all, and we may as well settle up on the noise deal, too, because it looks like some blasting's gonna be called for." She tended to fall into her father's tough speech patterns when she felt threatened. Normally, Cassie tried never to think about Boss McClean during the course of her workday. But this morning she'd thought of him twice already. Not a good sign.

Her aunt Rosemarie always said that Cassie's father was not a bad man. Only weak. And Cassie had to admit, his legacy to her, good and bad, had certainly amounted to a lot more than blunt language and hot temper. From him, and from her grandfather, she had learned the nuts and bolts of the building business, had absorbed it into her very cells. But her grandfather had shown her the rewards for doing things right, while her father had shown her the penalty for doing things wrong.

"Dynamite?" Jake Coffey repeated, and his dry lips looked paler.

But the haughty answer Cassie might have tossed back died in her throat, because even as the booming vibrated through the woods again, they both heard a horrified scream above it, followed by frantic shouting from the men up on the roof.

Cassie whirled to see Tom Harris, the youngest of the stonemasons, skidding down a valley of the roof like a puppet whose strings had snapped. The young man's face looked shocked, disoriented, as he tumbled sideways with such force that he knocked toe boards loose on his way down. The other men scrambled along the shingles grabbing for him, but he slipped from their hands and went flying over the edge, hitting a high scaffolding before bouncing down thirty feet onto a jagged pile of limestone below.

Cassie emitted a choked cry, then raced to the fallen man. She threw herself to her knees on the mound of rocks, tossed aside her sunglasses and shouted, "Tom! *Tom!*"

The young man, an apprentice barely out of his teens, lay perfectly still, white-faced, with eyes closed. But he was still breathing. Blood pooled onto the limestone from the back of his head. Cassie jerked off her flannel shirt and pressed it against the gash.

"He grabbed ahold of a live wire up there!" Darrell Brown shouted as he crabbed his way down the scaffolding toward the ladder braced against it. Other men were crawling down behind him like ants off a mound.

From inside the structure, the banging of hammers, the whining of saws and the loud rumbling of a rock radio station all ceased. The framing carpenters rushed out and gathered around with the stonemasons.

High up on the house, a new man—a loner named Whitlow—stood and pointed with a long piece of board at a thick white wire. Up there, Cassie knew, the dangling wire was the power to the decorative lighting that would eventually illuminate the massive chimney.

"That one shouldn't be hot!" she argued sense-lessly.

"This thing's hot, all right," the carpenter called back. He casually flipped it with the stick, and sparks flew.

The man's fearlessness with the arching wire snapped a red flag in Cassie's mind, but she was too distracted by Tom's condition to puzzle its meaning.

Why the hell was that wire hot? It wasn't like her electrician to make a mistake and switch the temporary with the main power.

"Somebody go kill that damn power," she ordered.

A gangly young man hollered, "Yes, ma'am!" and sprinted away.

"Somebody go down to the site trailer and get the big first-aid kit."

Again Cassie's order was obeyed with a "Yes, ma'am!"

Jake Coffey had dropped to one knee on the other side of Tom and was pressing two fingers against the victim's neck. "His pulse is okay," he said quietly.

Cassie fumbled around in the bib of her overalls, pulled out her cell phone and punched 9-1-1. Electric shock was a worry, but she was more concerned about the effects of the fall. She told the dispatcher the problem quickly, while Darrell scurried over the stones toward them.

"No," Cassie shouted into the phone. "There's a shortcut, a private gravel road—" she looked point-edly at Jake Coffey "—through Cottonwood Ranch."

Jake nodded. His dark brown eyes were alert, concerned. His mouth looked grim.

"How far is the turnoff from Highway 86?" She searched Jake's face imploringly while the dispatcher held.

"Let me." He took the cell phone from her. "It's two-tenths of a mile. Hard to see. I'll phone someone at the ranch and tell them to park one of our red trucks out there and flag the paramedics."

He handed Cassie the phone. "They want us to stay on the line."

She nodded, pressed the phone to her ear and looked down at Tom.

"Think he broke his neck?" she heard Darrell calling to Jake Coffey, who was sprinting toward his pickup.

"We'd better not move him, just in case," Jake called back. Cassie looked up and saw him pull out his cell phone. She turned her full attention back to Tom.

The men stood in a circle of stunned silence, watching as Jake, Darrell and Cassie covered Tom with emergency blankets, then padded the man's limbs against the sharp rocks as best as they could. They bandaged his burned hand, and then there was nothing to do but wait on the ambulance.

In the distance the rock crushers resumed their methodical work, the operators oblivious of the tragedy up on the hill. The sound filled Cassie with a mixture of guilt and nausea. She wanted the noise—that aggressive sound of progress—to stop. She knew there was no rational reason for work all over the development to halt. Still, her ambitious concerns of only moments ago seemed utterly callow now.

Please let him be okay, she prayed as she studied Tom's unconscious face. "Hold on," she told him gently. "Help is on the way."

She kept up this litany of silent prayer and verbal reassurance while they waited for the medics.

Time stretched taut, and she glanced up once to find Jake Coffey, wearing his sunglasses again, obviously studying her. When he caught her glance, he removed the shades, poked them into his breast pocket and squatted down on his haunches next to her.

As their eyes met in mutual concern, her fear mysteriously seemed to abate and a strange lightness overcame her.

"Is there anything else I can do?" Jake said quietly.

His face, the face she'd viewed as an angry opponent's only moments before, was the face of a compassionate ally now. She looked away because she felt the sting of tears and she didn't want to cry in front of the men...or in front of Jake Coffey. She shook her head and turned to stroke Tom's unburned hand.

Jake stood up again. "Fellas." He addressed the men gathered around. "We'd better move all these pickups out of the way." The circle of Levi's and boots disappeared from Cassie's view, and then she heard engines roaring to life. She only glanced up from Tom's face one other time, to see the vehicles pulling away from the cul-de-sac. At the same time, she caught sight of men jogging down the hill from the other building sites.

None of them could do anything to help Tom, she knew, but she felt a wave of gratitude for the caliber of the subcontractors and workmen she employed. These men were the finest of craftsmen, and they knew the meaning of teamwork and cooperation. They were always on schedule, always fair, always professional and honest, and not one of them would let a man lay fallen without rushing to his side.

She heard the sirens then. "Here comes help, Tom," she reassured the young man and squeezed his hand.

ONCE TOM WAS STRAPPED into a neck brace and safely loaded into the ambulance, Cassie turned to find the men still grouped around the cul-de-sac. An air of helpless frustration was setting in.

"Let's get back to work!" Darrell Brown bellowed at the assembly. He waved a beefy paw, and slowly, as if unfreezing from a carved tableau, the men responded.

"Ms. McClean, I'm so sorry this happened." A deep voice spoke quietly from behind Cassie. She turned. She hadn't noticed Jake Coffey still standing there.

She tilted her face up to him and tried to speak, but could only give her head a forlorn shake. He studied her, and his eyes were sad. They were also very kind, as if the earlier animosity between them had never existed.

He sighed. "What a terrible thing to happen."

"I can't believe it," Cassie admitted, and looked away.

Their sudden bonding over the accident came as a surprise to Cassie. And those few seconds of eye contact also brought another completely unexpected sensation. A thrill of attraction pulsed through her middle as she realized again that Jake Coffey was undeniably good-looking.

Cassie, who spent her days solely in the company of men, was seldom genuinely attracted to one. She often wondered if living in the world of construction had left her abnormally inured to male magnetism. But her honesty—her most valued trait—prevented her from feigning attraction when there simply was none. Even so, she secretly worried about herself: at age twenty-seven, she remained stubbornly alone.

And yet, she enjoyed men—enjoyed their world, their ways. She just couldn't seem to develop an intimate relationship with one. And ordinarily she wouldn't even behave normally around a guy this attractive, but for some reason she wasn't acting like an awkward schoolgirl now. She supposed she was too shocked to be anything but totally raw, totally natural.

This man standing beside her was certainly handsome. But there was something else about him. She glanced up again to find him still looking at her, with the tiniest frown line of compassion forming between his brows. She decided it was that protective, caring look that was definitely causing a physical stir deep inside of her. The realization gave her a spark of sheer wonder, of amazement. Of all things. She might actually have enjoyed discovering these new sensations if she weren't so worried about Tom. She couldn't let herself feel such things—she shouldn't even acknowledge such things—at a time like this.

She looked away, toward the ambulance now winding its way down the hill. Darrell Brown punched numbers into his cell phone as he paced the ground where the ambulance had briefly stopped. Contacting Tom's family, Cassie supposed.

She glanced up at Jake Coffey. "I've got to get to the hospital," she mumbled. *The hospital.* Would Tom even make it that far? She had never seen a body look so limp. Imagining the possibilities, she started to tremble and clutched her arms at her waist. She felt like she was going to cry. "Excuse me," she said as she moved around Jake Coffey.

He gave a hoarse whisper. "Of course." And he stepped aside.

She glanced back and saw that he was still studying her with that look of concern. She stopped in her tracks and drew a great shuddering breath.

His lips opened and he hesitated, as if he wanted to say something important but wasn't sure how. Then he simply said, "I hope the young man will be okay."

"Me, too." Cassie's tears threatened to spill over and she covered her mouth with her hand.

Jake stepped forward and wrapped warm fingers above her elbow. "Are you okay?"

Cassie nodded, then shook her head as the tears came. She swiped at them and glanced up at the rooftop, where the wirey young carpenter who'd handled the hot wire was standing, braced at the edge, staring down at the two of them. She turned her face away from the house so the men couldn't see, and Jake pulled her around in front of him, shielding her from view with his huge shoulders.

Cassie dropped her eyes, ashamed of her unprofessional behavior, but he said, "It's okay to cry."

She shook her head. "It's just that so many things have been going wrong lately. One little thing after another. And now this." She swiped at her eyes again.

To her astonishment, he produced a clean red bandana from his back pocket. "Here."

She took it and swabbed her cheeks. "Thanks." She handed it back.

He stuffed it back into his jeans. "Accidents happen, Ms. McClean, especially on construction sites."

Cassie sniffed. "I know that. But ever since I started this development, it seems like it's been one calamity after another. I admit I'm a bit of a perfectionist, and I've planned and saved and dreamed about this project for so long…but I'm beginning to think my dream is turning into a nightmare."

"Look, I don't want to add to your stress today," he offered gently. "We can finish our business another time."

"Okay," Cassie said. But she was so upset that she couldn't even recall what business, exactly, they had been discussing. *Dynamite.* Oh, damn. She had pitched that word out like a lit stick of the stuff. And she hadn't remained civil like she'd planned, not at all. And now she'd started to shake and cry like a fool because one of her men got hurt. Jake Coffey had certainly seen her at her worst, and now, she'd have to face this man—this *handsome, intimidating* man—in civil court, the day after tomorrow.

Seeing him again felt like the last thing she needed. And yet, as she watched him walk away, it felt like the only thing she wanted.

CHAPTER TWO

JAKE COFFEY STEERED THROUGH THE LABYRINTH of
streets in The Heights, fighting down a strange mixture of low arousal and high confusion. Since the day
the sign went up announcing The Heights, he and
architect and home builder C. J. McClean had been
on a collision course. He'd spoken to her on the
phone several times. But nothing in her smooth, confident, businesslike and occasionally caustic voice had
indicated that Ms. McClean was so young...and so
very beautiful.

What a face! Even without a speck of makeup, it
was a face so fresh—so *beguiling*—that no healthy,
normal man with two eyes in his head was likely to
forget it.

Her eyes, he'd noticed the instant she removed the
sunglasses, were deep set, blue as a cloudless
Oklahoma sky, full of intelligence and fire. And when
they'd filled with tears, he'd had to fight the urge to
cradle her in his arms.

She sported the kind of thick, bushy blond ponytail
that he was a sucker for—a wild, unselfconscious
mane that broadcast vitality. That straight, little,
barely freckled nose enhanced her look...and to top
it all off, she had those full, ripe lips. She was his all-

American type, all right. The kind of lively doll he'd tried to impress at high school football games and rodeo championships ever since he was a randy kid.

His type. Complete with that fit, curvy little body. Even those ridiculous overalls couldn't disguise her curvy bust, especially after she'd stripped off that baggy shirt to help the injured man. With only a thermal undershirt hugging her torso, it was easy to see that Cassie McClean had the goods. What was a woman like that doing sashaying around among construction crews all day long? Breaking lots of hearts, he bet. He'd done enough checking to know she wasn't married, but he wondered if she had a steady boyfriend.

What the heck was he doing, thinking about her in this vein? He didn't know a thing about C. J. McClean, except that she had the kind of rare good looks he'd once been a complete sucker for. And behind that pretty face, she had a mean-as-a-junkyard-dog business style.

Cowboy, he reminded himself sternly, *for the foreseeable future, you've taken yourself out of circulation.*

He'd sworn off dating as long as he had Jayden and Dad and the horses to worry over. And besides, since his divorce, he'd discovered that it was damn crazy out there in singleland. Scary, in fact. Cute little numbers wrapped in spandex could turn into a sane man's nightmare after only a couple of casual dates.

The last sweet young thing in his life had, in fact, ended up being a genuine stalker. Sitting outside the ranch gates in her darkened car. Calling late at night and scaring Jayden with her whispery questions: "Where's your daddy tonight, honey?"

After he'd finally gotten rid of that weirdo, he decided he would live without women for a while. At least until Jayden's life was more stable. Truth was, being single wasn't an impossible lifestyle—if a man kept himself real, real busy.

Your life might not be fun— he recited his familiar self-lecture *—but it's sane. It's healthy. It's simple.* Well, okay, maybe not simple. He gripped the steering wheel and gritted his teeth as he drove past the rock crushers. They banged so loudly they made his truck windows vibrate. It took enormous self-control not to flip the bird at the cussed things.

What was this business about dynamite?

He grabbed the cell phone off the seat and dialed his attorney.

Yes, Edward Hughes reported, they'd just now received a fax from C. J. McClean's lawyer. She'd filed a countermotion to force open the road and she'd apparently beaten them to the draw on the noise injunction by planning to bring forth evidence that the noise was not excessive.

"Not excessive!" Jake hollered into the phone. "Listen to this!"

He rolled the truck window down to give Edward the full benefit of the crushers. "And apparently," he said as he rolled it up again, "she plans to do some blasting with dynamite to finish the job."

"I know. I know," Edward Hughes groaned. "But my guess is they've got enough crap in this motion that the judge will be forced to conduct a trial. And there is no way the court can hold a trial before a week from now, because Jewett is in the middle of a big criminal case.''

''Can't some other judge do it?''

''No. The district court is one judge short. Judge Baker is recovering from a heart attack.''

Jake sighed into the phone. *He* was headed for a heart attack if he didn't get a grip. ''A week from now, none of this will matter. If she starts dynamiting, my mares all will have lost their foals by then.''

''I expect she'll have succeeded in getting her rock out of there in a week and the whole thing'll be moot. Pretty sharp maneuvering. Is that McClean woman a total hellcat or what? Chip off the old block, I say.''

''How's that?''

''She's Boss McClean's daughter.''

''That name rings a bell.''

''The old man went to prison a few years back for insurance fraud...and there was something else. I can't recall. But he was the same way. Anybody who got in Boss's way paid for it.''

Jake did recall a trial, years ago. ''His daughter sure seems to want her way about everything, and pronto,'' Jake confirmed.

''Yeah. As in, yesterday,'' Edward agreed dryly. ''The court appearance has been set for the day after tomorrow. That they managed to schedule a hearing on Judge Jewett's docket so fast is amazing. Must have some pull.''

''Figures. Apparently, she doesn't intend to lose a single day getting her damn fancy houses built. Says she has to beat the first freeze.''

"You talked to her again?"

"I'm just now driving back from a little jaunt up to *The Heights.*" The last two words were soaked in sarcasm.

"Well, then, did you explain the value, the rarity, of an Andalusian foal? And did you tell her the amount of money you'll lose if your thoroughbred quarter horses foal before January first? The risks?"

"Didn't get a chance. She was too busy explaining to *me* that I could simply move my horses. I said maybe I'd have to get the sheriff out there and she was telling me to meet her in court, when all of a sudden one of her men got hurt."

"Somebody got hurt? Was it serious?"

"Some guy grabbed the business end of a hot wire. The fella survived the shock, but he took a real nasty fall. Can't say how that'll turn out."

"Hmm," the attorney mused. "That's awful. In the meantime, maybe we can get the judge to give us another temporary restraining order—at least on the dynamite. That'll buy you some time. If we can hold off for a couple of weeks, you might not actually lose a foal, even if one does come early. I hate to say it, but maybe Miss McClean will be so distracted by this accident that she won't show up, and the judge'll favor us."

"Oh, *she'll* show up. She's one of those tiny, determined types that likes to make a man sweat."

"Nevertheless, you don't have to be present. If you're too busy with the mares, I'll get the noise stopped one way or another."

That's what Jake liked about having Edward

Hughes in his corner. Nobody had to tell Edward
what to do. Without Edward, Lana and her daddy
would have pounded Jake into the ground by now,
and where would that leave Jayden?

"I'll show up," Jake assured his family friend and
longtime attorney. "I want Ms. McClean to understand that this is as vital to me as it is to her and that
I won't back down any more than she will."

And the truth was, he was itching to see C. J.
McClean again. Hell, just admitting that to himself
made him realize he was in more than one kind of
trouble with this woman already.

WHEN JAKE DROVE HIS TRUCK under the iron gates at
the head of the long driveway leading to the ranch
house, he immediately spotted a whole other kind of
trouble.

Lana Largeant's champagne-colored Lincoln Navigator was parked up by the house, sparkling in the
sun, looking like one of her daddy's men had just
given it a fresh wax job. He eased his dusty truck past
the showy vehicle and saw that it was deserted, meaning Dad had let Lana into the house, despite Jake's
instructions not to.

He suppressed the familiar irritation at his father.
The poor old man couldn't remember what day it was,
much less keep the complications of Jake's relationship with his ex-wife straight. Lana treated Dad like
a dear old pet, and his confused mind lapped up her
attention.

At least Jayden was at school. This time Lana

wouldn't be able to work her manipulative magic on their daughter.

Another reason not to get involved with some cute little number, he reminded himself as he jerked the parking brake. Relationships brought all kinds of entanglements—like unplanned pregnancies that could complicate your life for good.

Not that he regretted having Jayden. Oh, no. That child was the only joyous thing about his life these days. Besides the horses.

What he resented was the tie Jayden had formed to Lana. As he climbed out of the truck, *that* fact coiled up in his gut, mean as a sidewinder. Over the past year or so, he had succeeded in setting aside his resentment of Lana for Jayden's sake, and, thanks to some long, honest talks with his brother Aaron, he had found a measure of peace about the whole deal. But Lana still found clever ways to disrupt that peace, keeping him lightly tethered, silently bound, through Jayden.

He always ended up asking himself the same circular question. How could he raise a daughter without giving the child the benefit of some kind of mother? Wasn't any mother—even a seriously flawed one— better than no mother?

But last year he'd sworn that if Lana called Jayden one more time when she'd been drinking, he'd order Edward Hughes to find a way to terminate the woman's parental rights. And, true to form, that's exactly when Lana had stopped her boozing. Just dried out. Like she'd read his mind or something.

But, sober or not, Jake didn't trust the woman. As

far as he could tell, Lana's life always revolved
around Lana, what she wanted, how things affected
her—and to hell with everyone else. The woods
seemed full of those self-centered types these days.
What he wouldn't give for one sensible, honest, decent, *unselfish...sexy* woman.

The screen door banged and Lana stepped out onto
the porch, into the morning sun. The newel posts and
white siding on the east-facing house glowed around
her slim silhouette. Lana's sleek blond hair and svelte
form—wrapped in some kind of clingy high-fashion
dress that was printed to look like army jungle fa-
tigues—created a sharp contrast to the simple homey
setting. She jutted a bony hip against a newel post
and shaded her eyes.

"Well, hello!" she called brightly, as if she were
surprised to see Jake walking up to his own home at
ten o'clock in the morning.

Instead of returning her chipper greeting, he sighed
and planted a boot on the bottom step. "Lana, what
are you doing here?"

She immediately adopted a stunned expression.
"Don't be like that," she sighed. "Just when Dad
and I were having so much fun, remembering when
Jayden got up on Arrestado and rode him all the way
down to the river. Remember that? When she was
only six?"

Jake narrowed his eyes at the woman. She had a
lot of nerve, persisting in calling his father "Dad" a
full two years after the divorce. And she had a lot
more nerve, bringing up the memory of the time she'd
been so drunk she hadn't even noticed that their

daughter had run off on the back of a dangerously high-spirited animal—commiserating about it with his addled father as if it were something cute, instead of the most terrifying day of Jake's life. Nothing pissed him off more than when Lana tried to rewrite history this way.

"Lana, look. This is not a good time."

"That Jayden!" Mack Coffey exclaimed from beyond the screen door. Poor Dad had always had a way of falling right into Lana's hands, even before the Alzheimer's had eaten away at his good sense. "That child always was a real cutter, even as a baby!"

Even with the shadow of the screen over his dad's face, Jake could see that Mack was overexcited—his cheeks flushed, his eyes unnaturally bright. Lana didn't give a thought to getting him all worked up like this, the same way she never gave a thought to feeding Jayden too many sweets.

Jake turned his attention away from the task of getting rid of Lana. "Dad, you look tired. Where's Donna?"

Before the old man could get his mind around the question, Lana answered. "I sent her to the store, Jake." She moved down the steps, closer to him. "I hope you don't mind. Y'all never have any of those cookies Jayden likes. And Dad and I need a pack of smokes."

"Dad—" Jake tried not to grit his teeth, but he was losing what little patience he had left over from the confrontation up on The Heights "—does not smoke anymore."

"Now see here, sonny." The screen door creaked

and Mack Coffey tottered forward. "I can have a smoke if I want to. I don't recall ever giving up that particular pleasure. That's your notion."

You don't recall anything, Jake thought, then hated himself for being mean-spirited. It was wearisome, caring for someone so fragile, someone who could be contrary and combative and confused all at once.

"Dad, it's chilly out here." Jake angled up the steps past Lana and clamped a friendly hand on his dad's arm. He had learned how to finesse his father without hurting Mack's pride. "Let's go inside."

Lana, naturally, followed Jake right through the door.

Jake steered Mack to his familiar rocking recliner by the window, then turned a level gaze on Lana. He was not about to give the woman an inch. "Okay, Lana, tell me what you want. I've got some skittish mares down at the barn that I need to tend to. I've already wasted half the day as it is."

Her eyes widened. "Nothing's wrong with the *Andalusians,* I hope!"

The Andalusians, prized mares from a province in southern Spain, were Lana Largeant's bread and butter. The mares had come from Lana's father's stock, and at the time of the divorce settlement, Jake had felt lucky, getting Lana to let him keep six Andalusians to breed along with his other Cottonwood Ranch mares, mostly thoroughbreds. In exchange for breeding the mares with his own rare Andalusian stallion, Arrestado, Jake had agreed to let Lana sell every foal that was born from certain mares.

An Andalusian foal could sell for as much as thirty

thousand dollars, so neither Jake nor Lana had ended up exactly broke, even after they split their operation. This arrangement had satisfied Lana, tenuously, for the past three years.

For his part, Jake had to bear the enormous overhead of getting Cottonwood Ranch back in the black. His father's slow deterioration was written all over the books in red. Jake didn't mind the back-breaking work of training and tending the stock on freezing cold nights and blazing hot days. But Jake felt now, just as he had during their ten-year marriage, that he did the work and Lana got the profits.

"The Andalusians are fine." Jake tried to sound confident. "Mainly, I don't want my quarter horses to foal before January first."

"Of course not! Lord knows, you can't run a yearling like it was a two-year-old." Jake wondered if Lana still imagined herself as his ally in the equestrian business. *It's in our blood,* she used to coo at him.

In the equestrian world, quarter horses turned one year old on January first, even if they'd just been born twenty-four hours earlier on December thirty-first. Thus, a breeder invariably lost money on any foals born late in the year. At sale, in races, those yearlings competed with horses that were actually a year older. With a horse's gestation running eleven months, two weeks, the timing was tricky. Jake always managed to keep his mares fertile and cycling through the dark winter, using constant barn lighting and every bit of available southwest sunshine. And he could always count on his two stallions, Arrestado and Pintado, to perform on cue.

By mid-February, babies were on the way. By Valentine's Day of the next year, Jake had new foals in the barn. By the following winter, the pasture was full of yearlings. Thus, the operation at Cottonwood Ranch renewed itself, year after year, in a cycle of breeding, birth and maturing stock that had garnered praise and prosperity for three generations.

Lana frowned as she went on. "But your mares never foal early. You're a great horse breeder, Jake—why would they?"

He jerked his head toward the noise in the distance as the *ka-rump* of the rock crusher echoed over the valley. "Hear that?"

"Yeah, I noticed it when I drove up. What the hell is it? Some kind of oil well operation or something?" To the west of Ten Mile Flats, an occasional oil well dotted the prairie.

"It's that damn upstart young woman's machinery!" In a flash Mack's face went from placid to agitated. He tried to push himself up from his recliner, but Jake stopped him with a calm hand on the shoulder.

"I'm taking care of it, Dad."

"What young woman?" Lana positioned herself in front of Jake.

Jake could see Lana's jealousies spiraling up as plainly as antennae.

"That woman up there on that hill." Mack flipped a weathered, shaky hand in the direction of The Heights.

Jake hooked his thumbs at his belt. "There's a developer building houses up on the old Sullivan ridge.

She's making a lot of construction noise in the process.''

"The builder is a *she?*"

"A woman architect. Name's C. J. McClean." Jake exhaled a pent-up breath. Why did he feel uneasy all of a sudden? "Calls her operation Dream Builders."

Lana eyed him, then lit up with a kind of excitement. "I've heard of Dream Builders! They run a big ad in the paper every Sunday. And they have TV ads on cable." She turned her head toward the picture window, gazing in the direction of The Heights. "You want me to tell Daddy to make this woman stop that racket?"

"I said I'm handling it." Jake's jaw clenched again. He was going to crack every filling in his mouth before this day was over. The last thing he wanted was Stu Largeant poking around in Cottonwood Ranch business. "You don't need to get involved."

"But we *are* talking about *our* Andalusians."

"You can only claim the foals, Lana, and only from Bailadora and Encantadora and—"

"How could I *ever*—" Lana's voice grew instantly acid "—forget about that...that *devil's* pact we made?"

Like her transparent jealousy, Lana's temper sprouted as plainly as horns popping out on her forehead. She whirled on the hapless Mack, who, Jake hoped, would have no memory later of the undercurrents that had just been unleashed in the room.

"Just for once, you would think your son could

forget his stiff-necked pride and let somebody help him.''

''Jake don't need Stu Largeant's kind of help.''

Mack, suddenly alert, suddenly lucid, surprised Jake this way at least once a day. That was the torment of Mack's disease. Jake could never be sure who was on board. Tough, sensible, loving Mack Coffey, or his withered twin, the frail man who couldn't remember how to put on his own socks.

Jake intervened. ''Lana, look. I've already talked to the woman myself. And I've talked to my attorney. I will get this settled. In the meantime, I want you to stay out of it.'' Jake hated to state it so bluntly, but he knew from long experience that you couldn't give Lana Largeant any wiggle room or before long she'd be ordering your hired help to run out and fetch her cigarettes.

''All right. If that's what you want.'' Lana snatched a stylish leopard-skin clutch off the couch. ''I was hoping to discuss something important with you— about Jayden—but I don't want to do it when you're in a bad mood. I'd better get going. Don't worry, Jake, I won't interfere with this...C. J. McClean woman.''

Jake nodded, but if he knew Lana, she'd head up to The Heights and have a look at C. J. McClean for herself, no matter what he said. And he knew she would run home and tell her rich daddy the whole story.

She thrust her arms into an oversize black micro-fiber duster. ''Tell Donna not to worry about my change.'' She said this to Mack. Then she flew out the door without bothering to pull it shut behind her.

Jake walked over and closed the door with a soft *click*. He removed his hat and hung it on a nearby coat tree. He gave a soft, mirthless snort of laughter when something occurred to him. Lana's clothes always gave some kind of clue to her mood. He wondered if the cutesy army getup meant she was gearing up for war. Again.

That's all he needed, more legal entanglements. Her mention of Jayden had caused a familiar twist of fear in Jake's gut.

"I wonder what Lana wanted. Did she tell you, Dad?"

But Mack was staring out the window, lost again in the cobwebby world of Alzheimer's disease. "Who?" he said, and his voice was croaky with fatigue.

"Nobody," Jake said.

"Where the heck is Donna?" Mack's gaze was fuzzy as it panned the room.

"At the store. She'll be back soon."

"She'd better be." Mack's voice cleared and he flicked out his pocket watch in the same crisp manner he always had. "It's gettin' on toward lunchtime."

Jake smiled. That was Mack—in and out.

BY THE TIME JAKE HAD FINISHED an apple and made a couple of business calls, he heard Donna's Jeep roaring up the drive. Donna Morales bustled in the back door by the kitchen, as was her habit, clumped through the house, and appeared in Jake's office doorway, out of breath.

"Is she gone?" she huffed.

Jake nodded, frowning.

"I'm sorry, Jake." Donna pressed a hand to her ample bosom. "But have you ever tried to tell that woman no?"

"Many times." Jake pushed his leather desk chair back and smiled.

"I swear—" Donna stepped into the office and flopped onto the leather sofa opposite the desk. "She makes me so nervous. I cannot imagine the two of you ever being married!"

Jake smiled again. What would he have done these past three years without Donna Morales? A licensed practical nurse, a mother of three perpetually hungry college-age sons, and an ardent Catholic, Donna whipped up the foods Dad loved, kept their rambling ranch house passably clean, and, best of all, was so honest and plainspoken that even Jayden had come to trust her.

Donna's quiet, reliable husband, Jose, had worked for Jake for years, cutting hay, cleaning barns, fixing fence and talking to the Andalusians in soothing Spanish. Soon after Lana packed herself off to her daddy's house, Jose had mentioned that the couple could sure use some extra income, with three boys studying engineering over at the university—and Jake, he had pointed out gently, could sure use Donna's kind of help.

At first Donna wore herself out, beating a path from the hospital to the ranch the minute her shift was over,

arriving just about the time the school bus dropped
Jayden at the road. But before long, Jake offered to
make her position full time. She and Jose had prayed
about it for about two seconds, then jumped at the
deal. Jose and Jake's main hand, Buck Winfrey, had
always been friendly, and they soon got into the habit
of hitting the ranch house of a morning, looking for
Donna's home-baked treats. Sometimes they'd grab a
quick cup of coffee with Mack. Donna called the
three older men "the boys" in the same tone she used
for her sons. Jake didn't mind the traffic in his home.
His life, Mack's life and, most of all, Jayden's life
would be awful lonely without that little ensemble
running in and out.

And in the past year, Donna had become a trusted
confidante to Jake where it concerned his father's de-
clining health. She seemed to be able to put a calm,
cheerful, down-to-earth slant on the discouraging
daily incidents that came with Alzheimer's disease. If
the woman had known anything about horses, Jake
decided, she'd be dang near perfect. Except that she
weighed two hundred pounds and her unkempt frizzy
hair was died the color of day-old coffee and her little
mustache was thicker than Mack's. But Jose seemed
to think she was a goddess.

"I shouldn't have left your dad alone with that
woman." Donna looked slightly embarrassed. "Honest to Pete, I don't know why I let her get to me."

"It's okay." Jake stood and threaded his arms into
the sleeves of his denim jacket. "Dad's asleep in his
chair. I've gotta get out to the barns."

"What'll I do with these?" Donna held up the plastic grocery sack she'd carried in.

"Here—" Jake held out his hand for the carton of cigarettes. "I'll give the smokes to Buck. He's not picky about the brand."

She handed him the cigarettes, then pulled out the expensive cookies. "And these?"

"Have the boys already been here?"

"Cleaned out my cinnamon rolls an hour ago."

"Then, I guess you and Jayden can have a little party when she comes home from school."

"Oh, not *me*. I'm on a *diet*." Donna winked.

"Yeah, me, too." Jake winked back. He grabbed another apple—his standard snack—out of the basket that Donna kept filled on his desk. "So how about a nice big pan of sour-cream chicken enchiladas for lunch?"

Donna flapped a chubby palm at him. "Behave yourself and get on out to the barns!"

As JAKE PULLED A GOLF CART up to the barns in the eastern pasture, he saw Buck Winfrey opening the south-facing barn doors. On a chilly day like this, Buck might even have the space heaters going. Jake trusted Buck, a veteran of the horse trade, with all such decisions.

Just inside the doors, two barn boys were blanketing this year's heavily pregnant broodmares for a walk in the sun. Jake was worried. The mares, normally placid, were dancing away as the barn boys held up the blankets. How high-strung had the quarter horses become? Jake had kept the Andalusians, thoroughbreds and quarter horses cycling this winter. Of those, the quarter horses were the biggest worry.

Losing an Andalusian or thoroughbred foal to prematurity would be costly, but early quarter horses, a full year behind the growth curve, might hurt the Cottonwood Ranch reputation for years to come. In the horse-breeding business, Jake himself was a rare breed, raising both racing and show horses. He valued his reputation, which was his father's, which was his grandfather's, as if it were an actual commodity.

The booming seemed considerably louder on this side of the valley. As he parked, Jake saw one of the old pickup trucks, loaded with hay, pulling around beside the barn. With his skinny arms raised over his head, Buck signaled the driver to go out far, past the water troughs. The farther he took the hay into the field before dumping it, the farther the mares would run for the feed and the longer they would stay out in the sunlight while they ate, getting needed exercise and sunshine.

"Buck!" Jake hollered, waving.

Buck ambled toward him, his cowboy's gait loose, easy, reflecting the wiry older man's attitude about life. He pushed a battered baseball cap back on his bald pate.

"What'd that McClean gal have to say about this damn racket?"

"She's taking me to court." Jake got out of the cart.

"Say what?" Buck cupped an ear against the intermittent noise of the crushers. "Taking you where?"

"To court!"

"Court!"

"Silly, isn't it?"

"What the hell for?"

"I expect so she can drive her concrete trucks through this ranch."

"By God, she will *not*," Buck asserted. He pushed his hat farther back and spit into the straw at his feet. Then he fished a cigarette out of his breast pocket.

"Let's hope not. But I've decided a court hearing could be useful. It'll give me a chance to ask the judge to shut down this noise permanently. I told Edward to ask for another restraining order."

"That'll show 'er."

"How're the mares?" Jake set off toward the barn.

Buck double-timed it to keep up with Jake's long legs. "Bailadora and Encantadora just about kick their stalls down every time that damn thing starts going *ka-boom*."

As he reached the barn door, Jake could hear the disturbed whinnying of his two most beautiful Andalusians. The plaintive sound made his chest tight. He opened the heavy steel door, and once inside the dim barn, the echoes of the horses' cries felt suffocating to him. Jake never broke stride on his way to the mares, but reached into a coffee can nailed to a post and grabbed a handful of sugar cubes on his way by.

He went straight to the mares, soothing them with his voice. "Whoa, girls. *Facil. Fah-ceel.* Easy. Easy."

The whinnying stopped, and first one, then the other, came to the stall's bars to nip a sugar cube off his palm. He popped one into his own mouth while he patted the mares' withers, each in turn.

Jake found that the ritual calmed him as much as it did his animals. For the first time all day, he felt his shoulders relax, felt his breath filling his lungs fully. This was where he found peace—in the barns, in the fields, with the smell of clean hay and healthy horseflesh around him. These beautiful animals, their solidity, their strength, their warmth, had calmed him ever since he was a small boy, reaching up into his grandfather's pocket for a sugar cube. Even as a man of thirty-five, with all the responsibilities a man could bear, Jake still found that a little time out in the barns, with the taste of a plain sugar cube melting in his mouth and the feel of horseflesh under his palms, could make the world seem sane again.

"It's the same for you, isn't it, my lovely ladies." He spoke to the horses. "A sugar cube and a pat from old Jake can soothe just about anything."

But even under his calming touch, the tension in the mares' muscles communicated loudly to Jake through his fingertips. How long could they go on like this? This constant noise was an untenable situation, one he'd never encountered on the peaceful Ten Mile Flats. If C. J. McClean started blasting with dynamite, he'd have an early, or perhaps even dead, foal on the ground before the week was out. He'd wager these mares would drop early, or he hadn't been a horseman for the past twenty years.

LANA LARGEANT WHEELED her Lincoln Navigator around the first bend in the road that climbed the Sullivan ridge and sucked in a breath. *Glorious!*

Even in their skeletal state, anyone could see that the homes in The Heights were destined to be first class. They rose up on the hillsides with the steeply pitched roofs and magical lines of the rambling English country manors that she'd grown to love when she and her parents had traveled to equestrian shows in Europe. The midmorning sun created long shadows over pockets of mist under the tall trees and along the deep sandstone creek.

Oh, my! The landscaping possibilities on this slope were endless. Already this developer, this C. J. woman, had erected curving rock retaining walls, gradual terracing and winding stone pathways, all of which lent a quaint, fairy-tale charm to the common grounds. The place embodied the kind of character and style that women like Lana lusted after.

Lana had always fancied this piece of land. Coveted it. When married to Jake, she had occasionally ridden her personal Andalusian mare, Isadora, up onto the hillside. Nowadays she didn't get over to this side of the Flats often.

Twice, she'd secretly contacted Helen and Caroline, the elderly Sullivan sisters and begged to buy the property from them. But the sisters had said that would never happen. So why, now, had the old ladies finally sold it to this C. J. McClean person? And how on earth had that woman managed to get the development under way so quickly? In a way, the overnight change in the place unsettled Lana, as if some interloper had sneaked in during her absence and stolen something from her.

One. Two. Three houses under construction, and pads cleared for six or seven more. She slowed the Navigator to a crawl, unconcerned that the construction workers might notice her. The Navigator was new, she was wearing her shades and it had been ages since her picture had been in the paper. As she circled the cul-de-sacs, she might have been any well-to-do woman out scouting for properties—not the daughter of Stu Largeant, the longtime mayor of the City of Jordan. Not the ex-wife of horse rancher Jake Coffey, who had apparently already been up here this morning, throwing his weight around with that McClean woman.

Lana wondered what this C. J. McClean looked like. Mack had called her young, but the woman couldn't be too young if she was overseeing a costly development like this. Unless, like Lana, she was using family money to make her way. Hadn't there been some McCleans in the home-building business in Jordan, way back when? Hadn't there been a scandal? Didn't somebody die or something?

The Heights. Already Lana was itching to live in one of the mansions on these slopes. Right above Cottonwood Ranch. Right next door to Jayden...and Jake. Daddy would definitely have to see this place. But at the thought of her father, Lana stopped her dreaming. Hadn't she told herself that the Navigator was the last expensive thing her father would ever buy for her? How would his control over her ever end if *she* didn't end it?

On her way back out of the brick gates, Lana passed a white pickup coming in. A burgundy Dream Builders logo was on the door and the woman behind the wheel looked petite, blond and definitely young.

Lana's curiosity strummed as she wondered if that was *her*. Lana Largeant fancied that she knew Jake Coffey awfully well. Knew when his blood was running high. And when he had mentioned C. J. Mc-Clean's name, Lana could already tell that the man's blood was up. Way up.

CHAPTER THREE

TWO DAYS LATER Jake Coffey and Cassie McClean stared at each other as they climbed the steps of the Cleveland County Court House. Their faces couldn't have registered more shock if they'd been naked as jaybirds instead of dressed in their finest business apparel. Both had apparently turned out in their best for this confrontation, although, Cassie surmised, in Jake's world business attire was by definition more casual, more Western.

Still, he looked so polished that he didn't even seem like the same man.

He wore cowboy boots again, although this pair, cut of a fine suede in a muted shade of cognac, could have taken him to lunch at the governor's mansion. Under a Western-cut sports coat in a dark khaki and olive windowpane blend, a cream-colored basket-weave Polo shirt contrasted against the tanned skin at his throat. The jacket was obviously made from a superior cloth—Cassie recognized the blend of silk and wool—and it coordinated flawlessly with his dark wool trousers, which had pleats that bulged subtly below his flat abdomen. His hair, which the battered Stetson had concealed at the job site, was close cropped—a clean, classic shade of chocolate brown that matched his eyes exactly, offset by a few tantalizing strands of gray at the temples and nape. To make the whole effect utterly devastating, the chill November wind carried from his person the scent of an aftershave that filled Cassie with a bad craving.

Cassie herself had pulled together her best power look: a pencil-slim suit of the finest red worsted wool, giant diamond ear studs, and a chunky solid gold watch. Oh, yes, and black heels. Very high black heels.

"After you," Jake said, when they reached the top step. He opened one of the heavy double doors and inquired, "Where's your attorney?"

"Inside. Yours?"

"The same."

Cassie was relieved when they were directed to a smallish office where Judge Jewett sat behind an ordinary-looking desk with a fake floral arrangement at one end. She had anticipated with dread the cold, mahogany-paneled courtroom of her father's trial. She imagined the judge, remote and punitive, high up behind a bench surrounded by seals and flags.

Her lawyer, Miles Davies, whispered near her ear, "We are meeting in chambers because the judge is in the middle of a big criminal case in the courtroom."

Cassie liked Miles. He was a kindly old eccentric. Her grandfather had considered him to be so competent and trustworthy that he had hired Miles to defend Boss fifteen years ago, and that was good enough for Cassie.

She and Jake were seated in comfortable armchairs

at right angles to each other. Their attorneys positioned themselves between Cassie and Jake, and the two older men shook hands, sat down and crossed their legs, balancing fat files in their laps. They seemed to know each other, chatting and joking until the judge came in. When they got down to asking for what their clients wanted, it was as if Jake and Cassie weren't in the room.

The legal mumbo jumbo made little sense to Cassie, although she and Miles had reviewed the procedure only an hour before. She could sense that he was making their case, and for her, that was enough. She wanted to get this thing over with, then go by the hospital and check on Tom Harris. After that, she hoped she'd have time to run home and change into work clothes and make a final check on the day's progress in The Heights. All the judge had to do was see the light and let her get on with her business.

But when it was his turn to talk, Jake Coffey's attorney, Edward Hughes, seemed to be making a convincing case, too.

Miles interrupted once, and a little bit of lawyerly yelling took place. All in all, the whole thing struck Cassie as going through the motions, something these guys, and the judge, apparently did every day.

For her part, she found this haggling and posturing most annoying because it interrupted the very real, very creative work she loved. And she blamed *him* for causing it.

She gave Jake Coffey a disdainful glance.

He didn't catch it. His handsome head was down as he listened to his snotty old attorney argue that the noise was clearly a nuisance and not merely a tort…or something like that.

At the moment, Cassie resented these two men with all her heart. Her own attorney was quietly leafing through his files. "What's going to happen?" she whispered, when the Edward Hughes guy finally stopped talking.

"The judge will probably go into chambers to make his decision," Miles muttered. "We shall wait here." He leaned forward and handed the judge a piece of paper. A copy of the noise variance, Cassie supposed. The judge had asked to see it.

She checked out Jake Coffey again. With a jolt, she saw that he was staring at *her*. And not exactly unpleasantly. He was slumped low in his chair with his long legs crossed comfortably, one hand resting loosely at his belt. The other hand—for some reason this gesture rattled Cassie—was covering his mouth. Well, not covering it, exactly, because Cassie could see the corners of a Cheshire smile peeking from behind his fingers. When he caught her looking at him, his brown eyes sparked for an instant, then narrowed in thought. Was that a dirty look? Or an admiring one? Did it mean he knew something she didn't? Oh, God, had the other side somehow won?

"I'm taking everything under advisement and will come back with my decision shortly." The judge got up and left the room.

Silence.

Jake continued to study her, continued to squint and continued to smile in that enigmatic, intimidating way.

Cassie squirmed. She hated courthouses, anyway—who wouldn't if their very own father had been taken away from them in one?—but this…this close-quarters examination by this…this *man*. Well, it was too much.

After what seemed like days, the judge returned.

"I am forced," Jewett droned as soon as he had resettled himself behind his desk, "to require difficult concessions from both parties in this case."

Everybody sat up straighter, giving the judge their full attention.

"If Mr. Coffey can extend the gestation of his mares for three more weeks, the foals will likely survive without damage—"

"Not really." Jake jerked forward. "Not at nine months—"

"Mr. Coffey, you've presented your evidence. Now, Ms. McClean, you understand that the jurisdiction of the City of Jordan ends at 60th Street, which happens to be Mr. Coffey's property line. So this noise variance means nothing to landowners on Ten Mile Flats." The judge lifted the paper and sent it drifting to the corner of his desk.

"Mr. Coffey has asked for jurisdictional relief regarding this noise. And I am of a mind to give it to him. This noise is clearly a tort, as it threatens the safety of valuable livestock. I am particularly concerned about any blasting with dynamite. However, if you can voluntarily delay the noise until the foals are viable, you'll likely save yourself a lawsuit for damages."

Jake cocked an eyebrow and pressed his lower lip out, as if weighing the merits of such a lawsuit.

Thanks for giving him ideas, Judge. Cassie narrowed her eyes in warning at Jake. He wasn't the only one who could dish out dirty looks.

"In the meantime, there is nothing preventing you from removing the rock in a more conventional, and far quieter, manner."

Nothing but money, Cassie thought, feeling her outrage beginning to build. Three weeks was a long time to pay interest on millions of dollars in construction loans and to pay rent on machines that were sitting idle. This was a compromise?

Cassie felt an encouraging nudge at her elbow, her attorney indicating that he thought this was an acceptable idea. She nodded her understanding at the judge. What else could she do?

"After three weeks, Ms. McClean's rock crushers may resume work, and if necessary at that time she may use the dynamite—"

Jake sat bolt upright. "But, Judge—" he started.

The judge held up a palm.

"But three weeks—"

"Mr. Coffey, that is the best I can do. I understand about birth dates and quarter horses, but we can't make Ms. McClean delay construction until January. For your part of the compromise, I suggest that at the end of three weeks you give up this restraining order—" the judge flapped another piece of paper "—and see your way clear to let her concrete trucks pass through Cottonwood Ranch. That will make up for some lost time, won't it, Ms. McClean?"

Again, Cassie nodded. It was apparent that nobody was going to walk out of this room happy.

Jake most certainly did not look happy. The deepening crease between his brows indicated that he wasn't at all satisfied. Well, tough. Neither was she.

Judge Jewett picked up his pen. "My final decision will be issued tomorrow morning at nine a.m., unless I hear that you two have settled it between yourselves before then. I encourage you to compromise and try to reach an equitable position between yourselves before I issue that order. You could save yourselves the distress of the trial."

The two attorneys smiled and nodded, but Jake and Cassie looked at each other like disgruntled juveniles being forced to shake hands.

Jewett rose when his courtroom deputy stuck his head in the door. "The attorneys in the criminal case are waiting in the courtroom, Your Honor."

"I'm coming." Jewett was gathering papers. "Now you two—" he aimed his pen at Jake, then Cassie "—sit down at a table and work this out." Then he left.

It was a decision worthy of King Solomon—that's what Cassie's attorney said when they got out in the hallway.

Cassie's jaw dropped. "King Solomon?" She turned on the old gentleman. "Miles, if you ask me, that was a crock of crap! A knee-jerk decision handed down by an overworked judge who doesn't want another trial on his docket. That—" she pointed toward the judge's chambers "—was what I call a lose-lose situation. Now Jake Coffey and I are probably *both* going to lose money on this! When you go before a judge, isn't somebody supposed to come out the winner?''

The fussy old gentleman looked offended. ''I have done the best I can for you, Ms. McClean.''

Cassie wanted to say something about how she supposed the *lawyers* would be the only ones making money, but she managed to bite that back. Still, then and there, she made up her mind to pay Miles every last cent she owed him and find herself a new lawyer who was more aggressive and less chummy with his pals at the courthouse.

But right then, Jake's attorney came up behind them and grabbed Miles Davies's shoulder before she could inform him of this. ''Miles,'' Edward Hughes said pleasantly, ''would you like to use my office for our negotiations?''

''How kind of you to offer, Edward.'' Cassie's attorney smiled. ''Perhaps we can, at least, work out something where both parties feel they are bearing equal financial risks in the—''

''I'd rather talk to Ms. McClean alone.'' The rich timber of Jake's voice stopped the discussion.

Cassie and the lawyers turned to face him.

''Uh, Jake, maybe it would be better if I were present—'' Edward Hughes started.

''Nope.'' Jake's dark gaze was fixed firmly on Cassie. ''The judge told us to work it out between ourselves. I'm good for my word. How about you, Ms. McClean?''

''I am absolutely a woman of my word.'' Cassie had no trouble asserting that. It was her lifelong code.

"Good. Then, we don't need the lawyers."

The two lawyers stood looking from Jake to Cassie, dumbstruck.

"I'm hungry." Jake put a palm on his flat middle. "How about some lunch?"

Cassie wondered what the heck this was all about. One minute they were sparring in court and the next he was inviting her to lunch. Was this a trick?

"The judge said to sit down at a table." He gave her a wicked grin. "There might as well be food on it."

Cassie frowned.

"Seriously." Jake tilted his head. "We only have until tomorrow morning, and in the meantime, we've got to eat."

This was true. Cassie always managed to find time to eat. Her appetite was as healthy as any man's. But most of her lunches were fast food, eaten in the cab of her truck while she studied a materials list. It was not often that she was dressed nicely enough to go to a real restaurant and sit down and have a decent lunch. Suddenly it seemed like a shame to waste her snazzy outfit.

"I guess we might as well eat while we talk this over, but it needs to be on this side of town. I've got to go by the hospital."

"Oh? The injured man?"

"Yes."

"Is Legend's okay?"

Legend's! A gourmet restaurant that had been hosting special events for Jordan residents for over thirty years. Cassie had loved that place ever since her aunt

Rosemarie had first taken her there as a child. Her fluttery aunt always called the atmosphere...*romantic.* Cassie preferred to think of it as tasteful, classy.

"Uh, sure. Legend's will work."

"Great." Jake gave the lawyers a little salute and put a light hand at Cassie's back, steering her toward the stairs.

Cassie glanced at the two older men, who were staring like stunned referees that had been told by the players to get off the field.

"How about if I drive," Jake said as he opened the stairwell door. "Once we've reached an... equitable position—" there was an unmistakable hint of humor in his voice "—I'll bring you back to your car."

As they descended the stairs, Cassie started to feel something. Something akin to magnetism. She didn't know if it was the synchronized physical movement—they stayed side by side, right in step the whole way—or the man's very nearness as he held her elbow on the way down. Cassie didn't even know if she had the right to feel this...this magnetism or whatever it was. For all she knew, he might be involved with a woman. The good-looking ones were never available.

All she knew for certain about Jake Coffey was that, right now, she was going to lunch at Legend's with him. And that prospect seemed at once frightening and thrilling.

CHAPTER FOUR

LEGEND'S NEVER CHANGED MUCH, and Cassie liked that. She liked the permanence of the quiet, sophisticated atmosphere. Layer upon layer of antiques, timeless art, and black-and-white photographs of patrons graced its shelves and walls. They'd never even removed the old private liquor storage lockers from Oklahoma's "bottle club" laws of earlier decades. The quaint, old-fashioned wooden bins were used to hold house wines now.

The owner recognized both Jake and Cassie, and stepped around the small maître d' podium to greet them by name. He seemed mildly curious to see them together.

Walking past the gleaming brass-and-glass case with the famous Legend's desserts on display at shoulder level, Cassie remembered how her aunt had always stopped to let Cassie choose a favorite. Sometimes it took the child a long time, as if her future depended on whether she ate strawberry genoise or Kahlúa pecan pie after brunch.

The lunch patrons—gussied-up older ladies, the local chamber crowd, professors from the university—were in high chatter. As they mounted the short steps to a balcony area and then threaded past the tables to a secluded corner, Jake smiled and nodded at a couple of folks. Cassie didn't recognize anyone, but she didn't really expect to since she seldom socialized outside of construction circles. The owner seated them at a cozy table by large windows that looked out on the patio garden.

A waiter came and took their drink orders. When he left, Jake smiled. ''The food here is great. And at lunchtime they're pretty fast.'' He tapped his fingers lightly on the table as if considering something. ''Maybe I should have taken you by to check on the young man in the hospital first.''

Cassie thought that was nice, considerate. ''That's okay. I'll want to stay awhile. You know, sit with his family.''

Their eyes met, as if they were suddenly reliving the event and again feeling the bonding that had happened as a result of it.

''I should have asked before now. Is he doing okay?''

''He's still unconscious. I'm afraid we don't know much about his long-term prognosis yet.''

Jake frowned and again Cassie noticed what a sensuous mouth he had. ''I hope he recovers all right. Have you figured out what went wrong?''

''Somebody switched the main and temporary wiring.'' Cassie squinted at the menu, not really reading it. That mix-up was most disturbing.

''How could that happen?''

''It shouldn't. Ever. The electrician swears none of his men could have done it.'' Cassie shook her head. ''I can't figure it out, but I'll get to the bottom of it.

There may be liability issues.'' Cassie bit her lip. Maybe she shouldn't talk about *liability*. This man put her so at ease that she'd almost forgotten they were suing each other. ''But Darrell carries full workmen's comp.''

''That's good.''

After the waiter brought water for Cassie and tea for Jake, Jake said, ''I happen to agree with you, you know.''

Cassie frowned. ''About what?''

''That was a crock of crap back there at the court-house.''

Cassie felt her cheeks turning pink. ''I should watch my tongue. I probably hurt poor old Miles's feelings.''

''You were being honest. The judge didn't want to bother with our dispute, and the attorneys let him put us off. I admire your honesty. It's what made me decide to take you to lunch.'' His brown eyes twinkled again, the way they had when he'd been watching her in the judge's chambers. ''Well, that was part of it, anyway.''

Cassie's cheeks grew hotter as she wondered exactly what the other part was. The way he was smiling at her, it should have been obvious. But she didn't dare imagine that this man was interested in *her*. She took a sip of water to cover her discomfort.

''Nevertheless, I should watch my temper. I just get so impatient when it comes to business.''

He smiled. ''I like your style. Like I said, at least you're honest. Honesty is a big deal to me.''

When she didn't respond to that, only sipped her

water again, he stopped grinning. "Anyway, I figure we could have done better for ourselves."

"I agree."

An uncomfortable silence passed. For some reason Cassie felt like she was on one of those miserable blind dates she occasionally endured to appease her friends.

"I really like this place," she commented lamely. Anything to end this endless water sipping and silence.

"You come here often?"

"No, not lately. But when I was a kid, my aunt brought me here for brunch almost every Sunday after church." Cassie smiled. "She always let me take of a little nip of her mimosa."

"Who is your aunt?"

"Rosemarie Cowan."

"Ah," he said, as if realizing something. "So you're related to Cowan Construction?"

"Yes. Cowan Construction was my grandfather's company—Rosemarie's father. My mother's father." The company was formerly very well-known in Jordan.

"Oh." Jake glanced out the window, then his gaze snapped back to her, assessing. "So you inherited the building business from two families?"

"I didn't inherit anything." Cassie wanted to be clear about that. She wondered if he was sizing up her assets. The assumption that she had stepped into Boss's shoes always rankled, but she had learned to keep her cool about it. Jake Coffey was not the first to assume that she had been handed success on a sil-

ver platter. "My grandfather taught my father the
building business after my parents married. When my
grandfather died, Boss changed the name of the business to McClean Builders. But then my father lost all
of it when—"

"I know that McClean Builders went under."

At her surprised look, he said, "I checked you
out."

"Then, surely you discovered that I started Dream
Builders on my own."

"Well, I didn't dig real deep, but I know about the
other two additions out east that you threw up in record time before you got your hands on the Sullivan
land."

"Those are fine, modest homes," she defended.
She did not build junk, as her father had, and she
resented any implication that she did.

"I merely meant that you sure work at lightning
speed for a builder. What's the hurry?"

Cassie ran her finger over the rim of her water
glass. "When I built Sandplum Creek and Meadow
Farms, I was struggling for credibility. The bankers
trust me now. If you consistently bring projects in on
schedule, or even ahead of schedule, they'll loan you
bigger money the next time."

He nodded. "Makes sense. So all the time you
were headed for The Heights."

She couldn't help smiling. "Yep. And now I'm
there, up on The Heights. And nothing is going to
mess up this project now."

"Certainly not some cranky horse farmer who
wants peace and quiet for his mares."

Their gazes locked, and they were suddenly the two people who'd recently had a confrontation from behind sunglasses.

Fortunately, just then the waiter brought a basket of hot, fragrant bread. They calmed down while they busied themselves buttering it.

After Jake swallowed a bite, he rolled his eyes. "The bread here is great. I've got a pretty decent cook, but she can't top this."

"You have a cook?" It occurred to Cassie again that she knew very little about this man, except that he could be awfully stubborn when it came to protecting his horse ranch.

"Yeah. Donna. A sweetheart. She's a very competent cook, but mainly she takes care of my dad."

"Oh? Your father lives with you?" Cassie felt a tiny prick of something akin to envy. Wouldn't it be nice, the generations living together in peace on the family ranch?

"Actually, it's the other way around. Cottonwood Ranch belongs to him. But he's got Alzheimer's disease." He stated it matter-of-factly, with regret but with no inkling of self-pity.

"Oh. I'm so sorry. I've heard that's very stressful for the family. Is your mother still alive?"

"No. She passed on years ago."

"Then, does...does the rest of your family help you with your father?"

She knew she was trying to get down to the question of whether he was in fact single, without actually asking. It made her feel nosy and manipulative, but she couldn't help herself. This was the first man she had been attracted to in a long, long time, and she had to know if he was romantically involved. She wasn't entirely sure he wasn't, in fact, married. Someone had said they thought Jake Coffey and his wife had split up about three years ago, but sometimes couples reconciled after a separation.

"My brother Aaron lives in Dallas. My parents were in their early forties when they had us. It was a miracle, according to my mother. But no matter how it happened, I'm sure glad they had Aaron. He's my best friend." His smile was warm, unselfconscious. "Do you have any siblings?"

"No, I'm an only child." And Cassie had always hated that. But she did have a gaggle of close friends from her aunt's neighborhood that had sustained her through the years. Three girls and one guy, Hermie. All into math and music and art. They'd all grown and gone their separate ways, far from Jordan, except for her and Stacey.

"But I still see my best friend since seventh grade about once a week," she said, and, again, mentally thrashed for a way to find out what she wanted to know without sounding like a ninny.

She glanced at his left hand. No ring, but that didn't mean anything, especially in a man who worked outdoors. Plenty of married construction workers left their rings at home for safety reasons.

"I'm divorced," he volunteered with a wry grin.

"Oh."

The waiter came back before Cassie could think of a way to find out if that meant he was actually available.

"Have you folks had a chance to look at the menu?"

They smiled sheepishly at each other, realizing that they'd been engrossed in each other instead of deciding what to order.

"I already know what I want." Cassie laid her menu aside.

"Why am I not surprised?" Jake's smile widened.

Cassie's smile grew more abashed. Maybe she had been a little too assertive when she met this guy, but that was business. She could separate business from pleasure, couldn't she? So, which was this? She glanced at the waiter.

"I'll have the chicken crepes."

Jake scanned his menu, then snapped it shut. "The prime rib. Medium. Plenty of horseradish on the side."

"Help yourselves to the salad bar." The waiter smiled and picked up the menus.

The salad bar at Legend's never changed, either. Eating here felt like coming home. Soon, she decided, she would have to bring Aunt Rosemarie here for dinner again. Cassie's work had been keeping her too busy lately, but that was no reason to neglect her dear aunt.

As they loaded their plates with tabbouleh, German potato salad, and the freshest of radicchio and field green salads, Cassie said, "I love this salad bar. My aunt used to let me pick out anything I wanted when I was a kid."

"Legend's is sort of a fancy restaurant for a little girl," Jake commented.

"I wasn't *that* little. I was already twelve by the time I went to live with her."

"Was that after your dad went to prison?"

He said it quietly, the way he said everything, and not at all unsympathetically, but Cassie nearly dropped her chilled glass plate. She looked around, relieved that they were the only ones near the salad bar. "Did you dig that up when you checked me out?"

"I'm a little older than you, Ms. McClean. And thanks to my father, I was reading the paper and paying attention to current events long before most of your contemporaries." Seeming to sense her discomfort, he added, "My lawyer told me. And it was all a long time ago, right?"

She squinted up at him, gauging him. He had maybe ten years on Cassie, but she hadn't expected him to be aware of her family's tragedy, their shame. Her cheeks burned as she turned her attention back to picking out fresh spinach with the salad tongs.

"Yes. It was a long time ago. Fifteen years."

When would she ever get used to the humiliation? After all these years. "But I still don't like to talk about it." She pinched up a few homemade croutons.

He reached across and covered her hand with his large, warm one, right there at the salad bar. She twisted and looked up into his eyes.

"I'm sorry," he murmured. "I shouldn't have mentioned it here." To cover the intimacy of his touch he made a small business of extracting the salad tongs from her fingers. "Thanks."

She turned and went back to the table.

When he joined her, he still seemed apologetic. He spread his napkin in his lap, avoiding her gaze. "You know, I really don't remember all that much about the deal with your dad. I think I saw a small article once in the local paper, that's all. I was in college at the time."

It had been all over the local TV news, on the front page—everywhere Cassie had turned, it seemed. The headline was still emblazoned in her memory. *Mc-Clean Sentenced To Twenty Years.*

"Oh? Where did you go to school?" She had long been adept at deflecting people from the subject of her father's incarceration.

"O.S.U."

"Of course. Animal husbandry?"

Jake shrugged. "It's my life."

"I don't want to harm your mares." She spread her napkin daintily on her lap. "You understand that, don't you?"

"But you don't intend to stop the noise, either. Just give me a little over a month. Just until, say, after Christmas. I can save a foal at ten months."

"Two weeks," she counteroffered, and forked some lettuce.

"Useless."

"Look. I shouldn't have to delay at all. *I* cleared the way—" Cassie's chin jutted forward over her plate "—*I* got the permits, *I* did everything I am legally required to do to continue construction, then *you* come along—"

"The judge is going to make you give me three

weeks, anyway. Why not add another week? I'll give you something in return."

"What? A pony ride? You don't have anything I want!"

"I have a road."

Cassie stared at him. Oh, yes, that stupid road. "I paid for the use of that, too, by the way." She was about to start sputtering, so she stabbed a chunk of salad, instead.

"Do you understand that one Andalusian foal will bring in thirty thousand dollars or more?"

"And do *you* understand what kind of money I'm flushing down the can by delaying for even two weeks?"

The white-haired couple at the table adjacent to theirs turned their heads, then smiled politely and resumed their quiet conversation. Apparently Cassie's and Jake's voices had risen above the babble around them.

They stared at each other, sharing the same stunned question, which Cassie voiced. "How come we keep jumping all over each other like this?"

He shook his head. "Amazing, isn't it? We seem to start out nice and civil and then..."

"And then we end up not so nice and not so civil." Cassie smiled.

"I guess it's because we've both got a lot at stake here," he said reasonably.

Cassie found herself warming to him again. He was an easy man—easy to be with, easy to talk to. "Look," she said. "Neither of us is going to be satisfied with what the judge decides. We might as well come to terms that suit us.''

He nodded.

She chewed a bit of salad, thinking. ''I operate on the principal that this is a win-win world. That there has to be a way to meet everyone's needs.''

''Me, too, more or less, but I'll tell you, Ms. McClean—''

''Cassie.''

He smiled. ''That suits you better than C.J. It's prettier.''

She hoped he realized that her blushing was a totally involuntary response. She foraged in her mind for a solution.

''I've got it!'' She brightened. ''I'll front the money to go ahead and pour Brett Taylor's slab without dipping into his construction loan. He's not ready to start, but a slab can sit there for a while. I'm gonna lose money, anyway, if I don't do *something* to keep things moving. There are so many levels on Brett's house, it'll take two weeks, at least. That'll keep my concrete guys busy. Brett won't mind if I start early, as long as he's not paying interest. He's in Nashville right now, anyway.''

''Brett Taylor? The country-and-western singer?''

''Yes.''

''Man. How do you come by such high-rolling clients?''

''I'm the best,'' she said with quiet assurance.

He gave her an admiring smile. ''I don't doubt that.''

His level gaze disconcerted her. She looked down,

fidgeting with her napkin. "Maybe by the third week—" she wanted to turn the conversation back to their compromise "—I can have my crushers operate every other day, or something. Would that help—letting the mares rest every other day?"

Jake nodded. "It might. Okay. Fair enough. And I'll open the road to you tomorrow and keep it open. Tell you what, I've been needing some rock to shore up the riverbank where there's erosion starting. If you promise to wait until after January first to start the dynamite blasting, I'll haul your red rock over to my place at my expense."

She smiled. That *would* save her some money. "Done."

"Agreed." He extended his hand over the table.

When she took it, Cassie felt an unmistakable spark between them. She slipped her hand away and tried to remember if they'd touched before. Out at the site when Tom got hurt? On the stairs. And there, she'd felt the same…spark. The same magnetism.

He must have felt it, too, because now *he* seemed suddenly uneasy. "Uh, now that that's done—" he forked some potato salad "—what say we try to have ourselves a nice lunch."

CHAPTER FIVE

THE SUN'S RAYS HAD BARELY SPEARED over the top of the Sullivan ridge when a rumbling blast—*berrooom-boom-ba-boom!*—rocked Jake from a deep sleep. Bailadora had not fared well in the night—Jose had awakened Jake twice—and he was exhausted. He sat straight up in bed, semiconsciously rubbing a hand over his eyes, then over his bare chest, wondering if he'd dreamed the disturbance.

But then he heard Donna's high-pitched voice and Dad's low gravelly one, out in the hallway, asking each other what the hell that was. He swung his legs out of bed, jerked on his jeans, padded to the door and yanked it open.

Donna, with a hand pressed to the bosom of her faded university sweatshirt, stood facing Mack in his rumpled pajamas under the weak light of the fixture at the end of the hall. "What in the Lord's name was that?" she asked shakily, as Jake approached them. "I swear, I nearly dropped the coffeepot."

Sudden explosive sounds, frightening under any circumstances, evoked even deeper fears and sad memories for many Oklahomans.

"Everything's okay." Jake put a calming hand on

Donna's shoulder and eyed his father. "Dad, are you okay?"

Mack nodded. "Is it that woman again?" he asked, seeming to have more wits about him at the moment than Donna did.

"What woman, Grandpa?" A sleepy Jayden belatedly emerged from her room. "What was that noise, Daddy? It sounded like an explosion."

"I believe that's what it was, princess." Jake clenched his jaw, fully awake now and realizing exactly what the booming had meant. Had she betrayed him? Why? He planted a reassuring kiss on his daughter's forehead. Her thick, tangled blond mane smelled like some fruity sweet shampoo, and Jake noticed that she slept, these days, in a baggy football jersey she'd probably kiped off some junior-high football hero. She was growing up too fast.

Another blast rocked the house.

Donna gasped, Jayden squealed, and they clutched each other. "That was definitely an *explosion!*" Jayden yelled to no one in particular.

"It's that gol-durned woman!" Mack hitched off toward the kitchen in agitation. "She's blasting that rock out up there!"

The other three caught up to Mack, just as he grabbed the old beige wall phone by the refrigerator.

"Dad." Jake tried to take it from him. "What are you doing?"

"I am calling the sheriff."

"No," Jake grunted, as his dad twisted his wrist away with surprising strength. "Would you give me the dadblame phone?"

Mack released it and Jake banged it into the cradle.

"Dad-dee! What is going on?" Jayden whined. The child rushed to the eight-by-eight black-and-white security monitor on the kitchen shelf as if the cameras outside could show her something. Cottonwood Ranch looked absolutely peaceful.

"I'll take care of this." Jake marched into the adjoining mudroom. "I talked to Ms. McClean yesterday and she agreed not to use the dynamite." He sat on the bench by the back door and pulled on his boots. "Something must have gone wrong. She doesn't strike me as the type to break her word." He grabbed a wrinkled flannel shirt off a hook, then his denim jacket, his cowboy hat. "Dad, *don't* call the sheriff. I will work it out with her. I have her cell phone number and I'll call her after I get to the barn."

"Who is Ms. McClean?" Jayden asked.

"You want some breakfast, Jake?" Donna called out from the stove.

"Thanks, Donna, but no time. I'd better get out to the mares."

CASSIE LOWERED THE SLOSHING COFFEE MUG to the cup holder and shook hot coffee off her fingers. *What the hell?* That was a dynamite blast! She gripped the wheel, stepped on the gas and squinted toward the base of the ridge, where morning shadows stretched and deepened the appearance of the rock formations. Sure enough, a small cloud of dust and smoke dissipated above the area where the red rock-infested lots lay. *Dammit!*

As she raced toward the lots, a second blast rocked the hillside.

At the bottom of the hill she found the men from BlastCat preparing to set another charge. Carpenters who had been headed to work on the upper lots had stopped to watch the show. A couple of them, wearing hard hats, had moved in closer to see how the charge was set.

She braked hard and jumped out, arms waving as she yelled, "Stop!"

The man who was obviously the foreman levered up from one bended knee, holding a long orange-brown stick with a plastic blasting cap already affixed. "Ma'am?" He gave her a wary look. "I'm afraid you can't be up here without a hard hat while we're blasting."

"I am C. J. McClean." When he looked confused by that, Cassie pointed at the logo on the door of her truck. "The owner of Dream Builders? And yesterday, I ordered this blasting postponed."

"But we were told to start at daybreak." The foreman reached in his shirt pocket to extract a folded paper. "I have the work order right here."

"Who signed this?" Cassie snatched the thing.

"The boss, ma'am."

"Didn't he get my fax? A stop order with my signature on it? Don't you people communicate?"

"What fax?"

The faces of the two other guys on the blasting team were starting to shift from confused to disgruntled and the carpenters had started to drift back to work. Cassie hated interrupting subs at work. It was frustrating and made her look disorganized, unprofessional. "I...I know we sent it to your office late yesterday, but...oh, never mind." She shoved the paper back at him.

She signaled the only carpenter still standing around, the one who seemed mesmerized by the dynamite. It was Whitlow, the skinny guy who had been up on the roof the day of Tom Harris's accident. "Whitlow, right?"

"Yes, ma'am. Donny."

"Follow me." Cassie marched to her truck. "Take this—" she pulled the spare key to the trailer from the glove box "—and run down to the trailer and see if there's a copy of a fax on the corkboard. If you find it, bring it right back here."

He stared at the key she'd put in his hand.

"Well, go on, Whitlow," she snapped. "You can take my truck."

"Yes, ma'am." He jumped in the truck, started the engine, killed it, goosed it too hard on the second start and lurched out of the cul-de-sac. She wished she'd sent someone else. That one was wound a little tight.

The BlastCat men were on their knees setting charges again.

"Just stop this operation, right now." Cassie waved her arms. "No more blasting."

The foreman stood...again. "Ma'am, I'll have to call the boss." The foreman took the paper from his pocket...again, and peered at it to verify that he was right. "We've got a schedule to keep."

"Then, call him." Cassie flapped a hand. Who was hiring whom around here?

She paced while the foreman punched the number into his cell phone. He mumbled into the mouthpiece. Cassie paced some more and rubbed her forehead.

"That was the main office. Said they didn't get any fax from Dream Builders. So this'll cost you—to stop today's work like this."

Cassie's jaw dropped. She had left the signed order tacked to the bulletin board in the site trailer. Mel Daugherty had offered to take it back to the office for Mary Lou to fax. That skinny guy, Whitlow, had been there and had heard the whole exchange. All of this had been arranged hastily so that Cassie could get back to the hospital, where Tom was not faring well. The boy had been put back on the ventilator, and Cassie had thought about little else throughout the evening. But Cassie trusted her people, especially Mel, who never dropped the ball, and Mary Lou, who would have had the sense to call BlastCat in person when she saw that stop order. Cassie checked to see that the paper was gone when she'd stopped by the trailer this morning, and she had assumed... Just then, Whitlow roared up in her pickup. He braked to a stop and raised his palms, shaking his head "no." There was no fax.

"Okay. Fine." She had to get down to Cottonwood Ranch and explain this snafu to Jake Coffey. Lord knows what he was thinking about her right now.

"Just go on home," she ordered the crew without looking back.

CASSIE INTERCEPTED Jake Coffey's pickup on the ranch road, tooting her horn for him to stop. They rolled down their windows as they braked their trucks alongside each other.

"I've got to get to my mares, Ms. McClean," he said, his breath puffing out in a cold cloud. He was unshaven and he looked tired and rumpled.

"I didn't do this!" She felt anxious, breathless, trying to explain. "I left clear orders not to blast!"

"It's moot now." His mouth looked pinched.

"Please!" she said quickly before he drove on. "Is there anything I can do to help?"

He gunned the engine of his truck, studying her with a smileless expression from behind his mirrored sunglasses. "I doubt it, but okay, follow me." He put the truck in gear and rolled away.

Cassie did a lurching turnabout and followed him down the bumpy gravel road to a cluster of barns about a quarter of a mile away. When she got out of her truck, the smell of horse manure from a corral assaulted her nostrils.

They entered the largest barn—a low, white metal structure—through a heavy steel door set in next to an enormous overhead garage door. Inside, the dim, cool morning air was disrupted by the sound of nickers and snorts from agitated horses. The place was lit by a few bare bulbs, and when Jake flicked on glaring fluorescent lights, the atmosphere quieted some.

Jake strode down a dirt corridor covered with fine gravel that looked like it had just been raked. Cassie followed him down the long line of stalls to an animal that was butting the boards of her stall. Even Cassie, who knew little about horses, could see that this mare was heavy with foal. The animal was pawing the ground, acting anxious. A short, dark-skinned graying man in overalls and a baseball cap was petting the horse.

Talking to the horse in soft, calming tones, Jake opened the barred door of the stall and disappeared below the bulging side of the mare. The short man followed him.

The horse put her nose against the bars of the stall, seeming to seek comfort, so Cassie slid nervous fingers inside to pet her. The huge nose, which felt like velvet pocked with cactus nettles, huffed and sniffed at Cassie's hand lotion. She smiled, but then the mare became agitated again.

"Looks like she's showing," Cassie heard Jake say from beyond the horse's flank. He didn't sound happy about it, whatever *showing* was.

She heard the other man talking in Spanish. To her surprise, Jake gave a short answer in Spanish.

"Pardon?" Cassie said.

"Means she'll probably deliver," Jake called to her. "She's in labor."

"From feeling only two blasts?" Cassie couldn't believe it.

"From that." Jake's disembodied voice sounded flat, disgusted, as if he was so angry that he couldn't let himself show any emotion. "And from the past three days of constant noise before that." Jake came around the horse, put a lead on her and said, "Excuse me." Then he opened the stall door.

"I'm Jose," the little man said.

"I'm Cassie."

Jake led the horse out, and Jose took off behind

Jake and the horse. "You want to come?" He beckoned Cassie.

Cassie followed...reluctantly. She had no idea how
to assist with a mare in premature labor, but she felt
she had to tough it out as a show of goodwill. No
telling what kind of legal mess this might create.

Jake led the horse to the other end of the barn,
where he tied her in a smaller, tighter box where the
floor was covered in clean straw bedding. Jose had
already brought in some heaters.

With gentle hands and a steady voice, Jake got the
horse down onto her side.

He took a cell phone from the pocket of his jacket,
punched a number and said, "Buck? Got a baby on
the way...'Course I heard it. It woke the whole house
up."

While Jake was placing another call to his veteri-
narian, the mare bolted back up, frightening Cassie
backward. She knew nothing about horses and she felt
like all she could do was wring her hands, but she
still didn't dare leave. She felt responsible for the
horse's condition. She fought down a sick tightening
in her stomach, fearing that maybe she had caused
irreparable harm.

Jose coaxed the mare into lying down again.

A blond child—maybe ten years old, maybe
twelve, Cassie couldn't begin to guess—poked her
head into the doorway at the other end of the barn.
"Daddy?" She pushed the big door open with surprising strength. Under a bulky, pink ski jacket, she
wore plaid pajama bottoms tucked into red cowgirl

boots. "Daddy?" she called again above the horse's frightened whinnying. "Is that Bailadora?"

"Jayden, go back to the house!" Jake ordered.

The child ignored him and rushed headlong into the barn, stumbling over her boots. "Bailadora!" she cried at the door of the box, and threw herself onto her knees in the straw at the thrashing mare's head.

"What's wrong?" she cried to Jake.

"She's foaling, honey."

"Right now?"

"I'm afraid so."

"What'll happen to the baby?"

"I'll do my best to save it."

"Who is that?" She cast a questioning glance up at Cassie, who was standing well outside the confined box.

"A lady from up on the ridge. She wants to help."

The horse huffed, tossed her head and then screeched out a series of frenzied neighs that twisted Cassie's gut.

"I'm calling Mom!" To Cassie's amazement, the child whipped a pink cell phone out of her jacket and punched a number. "Mom! Bailadora's foaling! Can you come?"

The horse struggled for another thirty interminable minutes, screaming in pain. Jake continued to try to calm her, managing a perfunctory introduction of Cassie and Jayden before an engine roared up outside the barn. A car door slammed and a tall, stunning blonde in knee-high boots, skintight jeans, and a red down vest burst through the open door.

"Mom!" Jayden jumped up and ran to the woman.

The woman hugged Jayden and shot Cassie a wary glance, then her eyes focused on the horse.

"Dammit!" she said, and pushed at Jake's shoulder. "Bailadora! Baby! What happened to her?" The accusing question was directed at Jake, but Cassie answered.

"I'm responsible." She stepped forward. "My crews started blasting with dynamite—"

"*Dynamite?* Who are *you?*" The tone of Lana's question made it perfectly clear that Cassie's presence here was suspect.

"She's that builder who set off the dynamite and did this to Bailadora!" Jayden exclaimed. "Grandpa told me." With her mother's attitude to embolden her, the child fixed a denouncing, indignant stare on Cassie. "He said he is spittin' mad at you!"

Cassie focused on the tall woman, who stood with her hand resting on the child's shoulder. "I'm C. J. McClean, from up on The Heights." Instinct warned her not to extend her hand. This woman exuded trouble.

"The *Heights?*"

"The Sullivan ridge," Jake explained tiredly. Above the horse's pained whinnies, his voice carried a rising note of impatience.

"Yes. It's my development up on the old Sullivan land. As I started to explain, the crews were removing embedded red rock with dynamite—"

"Contrary to your instructions," Jake interrupted. "This mare is in advanced labor, Lana, and all we can do now is try to save the foal."

Lana stripped off her vest, and while she rolled up her sleeves she skewered Cassie with an angry glare.

"I'm sorry. I didn't catch your name," Cassie said levelly. She wanted to know what interest this woman had in this situation, although she could guess. The child had called her "Mom."

"I am Lana Largeant Coffey, and if my foal dies, Dream Builders will pay."

Dream Builders? Cassie was certain she hadn't said the name of her company. An uncomfortable feeling crept up her neck. It occurred to her that this woman had become hostile entirely too quickly. Of course, there were signs posted out at the addition. But they were small and discreet, not something you could see from the highway. This Lana Largeant *Coffey* would have to drive up the hill to see the signs. But Cassie didn't have time to worry about why Lana would go out of her way to check out Cassie's operation. A foal was about to be born.

THE FOAL DIED.

A man named Buck Winfrey arrived. The vet arrived. And though everyone worked to save that expensive little foal, the baby was just too small, too weak, too early.

When the tiny front hooves poked out, wrapped in what the vet called the *caul,* Cassie thought she might be sick. She pressed a hand over her mouth, fighting down nausea.

At the mare's head, Lana kept the horse calm as the foal quickly birthed. Cassie had to admire the woman's confidence and skill. In one quick slip, as if the baby were diving out, the nose, forelegs, head and shoulders appeared. Jake maneuvered the back legs free, and broke the membrane around the nose, but Cassie could see no sign of life, no effort to breathe. Buck started the heaters in the area, and Lana and Jake dried the foal with towels, talking to it, willing it to live. "Come on, baby, come on, sweetheart," Jake repeated over and over.

"Are its feet okay?" Cassie mumbled without realizing she had spoken out loud. The soft fingerlike projections jutting from the sole of the foal's hooves looked wrong—grotesque—to her.

"That's normal," the vet said in a quiet voice near her shoulder. "Those bumps protect the mare's uterus from injury, and they go away as soon as the baby stands up."

"But this foal's not gonna stand up." Lana looked up from the limp baby, sending a blaming glare Cassie's way.

"Jayden." Jake seemed to be the only one who remembered that the child, deathly quiet, was still there. "Why don't you go back to the house now?"

"No."

The child's parents exchanged a long-suffering look.

"I am Doctor Toomley." The vet, a pleasant-looking young man, fixed an attentive stare on Cassie.

Jake glanced up, and Cassie crossed her arms over her middle, feeling like she could stand anybody's accusatory look right now except his. "I guessed as much," she said to the vet, hoping he would stop looking at her.

"And you are?" the vet asked.

"Nobody. I'm just a...neighbor."

Lana sent more daggers Cassie's way, and the vet looked back and forth between the two women, puzzled.

Things got quiet—it was as if the mare had given up—and Jake continued to swab the foal's nostrils, though other than an occasional involuntary shiver, there were no signs of life in the small body.

Lana and Buck worked to keep the mare lying down.

The vet explained what was going on to Cassie. "We have to leave the cord alone so the blood goes into the foal. If Bailadora stands, she'll tear it."

Cassie gave him a sick wince and a nod, and he smiled engagingly.

Cassie was more than a little annoyed with this guy. As far as she could tell, this vet seemed to think he was here to expound on science and flirt with her. Jake and his ranch hands...and his ex-wife were doing all the work.

The vet did step forward long enough to cut the cord and pronounce the foal "a loss," and that's when Jayden started to cry. The child's mother gave Cassie one more accusing scowl before she jumped up and spirited her daughter out of the barn.

"I'm so sorry," Cassie said later, when she was finally alone with Jake in the barn. The place was quiet now, except for the chirping of birds, flitting overhead in the rafters. He was stooped over, ministering to the mare, and Cassie was speaking to his back.

"It happens," he said without looking up. "But

not to my mares.'' He sighed as he put fresh water in front of the mare, coaxing her to drink.

''Your daughter seemed so upset,'' Cassie observed sadly. The guilt over this whole mess was killing her. It seemed she had guilt mounted upon guilt mounted upon guilt these days. How could she ever have imagined that building her dream would cause so much damage?

''She's seen a foal born before, but she's never seen one die. Jayden's a good kid, but she's a little high-strung.'' Jake stood and spread a blanket over the mare. ''She gets it from her mother, I think. Both of them love their horses.''

''Your wife—''

''Ex-wife.''

''Your ex-wife,'' Cassie corrected, ''seemed to have some investment in this foal.''

''Any foals from Bailadora belong to her after they're weaned. It's part of our settlement. In Lana's mind, she lost about thirty thousand dollars this morning.''

''And in your mind?'' Which was all Cassie really cared about.

''There is always a risk. A mare can lose a foal for a lot of reasons. Lana knows there are no guarantees.''

''I see.'' But Cassie worried. What would this woman do if she thought that the dynamite blasting alone had caused her foal to die? More legal trouble, undoubtedly, lay ahead. She made a mental note to track down that fax. It might be crucial in proving that she had tried to stop the blasting.

"You look pale." Jake, still squatting beside the mare, was observing her over his shoulder.

"I'm all right. I've just never seen anything like this before."

"It's not always like this." Jake stood. "Most of my foals are born healthy, they stand, they nurse. Some even arrive out in the paddock, if it's warm enough."

Cassie nodded, her eyes fixed on Bailadora. She had seen the foals with their mothers, during the long months when she had been getting the addition prepared for construction. They were beauties, with shiny coats and strong, frisky legs. And now, because of her, one of those beautiful little creatures was dead.

CHAPTER SIX

CASSIE NEVER DID find that fax.

She ransacked the small fifth-wheel trailer that she had installed at The Heights to serve as a construction headquarters. She checked the clutter of papers on the pop-up table she used as a desk. She checked inside all the compact cabinets, in the trash can, even under the miniature sink. She looked behind the stained coffeemaker, underneath her dusty laptop, inside her briefcase. She unrolled three sets of plans to see if the fax had ended up there, even peering down inside the cardboard tubes.

The bulletin board she had installed over the table was bare except for a scrawled note from Darrell Brown reminding her to pay Precision Stone for extra materials by the end of the week. She even looked in the small airplane-washroom-size bathroom. Nothing.

When she asked Mel, the framing sub, what happened to it, he looked perplexed. He said he'd gone to the trailer to get it after his crew had knocked off for the day, just like he told her he would, but he found nothing on the bulletin board, except the note from Darrell.

Cassie stared up at the second story of the house

where Whitlow was hammering listlessly at a brace. "I don't suppose he'd know anything about it."

"Him? That boy ain't all there, if you ask me."

"Ask him."

He turned to the skinny man. "Donny! You went in the trailer with me. Did you see a paper on the bulletin board?"

The young man gave Cassie an unpleasant squint and shook his head.

"Where's my spare trailer key?" Cassie hollered up, suddenly remembering that the kid still had it.

Whitlow hooked his hammer into his leather tool belt and started fishing in his pockets. After he'd dug in each one twice, he shrugged and called down, "Sorry, ma'am. I guess I lost it."

Mel shrugged, too. "Told you he ain't all there," he muttered. "Sorry about that fax, too. I just figured you'd taken care of it yourself."

A couple of Mel's men who were standing nearby had stilled their hammers and listened in while Cassie was questioning him and going on about the importance of the fax. The death of the foal due to the blasting became the intermittent gossip among the construction crews for the rest of the day. When Mel Daugherty had casually informed Cassie that there had even been some light betting that C. J. McClean and that horse rancher fella "were fixin' to mix it up again," she had snapped the poor man's head off.

"Jake Coffey and I are not about to 'mix it up.'" Cassie drew a frustrated breath, gaining control. "Don't you men have more interesting things to talk about?"

"No, ma'am—" Mel grinned "—not really." Under her unsmiling gaze, his grin dissolved into a frown. "Aren't you kinda worried about what Coffey will do now?"

"No. I am not."

But, in truth, Cassie *was* worried. What if Jake or his ex-wife filed a lawsuit for damages, as the judge had suggested?

But Jake Coffey didn't file any suit. He remained true to his word. The next day, concrete trucks were allowed to pass over the Cottonwood Ranch road, as promised.

The circle drive and the slab for Brett Taylor's three-car garage were poured by sunset on the second day. Feeling the need for the satisfaction of seeing something completed, Cassie drove to the upper cul-de-sac to inspect the results. The men had already left. Good. She desperately needed some peace and quiet. She got out of her truck and took a moment to appreciate the stirring sunset that reached into the vast sky with long fingers of electric red and atomic orange.

When the rays had faded to a quiet blush, she trudged up the lot, skirting the edge of the freshly finished driveway. The surface looked perfect. But when she got to the garage slab, her mouth dropped in horror. The once-smoothed expanse of concrete was a complete mess—churned up, full of... hoofprints! Had a deer wandered in from the woods? She swiveled her head, looking for the offending beast.

She knelt to test the firmness of the concrete. Crap!

Set hard already. It was expensive as hell to jackhammer set concrete out, and if they took out only part of it, she knew Brett Taylor would not appreciate ragged seams in the floor of his dream house, even in the garage. She inspected the damage. These hoofprints were bigger than a deer's.

Behind her, from out of the woods, a horse's neigh echoed. She walked cautiously in the direction of the sound. Before long she spotted the animal, a massive, solid white horse—a stallion?—with his hooves caked in concrete up to the fetlocks. His graceful form strobed in and out of the black tree trunks, looking like some kind of ghost.

"Whoa, boy." She extended her hand and inched toward him, but the horse gave her the eye, whinnied and galloped off through the trees.

She took off downhill after him, running and dodging brush until she grew winded and was forced to slow and follow his tracks down the remainder of the slope. The path led her straight to a section of downed V-mesh fence…Cottonwood Ranch fence. The horse had already gone back through the opening, trotting away in the distance, across a huge open field. Farther off, Cassie saw the barn where she had stood only two days ago, feeling so guilty.

She inspected the fence. A human, not a horse, had definitely done this—she flicked the severed ends of the V-mesh wire with her leather glove—with a simple pair of pliers or wire cutter. In places, she saw boot prints—the wire had been stomped down into the mud. Who could have intentionally let that horse out where it would do so much damage? Why would anyone do that? Jayden Coffey's angry young face came to mind, but the boot prints were much too large for a child's, too large for a woman's, in fact. That ruled out the hostile ex-wife. And Jake—Cassie couldn't imagine that man doing something underhanded. Everything she'd seen of Jake Coffey so far told her he was completely honorable.

Nevertheless, she would have to get to the bottom of this sabotage and protect her interests. She walked back up the slope, using her cell phone to notify the cops.

ON HER SECOND TRIP up the Cottonwood Ranch driveway, Cassie felt angry, sad…and very confused. If this farm had belonged to anybody but Jake Coffey, she'd be calling her newly retained lawyer instead of coming down here to find out Jake's side of the story.

A heavy-set woman with unnaturally black hair answered the door. The competent cook, Cassie supposed.

The woman tilted her curly dark head and smiled. "Hello."

"Is Mr. Coffey here?"

"Both of them are." The woman spoke with a pleasant, kindly tone.

"Oh. Yes." Cassie bit her lip. "I meant Jake."

The woman smiled. "May I tell him who's here?"

"Cassie McClean."

The woman's pleasant face clouded, ever so slightly. "Oh. Ms. McClean from up on the ridge. I see. Would you…would you like to come in?"

The woman stepped back, and Cassie entered a

spacious ranch-style living room. The atmosphere was clean but sparse and masculine, with comfortable-looking, functional tan-and-brown furnishings arranged for easy conversation. The drapes, a yellowed oak-leaf pattern, looked like they'd been hanging at the huge picture window for several decades.

"Make yourself comfortable. I'll get Jake." The woman disappeared down a short hallway lined with oak wainscotting. The homey aroma of simmering chili wafted from that direction, reminding Cassie that she was starving.

Jake appeared in no time, clutching a paper napkin with chili stains on it. "Cassie?" he said.

She folded her arms. "I think, if you'll check out in your northeast pasture, you'll find you've got a stallion with concrete all over his hooves."

Jake frowned. *"What?"*

"One of your horses—a big white one?—got out onto my property and made a fine mess of a freshly poured slab of concrete."

"Arrestado?" Jake mumbled. Then he frowned at Cassie. "But I don't keep horses up in the northeast pasture. We grow feed out there."

Cassie sighed. "He's out there. I chased him myself. And what's more, someone intentionally cut down the section of fence that he came through."

"Somebody cut my fence?" Jake scratched his head. "I don't get it."

"You need to talk to your men. Some guy's boot prints are all over the place. I'm sorry, but I'm going to have to have the police investigate this."

"Of course. Do whatever you have to do." Jake

seemed distracted. "But I can't imagine that anybody from Cottonwood Ranch would let a horse get out, for Pete's sake. Certainly not Arrestado."

"I hate to say it, but what about—" Cassie leaned toward him and softened her voice "—your father?"

Jake frowned. "Oh, come on. You don't think this was intentional—because of the foal?"

"I don't know what to think. Your daughter did say your dad was angry at me."

He shook his head. "Even in his addled state, Dad wouldn't do anything destructive. Besides, it would be physically impossible. Dad can't drive anymore, not even the golf cart. And he couldn't possibly walk that far."

Cassie sighed. "Well, it's pretty clear somebody did this on purpose. I've gotta get back up there. The cops are coming out from town. They said it would be thirty minutes or so."

"I'm going with you."

"That's not necessary. This is my problem."

"And it's my fence," he countered calmly, "and my horse."

THEY PULLED OVER in the pasture, and Jake whistled for the horse. The stallion, still not that far from Cassie's land, galloped up to Jake like a kid expecting candy.

"Stay back," Jake warned. "A stallion will bite a human, particularly a woman."

Cassie stood back with her hands jammed in the pockets of her jacket, while Jake approached the horse. Once he got ahold of the bit, he slipped the animal a sugar cube out of his pocket, then he ran his hands over the animal and inspected his concrete-encrusted hooves.

Despite her anger over the destruction the animal had done, Cassie had to admit that he was a fine specimen. He had a highly intelligent turn of his head, and large, kind eyes. He seemed to enjoy Jake's attention and stood remarkably still for the examination.

"The grass wiped most of the cement off." Jake sounded relieved. "But I'll have to take him back and clean these hooves soon." Jake raised his head, looking in the distance, surveying the perimeter of the pasture. "What the hell—excuse my French—is Arrestado doing way out here?" He seemed to be talking to himself, not Cassie. "We did run him with a couple of maiden mares in that north paddock over there—a stallion that runs with his mares has a higher fertility rate than one who covers in hand."

Cassie realized he was addressing this last remark to her. "Covers in hand?" she said to show that she was listening.

"Uh, you know. Mates under a trainer's supervision. My thoroughbreds cannot be artificially inseminated, anyway, and Arrestado had a taste of a real mare early on, so I just got rid of the dummy mare."

"Dummy mare?"

"Never mind." Now Jake's cheeks pinkened.

"So you had him running wild in order to... mate?" Cassie felt her cheeks heating up more, but she found this fascinating.

But Jake didn't seem to notice. "No, just to give him ideas." He looked off in the distance, pensive.

"I suppose he could have followed a mare up here. Did you see another horse?"

Cassie shook her head.

"Well, the important thing is, he's okay. Let's see the downed fence before it gets too dark."

They drove as far as they could, then climbed the hill together and found the hole in the fence where it adjoined Cassie's property.

"Those are human footprints, all right," Jake agreed.

"I want the police to take castings," Cassie stated.

"Absolutely. I want proof that my people didn't do this. Let's see the damage."

"Who else would have any reason to destroy my slab?" Cassie argued, as they picked their way through the underbrush toward the building lot.

"You haven't had a run-in with anybody like environmentalists or such? There was another builder out on the highway who had a little trouble with the horny toad folks."

"The *horny* toad folks?" Cassie looked skeptical.

"The fields around here are the horned toad's natural habitat." Jake moved a low limb aside for her. "The little guys each need about two acres to scurry around on, looking for females and food, sorta like every other guy on the planet, I guess." He smiled.

Cassie didn't. Her cheeks hadn't stopped burning from his previous reference to mating.

Jake cleared his throat. "Anyway, some graduate students from O.S.U. came out here once to study the effect of grazing on the horny toads. Some people from the Horned Lizard Conservation Society got into the act. They were a little pushy, as I recall. Wanted us to stop using pesticides before all the facts were in. But the O.S.U. guys proved that with pesticides, you get more crops, thus more grazing. More grazing means less grass and more seed-producing annuals, so you have more harvester ants—the staple of the horny toad diet."

Cassie turned a quizzical look on him. She'd lost something in the translation.

Jake smiled. "Simple math for the horny toad. More food. More females."

Cassie favored him with a tight grin. "How nice for the horny toad."

Jake cleared his throat again. "Yeah. Anyway, they decided the sprawl of development was a bigger threat than our horse-grazing practices. They really don't like to see new developments going in around the habitat."

"Even so, environmentalists doing this kind of damage? Seems a bit far-fetched."

"You're right, but I'm telling you, this isn't the work of anyone on Cottonwood Ranch. Arrestado could have been hurt, getting tangled up in the fence or getting mired in concrete and twisting a knee. Nobody would do that to him. He stands to stud better than any other show stallion in the country."

Cassie could hear the unadorned pride in his voice, and she clearly understood that he didn't like this trouble any more than she did. "What about your ex-wife?" Cassie hated to imply it. Or did she? She really did not like that woman. "Would she resort to sabotage?"

"Lana?" Jake's voice changed—Cassie could hear the doubt there, and a creeping edge of something like fear. "Lana has been a little unstable in the past. But...this? I doubt it. Anybody else upset with you? What about that Spirit Tribe bunch?"

"The Spirit Tribe?" As soon as Cassie turned to say it, she stumbled into a gopher hole.

Jake lurched forward, catching her arm with both hands. "You okay?" he said.

"I think so." She massaged her knee. *Except for the fact that every time you touch me, my skin feels electrified.*

He looked down at his hands, still on her, and released her as if reading her mind.

Silence stretched, while around them the quiet sounds of evening in the woods punctuated the moment of contact. They stood with their breaths mingling, creating fog in the cool evening air of autumn, emphasizing just how closely they stood, alone together in these woods.

Cassie stepped back. "Thank you." She cleared her throat.

"Sure." Jake cleared his. "Let's be careful out here. It's getting pretty dark." He took a penlight out of the pocket of his jacket and flicked it on.

Cassie turned to continue the trek uphill. "So, what is the Spirit Tribe, and what do they have to do with me?"

"The Spirit Tribe is a Native American activist group, mostly students over at the university. They raised a stink over this land once before, back when the Sullivan sisters owned it. I kinda think that may

be why Helen and Caroline never did build anything
out here.''

"Hmm." Cassie searched her memory. "Matter of
fact, I believe that's the group that contacted me when
I first bought the land. But they used some lawyer.
Ben Morehead. They wanted to stop me from building houses up here, specifically on Brett's lot. Said it
was an old Pottawatomie burial ground.''

"Man. You have certainly had your legal battles
over this place.''

She turned to him. "Nothing worth doing right is
easy.''

Even in the gathering gloom, she saw his raised
eyebrow and his mouth that turned down in a faint,
ironic smile. "Well, now, some things worth doing
are easy...or at least they should be.''

Cassie faced back uphill and was grateful for the
darkness, because she could feel her cheeks heating
up again. Was it her imagination or had he been awfully suggestive with her this whole time? She told
herself she had probably taken a perfectly innocent
remark and sexualized it. She'd been having a lot of
these thoughts lately, ever since she met this man.

When they reached the lot at the top, they stopped
to rest. Then Cassie pointed. "Over here.''

Jake fanned the beam of his flashlight over the ruined concrete.

"Hardened already?" He stopped and stooped,
putting a hand out to test it.

"I'm afraid so." Cassie sighed.

"I'm sorry." He stood and faced her.

"We seem to be saying that to each other a lot lately."

He smiled. "Well, I guess it's better than saying, 'To hell with you.'"

She laughed. "Yeah."

They studied the concrete.

"Fourteen hundred pounds of freaked-out horse can sure do a lot of damage."

"I have no intention of making you pay for this," she offered, "since you aren't going to hold me accountable for the lost foal."

"I told you I won't. You said you tried to stop the blasting. Besides, the mare could have miscarried for other reasons. The foal was born dead, technically. It never tried to stand."

Cassie was suddenly grateful that the annoying vet had been present.

"But there's no telling what Lana might do," Jake said.

"You don't think she's behind this?" Cassie waved the flashlight.

Jake sighed from the depths of his broad chest, and Cassie sensed a great sorrow in him.

"I suppose she could have ordered one of her daddy's men to do it."

"Is she a vindictive person?"

"Sometimes. And jealous."

"Jealous?"

"Yeah. Of you. I think she can sense that I'm attracted to you. It wouldn't be the first time she went on the attack because I'd shown interest in a woman."

Cassie stood stock-still, heart drumming with this sudden knowledge. He *was* attracted to her! She'd sensed it, of course, but could hardly believe it. A very handsome man—a nice, decent, hardworking, *sexy* man—was attracted to her! She wanted to go off whooping through the woods like a banshee, but instead she stood there, very still, trying to be cool, trying to think of something to say. *It doesn't have to be clever,* she told her stubbornly wooden mind, *just something normal will do.* But nothing came. Finally, she closed her gaping mouth and said, "Well."

"And I am very interested in you," he encouraged. "I mean, I'd like to get to know you."

She looked down, aiming the flashlight at her ugly, muddy work boots. In her worn, grimy overalls, she felt as plain as the dirt clods at her feet. What to say? Oh, heavens, what to say?

"What do you think?" he asked after he'd let her study the ground for a couple of moments.

"Well," she repeated.

He was getting exasperated, she could feel it—or maybe that was just her inbred reaction to her father's perpetual impatience. She looked up, checking his mien. He was smiling, and, in fact, looking as patient as a saint.

"I...I think...okay. I'd like that—to get to know you, too, that is. That would be nice, in fact." She smiled, but immediately frowned. "But not now. Well, I mean, how should we do this? I mean, I'm so busy. You're so busy. Do you want to call me? Do you want to go somewhere, like, right now? Oh, but I can't. I'm...I'm dressed in my work clothes." She plucked at the bib of her overalls while her mind screamed, *Shut up!* Sheesh. She hadn't been able to find her tongue a second ago and now she couldn't stop babbling.

He was still smiling, thank goodness. Down the hill, the blue and red of a squad car's lights flashed as it bounced off the entrance gates to The Heights.

Jake turned his head. "Here come the police. Why don't we just go on a date soon? I'll call you."

"A date?" Cassie repeated. He shot her a curious look, and she realized she'd said the word as if it were a death sentence. It wasn't the idea of a date that scared her. She'd had her share. What was mind-boggling was the idea of going on a date with Jake Coffey. This was happening so fast! "Uh, okay," she amended, "call me."

The police officer, a patrol cop, did not want to call a lab guy all the way out to the country to make plaster castings of the footprints.

"I insist on it," Cassie asserted. "I want to know who did this."

"It's a waste of time. They book the castings into evidence and nobody even looks at them. Nine times out of ten, these vandals are juveniles and you can't prosecute them, anyway." The cop was scribbling on a clipboard.

"Look." Jake stepped up, his chest puffed. "The lady wants the castings done and so do I. We both pay plenty of taxes. I know the mayor. Do I have to call Stu Largeant at home to see that this gets done?"

The cop called the lab guy.

"You do keep those for a while, don't you?" Cassie badgered when the job was done.

In the glare of the alley lights, Cassie caught the sidelong glance the cop gave the lab guy, as if she were a gigantic pain.

"Yes, ma'am. We keep them until the case is solved."

"I've had a string of weird incidents out here, and I'm starting to suspect sabotage," Cassie explained.

"Yes, ma'am," the cop repeated with extreme patience, as if he had his doubts, about the incidents and about her.

But Cassie didn't have doubts. Her housing development was definitely being sabotaged.

And from the worried look on Jake Coffey's face, she could tell he shared her dark suspicions.

CHAPTER SEVEN

THE FOLLOWING WEDNESDAY Cassie was again heading out at sundown to check the final finish work on the first level of Brett Taylor's enormous slab. The garage floor was still being jackhammered out.

She got detained—always frustrating—when she stopped at the trailer. And tonight, especially, she had little patience for this delay because she had another date with Jake—her third since Friday. An ordinary movie on Saturday. An ordinary dinner out Sunday. And then it seemed like he wanted her with him all the time.

Tonight she was going to sit up in the bleachers with him at his daughter's volleyball game. Even sitting in a noisy junior-high gym sounded good when she was going to do it with Jake. He was funny and charming and warm and witty. And he was a killer of a kisser.

He'd asked what she was doing for Thanksgiving tomorrow. Cassie hated to tell him her dismal plans. For Cassie, holidays were long, aimless reminders of how sad and empty her life would be without the distraction of Dream Builders. Tomorrow she would endure her aunt's incompetent cooking, eating the dry turkey and lumpy gravy that Rosemarie insisted on

making every year. Then they'd box up some of the
food and make the obligatory trip to the minimum
security correctional facility in Mayer, two hours
away. Boss would eat, claiming it was delicious. They
would give him his holiday cigar, make small talk for
an hour, and drive back to Jordan with the sun sinking
at their backs. Cassie would drop off her aunt and
return to her big, empty house after dark, thoroughly
depressed.

But before the Thanksgiving break, there were urgent material orders to sign and a revised contract
with the framing sub to complete. Mel was waiting
in the trailer and wanted his answer right away. Everything in the construction business was an emergency.

By the time Cassie drove her truck up the hill to
the far cul-de-sac, the sun had tipped low behind the
distant trees along the river off in the west. She dug
out her big halogen flashlight from behind the seat.
The men had gone. Normally, Cassie liked to wander
around a jobsite when it was quiet, deserted. That
ritual was always, for her, a moment of satisfying
peace in an otherwise hectic day. Now, the quiet
made her uneasy.

Somewhere at the bottom of the cul-de-sac, Sugar
and Brutus, her two Doberman pinscher guard dogs,
were prowling around. She reminded herself that she
could always whistle for them if she needed them.

And nothing had gone amiss for a week. Tom Har-
ris had finally woken up and had talked to his mother.
He was showing signs of feeling in his legs—thank
God. She hadn't heard a peep out of Lana Largeant—

or her lawyers. The red rock was coming out of the hillside, albeit slowly, and being dumped truckload after truckload along Jake's area of the riverbank, just as they'd planned. Things were looking up.

She jumped out of the truck, switching on the light to cast irregular black shadows over the muddy ruts and litter left by the concrete crew.

The postdusk chilliness had already set in, and as she picked her way across the lot, she regretted having left her jacket in the truck. But this was just going to be a quick check. She hoped it didn't freeze tonight. The last thing she needed was six thousand square feet of concrete going to scald.

As she got to the top of the driveway, her steps slowed, then halted completely as the shock hit her.

Oh, God. Not again.

She panned the light over the damage. Someone, *someone*—but who?—had vandalized this slab, too.

She looked over her shoulder into the dark woods and shuddered. Not from cold this time, but from genuine fear. She put her fingers to her teeth and sent up a piercing whistle for Brutus and Sugar. She knelt to test the set of the concrete. Still warm and damp, but definitely setting up.

She fumbled with shaking fingers in the bib of her overalls, and when she finally retrieved her cell phone, she clutched it for dear life. She dialed Jake's number.

"Hello?" For some paradoxical reason, his calm, quiet voice brought forth her tears of fear.

"Jake—?" she choked.

"Cassie? What's wrong?"

"It's happened again."

"What? What's happened?"

The huge dogs bounded up, barking and bumping against her legs protectively, making her voice quake. "The concrete...someone tore into my freshly poured...concrete again." As she said this, she fanned the halogen light over the damage—sticks, cola cans, the white plastic debris the plumbers had left, all jammed into the semiset slab.

"Oh, no. Not again—" Cassie's sharp gasp interrupted him.

"Cassie! Sweetheart!" he shouted. "Are you okay?"

"Yes, I am. But...but, oh, Jake. This is really creepy. There's something written in the concrete. Can you come up here?"

"I'll be right there. Are you alone?"

"Yes. But I've got the dogs." Her teeth had started to chatter slightly, but she hoped Jake couldn't detect the fear in her voice. Her panic wouldn't help anything.

"Do I need to call 9-1-1?"

"No. I'll do it. I'm okay and the damage is done."

"Get back in your truck and lock the doors. I'll be right there."

"Th-thanks." She punched off.

She calmed the dogs, made them sit on the ground next to the truck, then climbed inside.

But Brutus and Sugar didn't sit still for long. No sooner had she locked the doors than the two massive dogs jumped up, sinewy bodies taut and ears erect as they barked toward the woods behind the slab.

Cassie started her engine and flashed the headlights on bright. She backed up the truck and pulled forward to aim the lights directly at the spot where the dogs focused their attention. She saw nothing—no movement, no unusual shadow, nothing. But the woods were dense, deep and dark. And the hair on the back of her neck and goose bumps all over her arms told her those woods were not unoccupied.

Anyone could be hiding out there. She revved the engine. The dogs stopped barking but held their alert pose. If the dogs really sensed a prowler, a threatening presence, surely they would charge, even though they were trained only to surround an intruder, never to physically attack.

She kept her eyes glued on the trees while she fumbled on the seat for her cell phone. She only flicked her glance down long enough to find the 9 and the 1.

Oh, Jake, she pleaded, while she waited for the operator to answer, *please hurry.*

JAKE DIDN'T THINK he had ever moved so fast. He found his keys, grabbed his jacket and hollered for Donna.

Donna came bursting into his office, bug-eyed at the unusual sound of Jake yelling.

"Cassie's got a problem," he explained as he brushed past her. "Tell Jayden we might be a bit late for the game, okay?"

Donna nodded. "What's happened?"

"Some more vandalism up on The Heights."

When he got to his pickup, he dug his cell phone out of the clutter on the seat and redialed Cassie.

"Cassie! Stay on the line with me," he ordered. "Why are the dogs barking?"

"I don't know! I thought maybe they heard or saw something, but they won't charge. They're just standing here beside the truck, barking every now and then."

Cassie stared up at the rising lot and the dark wall of woods beyond. An enormous yellow moon had mounted the ridge, lighting the damage, making the message that had been scrawled with a large stick across the concrete seem all the more ominous. Deciphering it, Cassie's mind kept flashing back to Jake's ex-wife and the dead foal. Surely the woman wasn't *this* twisted.

Finally the dogs broke stance and bounded into the woods, but in no time they returned, completely docile.

Cassie was reassured by the continuous whine of Jake's pickup engine as he shifted and roared up the gravel road.

"Are you inside your truck?" he said.

"Yes." She was gunning the engine, with the heater blower on full blast. The warmth was reassuring.

"You called the cops?"

"Yes."

"Tell me what happened," he said.

"You'll just have to see it."

HE WAS EXTRAORDINARILY QUIET, even for Jake, as he surveyed the mess. "Man—" he released a pent-up breath "—somebody was working fast."

"Yeah. But this isn't the worst part. Come here." Cassie took his hand and led him to the disturbing message. She didn't let go of him—only squeezed his fingers tighter as she panned the pale light over the large letters that had been scrawled in the wet concrete.

U Die 2.

Jake reached up and pulled her to him, pressing her head into his warm shoulder. And she let him. Nothing had ever felt so good as being enfolded by his strong arms and held against his broad chest. She started to tremble and he hugged her tighter.

"You die, too," she whispered, and squeezed her eyes shut. "Do you think there's someone out there who actually wants me to die?"

"Why do you think this is meant for you?" He said it softly.

"Who else could they mean?"

"Maybe this is about Brett Taylor." His voice took on a note of hope. "He's awfully famous. Maybe he's drawn himself a stalker. That's kind of common. I even had one once. A woman stalker can be as sick, as scary, as any man."

"You had a stalker?" Cassie tilted her face up. This startling revelation momentarily distracted her from her own problems.

"Yes. A few years ago. When Jayden was nine. Shortly after my divorce. I was lonely and not too bright about women. I still thought pretty on the outside meant pretty on the inside."

"What happened?"

"Nothin'. I told her to get lost like I meant it." He

frowned down at her. He hadn't taken the time to put on his ever-present cowboy hat, and in the light of the rising moon, the shape of his uncovered head looked incredibly masculine. "Right now—" he traced gentle fingers along her cheek "—I'm worried about you. You're shaking." He opened his jacket and wrapped her inside.

Cassie could hear his heart drumming as she rested her ear against his chest. She wasn't sure she'd ever heard another person's heartbeat, not like this. Not the way his sounded, as if each steady beat was communicating something important to her. His strength. His concern. Breathing in his clean, masculine scent calmed her enormously.

"The police will be here soon." His voice reverberated through his chest.

Cassie wanted to stay in his arms forever, but she had to face this situation. She eased herself away. "Yes." She sighed and smoothed her ponytail. "I only hope they kept that plaster casting from last week."

They had. And Cassie tried not to be too bossy with the cops this time, though her anxiety level had risen by several notches.

Jake stayed through the whole ordeal. The police secured the crime scene. Collected evidence. Took more plaster castings. Questioned Cassie. Questioned *him.*

The patrol cop who had answered the first call had actually sauntered over to Jake's pickup and said, "You seem to be around every time we get called out here, Mr. Coffey. What's the deal?"

Jake hooked his arm over the edge of the window. "I didn't scrawl a death threat in the lady's concrete, if that's what you mean," he answered dryly.

"I didn't say you did. I just wondered what you're doing up here."

"Ms. McClean called me when she discovered this." Jake jerked a thumb toward the slab.

"You know her well?"

No, Jake had to admit he didn't know her all that well. Attraction was not the same as knowing. But he did have a feeling about this woman. She certainly had strength and decency and heart. He'd seen all that for himself. And on their few dates so far, her personality had delighted him, enchanted him.

"We're friends." He wished he could claim they were more.

The cop crossed his arms over his chest and frowned at his shoes. "Seems to me, if somebody did this damage after the crew left but before the concrete was dry, they had to be, you know, kind of waiting in the wings. The timing's pretty suspicious."

"What are you saying?" Jake hated subtlety, hated mind games.

"Has Ms. McClean mentioned any financial difficulties to you?"

"Huh?"

"You know, wanting to collect insurance money, anything like that?"

"You're insinuating that she sabotaged her own property?"

"No. Just trying to look at every angle."

"If you really want all the angles, maybe you

should check out a group that calls themselves the Spirit Tribe.''

"The Spirit Tribe?''

"That radical group of Native American students that staged a protest with drums and dancers after the teepee incident over at the university?''

The cop nodded. "I remember.''

"They've committed little acts of vandalism before, haven't they?''

"Threw some paint around over at the university, as I recall. What have they got to do with this?''

"They tried to stop Ms. McClean from building on this site months ago. They claim this is an old Pottawatomie burial ground. As soon as Cassie started doing the work on this particular lot, the trouble started.''

"That's not what she said.'' The policeman jerked his head toward Cassie, who was walking the edge of the slab with the other officer. "She said the trouble started the day *you* came up the hill.''

WHEN THE POLICE HAD FINISHED their work it was late, and Jake walked Cassie over to her truck. Without the high-wattage alley lights on the patrol cars, the addition was pitch-dark except for Cassie's flashlight.

"Are you okay now?'' Jake asked.

"Yes. Honest. I am. I'm just so sorry about Jayden's game,'' Cassie said as she climbed into the cab. She *was* sorry. She had looked forward to getting to know his daughter under happier circumstances than their first meeting. "Will you tell her so?''

"Sure." He grabbed her arm before she could close the truck door. "Cassie."

"Yes?"

"Am I complicating your life? I mean, are you sorry we met?" He moved in closer, angled his head into the light from the interior.

"Why would I be sorry we met?"

He released her arm and hooked his hands on the drip molding above the door, ducking his head farther inside. "That younger cop came over to my truck and said you had told them the trouble up here started the day I came up the hill."

Cassie's arrested look told him she had, indeed, said that.

"I didn't mean *because* of you! I meant, the day I met you was the day all the trouble started, with Tom getting hurt and all, but I didn't mean that you were the *cause* of all the trouble. I don't know who's behind all of this, but I know one thing for sure, it's not you."

He looked down at his boots, relieved. "I just needed to hear that."

"Jake, really." She curved a hand over his arm. "I am starting to think that—because of you—that day was actually…it was one of the best days of my life."

He looked up, at her hand where it rested on his arm, then into her eyes. How could a man feel so strongly about a woman after knowing her such a short time? It didn't matter. He felt what he felt. And what he felt was—well, he hated to put so strong a word on such recent tender feelings, but it looked like what he felt for Cassie McClean was the beginning of love. The real thing. And after all this time without these feelings, without love, he found he was powerless to resist it. He didn't want to resist it—or her.

"Could I hold you again?"

She twisted off the seat and practically threw herself into his arms. He clutched her body to his and pressed his cheek against her thick hair, already cherishing the feel of her, the scent of her.

"Have you ever felt this way about anybody before?" he croaked. "Tell me."

"No. Have you?"

"No. Every time I'm around you, all I want to do is touch you, hold you. Like this." He encircled his arms under her jacket, fitted them firmly around her and angled his mouth over hers, branding her with a hot, open kiss.

When they broke off, she whispered, "Oh, man! The things you do to me! Look at us. Here we are kissing this way, and I thought I would never even be able to carry on a conversation with you."

"Really?" He planted a joyous kiss on her forehead. "Why did you think that?"

"You're too handsome."

He frowned, dubious of her reasoning.

"I'm not kidding. I've always had a thing about good-looking men."

He slid his hands higher, bringing his thumbs up around her rib cage. "Is that so? A *thing?*" He tightened his embrace until she was drawn firmly, sexually, against him. "Then, I guess I'll have to plead guilty to handsomeness."

"Not that kind of *thing!*" She slapped his shoulder,

but he didn't loosen his hold. "I had a hang-up kind of thing. Handsome men make me so nervous. I can never be myself around them, can't relax. Especially around *big* handsome men."

"But I'm different somehow?" Jake used his hands to settle her hips seductively against him. "Different, that is, from most—" he lowered his head, found a soft spot on her neck, and planted intermittent kisses between words "—big…handsome…men." He was suddenly enjoying this, he really was.

"You're making me forget," she said breathlessly, "what I was going to say."

"You were saying you can't be yourself, can't relax," he murmured low against her throat. "Around handsome men."

But she was, in fact, relaxed, right now. More like melting. He could feel it in the way she seemed to sink deeper into his arms when she released each tentatively held breath.

"It's just that you, um, you're so calm, so easygoing. I never feel uptight around you." She gave a feathery, weak little laugh as he opened two snaps of her denim jacket, hitched her higher and ran his tongue in a circle at the very top edge of her left breast. "I mean, I can talk to you."

"Just talk? Isn't there something more to it?"

He pressed his lips lower, simultaneously stroking his thumbs upward, inside her overalls, below the lower swell of her breasts.

"Oh, yeah, there's more." Her voice was strained with trying to resist him.

But right then, Jake stopped his teasing. It was as

if a dam burst, and he decided to take her, devour her. He ripped open the remaining snaps of her jacket and pushed her against the cab of the pickup. He grasped her under the arms, positioned her up on his massive thigh, and pinned her back, while he simultaneously kissed her and caressed her front with one large hand.

Cassie broke the kiss, threw her head back and dug her fingers into his shoulders, pushing, powerless, but also gripping, urging, wanting more.

She clung to him, with her arms high, giving his hands the freedom to feel their fill. But even so, when he began to try to unclasp her overalls she asked, "Jake, what are you doing?"

"I'm touching you the way I wanted to touch you the first time I saw you in these ridiculous overalls," he growled. Then he pulled at the things until they were out of the way of one luscious breast. He fastened his mouth there, over the thermal shirt and the thin bra that were saturated with the heat of her.

Cassie groaned in a half-mad way that gave Jake a secret rush of satisfaction. He wanted her to ache with the same desires he felt.

But in the next instant she stiffened. "Jake. Not here."

He couldn't help it—a low groan bubbled up. "What do you mean, not here? It's dark and there's not another soul for miles." He pressed her back and continued touching her.

"Exactly. It's creepy. Not what I want for our first time."

"Was that where we were headed?" Jake halted

and took his hands away from more intimate areas, anchoring them gently at her waist. "A first time? Are you ready for that?"

"Maybe." Cassie seemed self-conscious. "Is that what you want?"

"It's what I've wanted from the first moment I saw you, if I'm honest about it. But..."

"But what?"

"But you're right, we want something more special than this, you know, for the first time." He felt suddenly sobered out of his earlier euphoria. He hadn't intended to throw her down right there on the pickup seat, for Pete's sake. He cared about this woman. He cared about building a history with her. He'd known right from the beginning that if they started up with each other, it might lead to a life together. At least, that's what he had hoped. He knew himself that well. He knew that once he had this woman in his blood, he would never want to let her go. Cassie McClean was special. She had all the heart, the brains, the class he'd ever dreamed of in a woman. "I know I'd like it to be special."

Cassie threw her arms up and pressed her breasts seductively against him, her enthusiasm magically restored by he couldn't imagine what.

"Special? How?" she teased.

"I'd like to take you to dinner, maybe dancing. I'd like to see you all dressed up again. Buy you flowers. Don't you want that?"

"I do. Ooo." She pressed an enthusiastic, smacky little kiss to his lips. "I do. I've never had a real romance. But this is so crazy! Talking this way, when we barely know each other!'' She wiggled against him.

"No, it's not.'' Jake tried to hold her still, so she would really hear what he was saying. "I already know plenty about you. We've been talking on the phone since last summer.''

"Oh, yeah. Threatening to sue each other. That was nice.''

"You know what I'm saying. I know you're hardworking, successful, and honest and fair. You have a soft heart. And you're the most beautiful woman I've ever seen, bar none.''

Cassie stopped her wiggling and looked deep in his eyes. By the light of the moon they looked black, sincere and vulnerable. There was not a shred of pretense in this man. If he said she was the most beautiful woman he'd ever seen, she believed him.

"Oh, Jake.'' She sighed, "How in the world did I ever find you?''

"I roared up the hill in my truck to give you a piece of my mind.''

They settled happily against each other while their earlier sexual yearnings grew into something far deeper, far more meaningful than frantic passion.

"Come and be with me for Thanksgiving,'' he urged. "It won't be the same without you. Nothing is, these days.''

"I can't.'' She turned her face away, not wanting to share the sad facts about her family life.

"You have to be with your family?''

She nodded. "It's not what you think, Jake. Not a

command performance. Not a warm and happy holiday, either. My family is...different.''

"I know about your father, remember?"

"Well, there's more. There's a lot more that you don't know. I guess we really should get to know each other better before we do anything...you know, anything too..."

Words scrolled through Jake's mind as he imagined they were scrolling through hers. *Impulsive. Committed. Serious. Passionate. Overwhelming.* He was certain that sex with Cassie McClean would be all of those things.

"When can I see you again?" he said softly, urgently.

"Friday?"

"Friday it is. I'll pick you up at your house." He eyed her overalls, ran two fingers under the strap. "Much as I love how you look in these, for this particular date, you'll want to wear something pretty."

CHAPTER EIGHT

AUNT ROSEMARIE'S HOUSE never changed. Tucked behind giant trees and overgrown hedges in a cozy corner on a dead-end street in one of Jordan's historic neighborhoods, the place had the steep-pitched roof and elfish details of an early-thirties bungalow. The stone at the foundation was mossy, the floors sagged, the doors creaked, but to Cassie this little cottage was home.

Aunt Rosemarie, almost six feet tall with a shock of white hair furling from a too high forehead, answered the door in her usual dither. "Come in, darling!" she cried. "I think something is burning."

Cassie could smell it. The crust on the pumpkin pie, no doubt. Every year Rosemarie burned it black. Every year Cassie discreetly picked it off.

Rosemarie hugged her, and Cassie hugged back enthusiastically. Ah, this dear lady. Her mother's older sister. A sweet butterfly trapped in a body of Amazon-like proportions. Cassie had inherited her mother's petite blond traits, while Rosemarie embodied the flip side of the genetic track—tall, rawboned brunettes who looked like descendants of cavemen.

Her aunt never bemoaned her looks, or her spinsterhood. In fact, she never complained about her single life at all. She just blithely made the very most of every minute of every day, and by example, had shown Cassie how to do the same.

Rosemarie had long functioned as the dedicated, efficient secretary at her church, but unfortunately, she was no cook.

"The pie!" Aunt Rosemarie threw Cassie backward and charged off to the kitchen with her enormous hands fluttering about her head.

Cassie stepped inside the arched foyer and noted each familiar landmark. The wrinkled cashmere sweater thrown over the newel post at the bottom of the stairs, the stacks of unread junk mail piled crookedly on the Queen Anne table by the door, a colorful array of quilting pieces blanketing the table in front of the fireplace. Above the burned smell, the familiar odor of gently decaying books and gone-by-the-way sachet settled on her. Ah, Aunt Rosemarie.

Every year the lace at the windows got more yellow, the leaves in the yard piled higher and Aunt Rosemarie grew more dear to Cassie.

They made it through the dreaded meal, with Aunt Rosemarie floundering about, slapping at smoke with her tea towel, muttering deprecations to herself...and waiting on Cassie like a nervous servant.

"Auntie, please. Sit. Let's just sip our tea. We have a long drive ahead of us." Cassie patted the faded needlepoint cushion on the dining chair nearest hers.

Rosemarie gave up and flopped into the chair. "You are so good, dear, to continue to see Boss this way."

"Well—" Cassie poured her aunt some tea "—you

taught me to visit the sick and the imprisoned. And he is my father—although he doesn't really seem like my parent, you know?''

"Oh, don't say that, dear. Boss loves you. If only you understood how much.'' Rosemarie quickly took a sip of tea, as if to silence herself.

"Still, sometimes I feel obligated to visit him, you know? Guilty, like I owe it to him or something. I can't explain it. Most of the time it's not so bad, though.''

"Boss's personality has indeed mellowed with age,'' Rosemarie added.

Cassie sipped her tea and nodded. "I do enjoy talking to him by myself, without distractions. He knows a lot about the building business. When I was a little kid—after Mother died—it seemed like he never had enough time for me. Then when he went to prison, he had nothing but time. I feel like we've actually become friends.''

"He's really proud of you. That's a very interesting thing about relationships, isn't it, dear? The ones where you invest one-on-one time—those are the relationships that grow.''

"You are such a wise auntie.'' Cassie smiled. She was thinking about Jake now.

"Let's talk about something cheerier,'' Rosemarie said, and placed her cup back on the saucer. "How are things at Dream Builders?''

Cassie filled her aunt in on the strange happenings out at The Heights. They continued to mull it over on the long drive to Mayer. It was quiet and comfortable inside Cassie's smooth-riding Avalon, and she found it easy to pour her heart out as they flew down the familiar highway, with the fall sunlight, soft and dreamlike, soaking the farms and fields that rolled by. Aunt Rosemarie, who could infuse almost any situation with reassurance, admitted that even she found the string of events disturbing. When Cassie could see that she really was worrying her aunt, she changed the subject.

"Auntie, can I tell you a secret?"

"Why, of course, darling! I adore secrets."

"I've met a guy."

The tires hummed along the highway as this news sank in. Then, Rosemarie's eyebrows shot up and her long, plain face lit in a beatific smile. "Oh, my. You mean a *man*. A real man? Someone you...like?"

"Someone I like very much," Cassie admitted. "Someone I care about. Someone...oh, you should see him. He's so-o-o good-looking. But I shouldn't even be talking about him yet. We've only known each other a few weeks."

"But my dear, this is wonderful! This is the answer to all of my prayers for you!"

"Aunt Rosemarie." Cassie took one hand off the wheel and squeezed her aunt's long fingers. "You are such a sweetie."

"My prayers are merely practical." Her aunt patted Cassie's hand with her free one. "Love, an intimate relationship, a good man to call your own—that has to be among the greatest of God's gifts. Just because I never had that, doesn't mean I don't want it for my girl. Is he good? Is he kind?" She patted Cassie's hand again. "Tell me all about him."

Cassie did. And in the process of recounting Jake Coffey's qualities to Rosemarie, she realized she'd developed stronger feelings for him than she'd admitted even to herself.

By two-thirty, the high chain-link fence with the sign that read Mayer Minimum Security Prison had come into view.

They passed the cows dotting the prison dairy farm, the guard at the gate—who had to inspect their purses, the trunk, the undercarriage of the car and the food they'd brought—and finally the library-chapel building. Cassie parked her car in the visitors' lot next to the cinder-block structure where her dad was housed. The long low shape of the thing, resembling a dreary nursing home, depressed the architect in Cassie.

They found Boss waiting at one of the turquoise Formica tables in the visiting area. Since it was Thanksgiving Day, the tables and plastic chairs were all occupied. One family was even forced to huddle near the vending machines.

Cassie found the conversational roar and the bare fluorescent lighting annoying, but she pasted on a smile for Boss, who, as always, lit up when he spotted her. He was wearing the required visiting day uniform, a solid green shirt and pants of a cheap polyester blend, with the prisoner's name and ID stenciled in bright orange over one breast pocket. Boss, always portly, had gained enough weight that Cassie noticed his prison garb was new, not faded like the other men's.

After he hugged them, Boss asked Cassie and Rosemarie if they preferred to sit inside or if it was too windy outside where there was more room on the park benches, swings and worn picnic tables.

"It's a bright fall day," Aunt Rosemarie chirped, "and I, for one, don't mind a little breeze. Let's go outside and enjoy it."

Boss signaled the little family by the vending machines to go ahead and take his table.

Outside they settled at a gritty picnic table, and Rosemarie ceremoniously set the rectangular Tupperware container full of Thanksgiving fare before Boss.

"Why, thank you, Rosie, honey," Boss crooned. "It is so kind of you to share with me this way." As far as Cassie knew, Boss was the only one who called Rosemarie "Rosie," but her aunt didn't seem to resent the nickname. It was merely Boss's way.

Families could only bring food into the compound on holidays, and only after it was carefully inspected. Even though Cassie was fairly certain her dad had eaten the prison's Thanksgiving feast, he unwrapped the plastic tableware—sans knife—rolled in a turkey-printed napkin, peeled off the plastic lid with his thick sausagelike fingers and dug into the food with relish.

"Anybody want a bite of pie?" he said when he'd eaten a convincing amount of turkey and trimmings.

Both women shook their heads.

Cassie produced a cigar from her purse. "Happy Thanksgiving." She smiled.

"Happy Thanksgiving to you, sugar." Boss accepted her offering.

"You look pretty today," Boss said as he lit the cigar and eyed Cassie's brick-red sweater set and charcoal wool slacks. "She should dress like a girl more often, shouldn't she, Rosie."

"I expect she will, too, now that—"

"Dad! I've been having some trouble on the job," Cassie blurted. She certainly did not want Boss to know about Jake. She wasn't sure why, but she wasn't ready to share this important information with her father.

Aunt Rosemarie blushed over her gaff, but Boss was focused on Cassie.

"What kind of trouble?"

"Some yahoo keeps messing up my fresh concrete."

"Messing up?" Rosemarie warmed to the diversion. "I would call a death threat far more than messing up."

"A death threat?" Boss coughed smoke and his breathing seemed suddenly unsteady.

"You…die…too." Rosemarie pronounced each word selectively. "Only not in words. The capital letter *U*." She used a long finger to draw one in the air. "The word *die*, and then the number 2. Ugly, isn't it?"

"Dad." Cassie held up a calming hand. "I called the police."

"Oh, and what did they do?" Boss muttered.

One good thing, Cassie thought, was that prison had taught Boss how to keep his voice low.

"Did they string yellow tape all over the place and take a doughnut break?"

An unfortunate side effect of going to prison, though, was Boss's increased skepticism. With each passing year he seemed more mistrustful of anything with "government" stamped on it.

"We'll catch the guy," she reassured him.

"They know it's a guy?"

"We're assuming so. They took castings of some big footprints after the first incident."

"There's been more than one?" Boss blew out smoke and leaned forward, looking like he might pop a gasket.

"It's very complicated, Boss, dear." Rosemarie patted his hand. "The damage was done on a famous rock star's building site, and there are some Native American students, the Spirit Tribe, who have been getting publicity for themselves at Cassie's expense. And Cassie's had some run-ins with some horse rancher and his children."

Leave it to Aunt Rosemarie, Cassie thought, to get the facts all backward. In fairness, she hadn't told Rosemarie that the horse rancher and her new love interest were one and the same man.

"It is really quite impossible—" Rosemarie finished her summary with satisfaction "—to tell who this cowardly vandal might be at this point."

"It could be anybody." Boss stopped puffing his cigar, as if distracted, disturbed. "Plenty of folks in Jordan will be jealous of Cassie's success. People who hate me, who'd hate to see my girl getting rich the way I should have."

Cassie despised this kind of paranoid, self-centered talk from Boss. It had always been this way with him. The feelings that his negative attitude stirred up in Cassie suffocated her, clouded her thinking. This aspect of Boss's personality seemed as inescapable as the scent of his cigar.

"Dad, I'm sure it has nothing to do with you," she countered.

"Why wouldn't it? I ruined some folks, Cassie. There were subs, some of them as low down as snakes, that I took down with me when I went bankrupt. And now the McClean name is out there again, prominent in the building business. The Heights screams money. Why wouldn't old resentments surface now?"

"Because that was all a long time ago," Cassie reasoned.

"Some things are never, ever forgotten," Boss muttered, and Cassie felt sorry for her father, living in the past, nursing his regrets and resentments. "Tell me the names of your subs."

"None of them ever even mentions your name to me," Cassie said emphatically. She didn't mean to be cruel, but it was true. Boss had no claim to her success, no part in it. Absolutely no part. She wanted—*needed*—to be very clear about that.

"Don't start that condescending talk with me, girl. I did what I did for good reasons and I wouldn't change a bit of it." Boss's face hardened into that look, the one that made Cassie want to slap him silly. "I tell you, I would *not*."

"Maybe we should go." Cassie stood and pressed the lid firmly onto the food container. No matter how many times she told herself that Boss's situation was pathetic, she still resented the fact that it was of his own making and that he never showed the proper amount of remorse for what he had done.

"Cassie…" Rosemarie's expression looked pained. "It's Thanksgiving."

"Go on home and leave me alone." Boss spat his words at Cassie, then turned to Rosemarie. "It doesn't matter, Rosie. In prison, Thanksgiving is like any other day."

Poor Rosemarie looked from Cassie to Boss with so much sorrow in her eyes that for one instant Cassie regretted her stubbornness.

"Take care, Boss," Rosemarie whispered, and patted Boss's hand before standing up beside Cassie.

Cassie had to bite her tongue to keep from saying, right in front of Boss, *Don't waste your pity on this old coot, Auntie. He'll never admit he was wrong.*

ON THE RIDE BACK to Jordan, a prolonged silence on the lonely stretch of road gave Cassie the courage to bring up a subject that had bothered her for a long time. "What did Boss mean when he said he had good reasons for doing what he did? Was he using my mother's death as some kind of excuse for going crazy, because if he was—"

"No," Rosemarie interrupted. "It has nothing to do with your mother." Rosemarie rearranged her long legs sideways in the seat, casting them toward Cassie. "When Amelia died, I have to say, Boss was very brave. The car wreck, the way it happened, was such a shock to all of us. And he just put it behind him and turned around and put all of his attention and energy on you."

Cassie sighed. Her memories of that time were vague, overshadowed by emotions too complicated to explain even twenty years later. She had been a stunned, frightened seven-year-old, but she did recall the constant murmurings of the adults around her. They had used words the child had never heard before, like *freak accident* and *split second of tragedy*. To Cassie, the way her mother's car had been swept off the road into a raging creek during a flash flood was something that, even now, she could hardly bear to think about.

"Are you ever gonna tell me what really happened back then, with my dad?"

Behind them, the southwest sun pulled a blazing Oklahoma sky downward behind it, and in the east a soft moon settled in for the night, inviting confidences.

"Yes, I think I am," Rosemarie said heavily. "And I think the time to tell you is now."

"Okay." Cassie gripped the steering wheel and drew a huge breath. This was her life, where she came from, who she was, and it was finally about to be revealed to her by the person she trusted most in the world.

She hoped she could accept what her aunt had to say. She hoped it didn't derail her from the narrow path of security she had built for herself.

CHAPTER NINE

"HOW MUCH DO YOU KNOW about your father's..."

When her aunt didn't finish, Cassie glanced over and saw Rosemarie biting her lip. Finally she released the word *"crimes"* on a sigh.

"It's okay to call them 'crimes,' Auntie. Cutting corners with cheap, bug-infested wood that causes a house to crumble within two or three years, skipping the insulation in the walls, omitting the conduit over inferior wiring—those are crimes in my book."

"I meant the manslaughter charge."

Cassie gripped the steering wheel. Damn little, that's what she knew. Boss refused to discuss it. Cassie had spent some time in the microfiche at the university. The local paper pretty much told the story. "A whole family died in a fire because of his greed."

"Not the whole family. A young boy survived. Badly scarred, I suppose. I never found out exactly what happened to him. I confess I was too focused on you to worry about the trial, or even that poor boy. All I could do was pray that there were people who were helping him to heal."

"Me? Why were you worried about me?" Cassie knew that the answer should be obvious. Who wouldn't worry about a twelve-year-old who was watching her father go on trial, face prison. A twelve-year-old whose mother had died only a few years before, a child who had recovered from a devastating illness, narrowly escaping with her life. But Cassie also had memories of being strong during that time. At least, in her mind she had been strong. She had kept her grades up. She had done her small chores in the big, cold, motherless house she shared with Boss and various live-in helpers. She had been quiet and controlled and absolutely no trouble—at least until she had moved into her aunt's house.

She could feel Rosemarie's eyes on her, weighing how much to tell. Rosemarie, Cassie now understood, had always executed a delicate balancing act. Giving Cassie a safe place to heal, to grow, while at the same time helping the child to accept harsh truths in small doses. And it seemed that balancing act was still going on. Now Rosemarie had more truths to tell. Poor Rosemarie. She had always avowed that Cassie was no burden, but how could it possibly have been otherwise?

She heard her aunt clear her throat. "When your mother died, you went through a bad time. You withdrew. We were all so worried about you. What do you say to a seven-year-old who persists in asking when her mommy is coming back?"

Cassie felt the sting of tears, remembering the pain, the anger that had caused her to stubbornly insist that her mother had to be coming back, that the accident had to be some stupid mistake, some horrible lie. Her world had felt so bleak, so confusing and dark after her mother died. Maybe it would have helped if she'd seen the body, the way her father had. But decisions were made that were beyond Cassie's control, and sparing the young child from seeing her mother's bloated body after the accident had been one of those decisions.

"I'm sorry," she said. As an adult, suddenly she wanted to atone for the pain she must have caused Rosemarie, who had lost her only sister. "I'm sorry I—"

"Darling, you mustn't say that." Rosemarie stopped her. "There is nothing to be sorry about. You were only reacting the way any child would. At least, that's what we thought at the time. You grew so thin. You spent too much time up in your tree house alone, brooding. Oh, I should have known. I should have seen it coming."

"Seen what coming?"

"Your illness."

"The leukemia?" Cassie took her eyes off the road long enough to check her aunt's face. She looked absolutely serious. How, Cassie wondered, could anyone expect to see a thing like that coming? "You think my leukemia was related to my mother's death? But it came on years later."

"I think it was a result of your whole little system gradually weakening because of your grief. I should have insisted on counseling, or something, before it came to that. Boss thought he could buy you nice things, take you to Disneyland, and cheer you up. That was his way, and you were his daughter, and so I kept my piece. But, even so, I should have intervened. I should have."

"Auntie, you can't blame yourself because I got sick." It was not the first time Rosemarie had been emotional and irrational about such things. Cassie even felt Rosemarie was a bit superstitious at times.

"Well, it's all hindsight now. We did the best we could. Boss was terrified. When you were diagnosed, I jumped right in to help."

"I remember," Cassie reassured her. Because she did. Her aunt had always been there, with balloons, teddy bears, funny books, cookies, hugs, back rubs. Cassie remembered clearly thinking that her aunt Rosemarie was some sort of angel.

"We were so happy when they found a match and you got your bone-marrow transplant. You cannot imagine our relief. Boss and I actually cried on each other's shoulders."

Cassie hadn't known that. She couldn't imagine her father shedding tears, much less on Rosemarie's bony shoulder. "We felt like you had been restored to us. We didn't even care that there would surely be consequences, later, because of all that radiation. At the time we were just glad you were alive."

Consequences.

Cassie looked out over the fading fall countryside and remembered the day, a bleak frozen gray day in January, just after her fifteenth birthday, when she and her aunt had returned home from an appointment with Dr. Stewart. Rosemarie had parted the lace curtains at one of the tall windows in the living room of her old house and said, "I wish it were sunny outside. Today, of all days."

Cassie had stuck her nose in a book the minute they

walked in the door. But when Rosemarie spoke to the window glass like that, Cassie looked up. Aunt Rosemarie was given to such comments, apropos of nothing, and Cassie usually ignored her, but today the sound of her aunt's voice was different.

"What did you say?" Cassie had said.

"Nothing." Rosemarie had pressed her long fingers over her carefully ironed collar, spread neatly against her nearly flat chest. "Nothing. Let's have some hot chocolate."

Rosemarie had rushed into the kitchen, and soon Cassie heard her fixing the hot chocolate in her bungling way. She carried it out on a lacquered tray and beckoned Cassie to sit on the saggy old camel-back settee next to her. Then she set about the heartbreaking task of making her niece accept the truth.

In the soft light of the car's interior, Rosemarie studied Cassie's profile and wondered if she was remembering that day in January. For Rosemarie that bleak afternoon was etched in her memory as the saddest and most profound day of her life. Her own sorrows and disappointments she could accept, but for her beautiful niece Cassie she wanted everything life had to offer. And on that day the doctor had confirmed that Cassie would be deprived of one of life's greatest gifts.

"The day you were born—" Rosemarie remembered how she had started. She closed her eyes, recalling the exact sentence with years-old regret. So clumsy. So ill prepared. She remembered seeing fifteen-year-old Cassie, with her keen ability to read people's faces, frowning at her, already suspicious, already seeing through this hot chocolate and fairytales routine. How did one explain such a devastating loss to a young girl? Oh, if only God would magically lift the burden of having to tell her! But the task had fallen squarely to Rosemarie. There was no one to help the child. No one but her.

Boss had already gone to prison by then, grieving his heart out. Angry at the insurance companies. Angry at the families who had sued him civilly. Angry at the district attorney who leveled the charges and hounded him to conviction. Rosemarie was not about to let an angry, bitter man, even if he was the child's father, tell Cassie news so devastating as this.

And her poor Amelia was dead. Rosemarie sent up a prayer, she knew not where. To her sister, she supposed, as if some essence of Amelia could be called upon to help this child, her only child.

The doctor had been somewhat clinical about it from the beginning, saying they would wait for the "onset of menses" before "checking hormone levels" and "beginning hormone-replacement therapy." To soften the blow, Rosemarie had asked the doctor to let her tell the child the outcome of the tests in her own way, in her own time. He had seemed relieved.

"The day you were born," Rosemarie had started again on that day, "was the happiest our family ever had. Mama was beside herself at the hospital, running back and forth from the nursery window to Amelia's room, gushing about your peach fuzz of blond hair and your tiny turned-up nose. Your grandpa...well, Daddy was so overjoyed, he started humming you a little lullaby, right through the window. He ran down to the gift shop and bought a big bunch of flowers, took them to Amelia's room and said they were for *you*." Rosemarie smiled. "Your grandpa was such a great guy.

"But I, well, I stayed glued to that window. I felt guilty for not being at Amelia's bedside when she might need my help—Boss and Daddy were certainly not nurturers. Men who work outdoors are so inept in a hospital setting. And Mama, she was an absolute twit—but I was unable to tear my eyes off this miracle." She lifted a strand of Cassie's honey-colored hair, still seeming awestruck by that miracle some fifteen years later. "I was not jealous of your mother. She was my baby sister—like my own baby, really...so much younger. I was always protective of her. But I did feel a certain melancholy that day. I guess it was a kind of sinking self-pity, an acceptance of a sad reality."

Cassie put down her mug of hot chocolate. This was not the way her aunt usually talked. Not at all. "Why are you so sad, Auntie?"

Rosemarie avoided the question.

"You see, I realized then that I would probably never have a pretty baby like you. Time, love, had passed me by. I was forty years old and I knew I would never marry. I knew I would never have babies. I've always known I'm not attractive, but I think, until then, I still had some hope."

"But you don't have to be a model," Cassie argued sensibly, "to get married, or to have babies." She and her buddy Stacey had avidly poured over the facts of life in an illustrated book that Stacey's mom had given her. "It all happens on the inside. It hasn't got anything to do with how you look. Anybody can have babies."

"No. Not anybody." Rosemarie kept her voice oh, so gentle. "Only fertile women."

Fertile. Rosemarie watched that word settle on Cassie. She had tried to prepare Cassie for this day ever since the damage was done. She had stimulated the child's imagination, fostered her creativity. Had taken her to cultural events, hauled her to piano lessons. Had made sure she was well-read, well educated. In short, Rosemarie had done her best to make sure Cassie had something, anything, to fall back on when the diagnosis came. Something that would make her life so full and joyous and beautiful that she might never feel the impact, the toll that had been taken on her little body. Sterility.

But now, here they were. Now, here was the moment of truth.

"You understand what these recent tests with Dr. Stewart have been about?" Rosemarie asked.

Cassie looked down at her lap and nodded. "To see why I haven't had my period yet, like all of my friends."

"That's right, darling. At least you had breast development, but the tests show that you will never have your period. You will never be like your friends…in that way." Rosemarie sighed, hardly able to bear the change in Cassie's facial features as the awful truth dawned. Lord, she wished this cup would pass.

"I wonder what it's like to have a baby?" Cassie raised sad eyes and looked off in the distance, through the thin curtains on that gray day, off to a place in the future where, for her, there would be no babies.

"Some women complain about it, as if it is a burden. But I think if she were here, your mother would say that giving birth to a child is one of the most beautiful things that can happen to a woman."

"But it's something that won't happen—" the tone of finality in Cassie's voice as she stared out that window nearly broke Rosemarie's heart in half "—to me."

Rosemarie swallowed, hoping she was saying the right thing. "Or to me, either, dear."

Rosemarie reached out and took her niece in her arms. She felt the slender young shoulders shake as the child started to weep. "It's a hard thing to accept, I know," she said after a moment, "but it's not the end of the world."

"I know." But Cassie's half child, half woman voice had the high-pitched, shocked, keening sound of one who had been mortally grieved.

"You have your *life,* dear, and God does not mean for you to waste it. Children or no children, you will find a way to serve others, to be happy and to live with love."

The two women clung to each other for a long time on that little settee, mourning their losses, creating a bond that would never be broken.

"Boss did the best he could, Cassie," Rosemarie said now. Inside the quiet Avalon, her aunt's voice brought Cassie back to the present. "He made… sacrifices."

Outside, a gentle autumn rain had started. The tires

hissed on the newly dampened road, and Cassie didn't speak. She felt like something big was coming. Rosemarie fidgeted in her seat, then pressed her hands together over her heart. Normally, Cassie loved these small dramatic gestures that came as naturally to her aunt as breathing, but on this evening, she wished her aunt would simply be out with it.

"Today, when Boss said he had good reasons for doing what he did, he wasn't talking about your mother. He was talking about *you*. You were his reason...or rather, your illness was."

It took a great effort for Cassie to maintain her composure, to not turn an incredulous stare on her aunt and shout, *Me? If he'd been thinking of me, he wouldn't have landed himself in prison! He wouldn't have been trying to get rich quick!* But instead she gripped the steering wheel, waiting. Because whatever Rosemarie had to say, it had taken a great deal of courage for her to edge this close to the topic. One wrong move from Cassie, one hard word, would send Rosemarie back into her shell of secrecy faster than a rabbit darting into foliage at the roadside.

"That's why he did it. You see—" Rosemarie sighed and lowered her hands to her lap "—Boss needed money because the limit on your health insurance had been exceeded."

"What do you mean?" Cassie was confused. Was Rosemarie saying that Boss had done desperate things, illegal things, because of *her*?

"He would have done anything to save you, and I guess he did. Thank the Lord, I was not aware of his activities, his business dealings, if you can call them that. He said he wanted you to have the best of care. He told me once that he was going to look those doctors in the eye and say that cost was no object, and mean it.''

''But surely there were options, the state hospital—''

''He did not want you in the state children's hospital. In those days, that was not a nice place, not even a safe place, at least in Boss's mind. He wanted to take you to M.D. Anderson in Houston, and he did.''

Cassie remembered the trips to Houston. Flying in. Three days of chemotherapy under a clinical trial. Flying out. Only to repeat the trip on the next cycle. For her, those days were a blur of unrelenting nausea, drugged sleep and white cotton blankets that smelled of the hospital autoclave where the nurses warmed them up.

''The airfare and hotel bills alone would have bankrupted an ordinary family. But it was the bone-marrow transplant that Boss obsessed over. In those days that was a new and very risky procedure, but as soon as Boss heard about it, he was like a bulldog. The insurance company wouldn't sanction it, wouldn't even fund the search for a donor. But Boss found a doctor in Houston—I believe he actually worked at the Hermann Hospital most of the time— I am not sure, it was all so long ago.

''I clearly remember Boss on the phone with the insurance company, yelling. I'll never forget his phrasing. 'I am sick of playing Mother May I with you bastards'—sorry, but that's what he said.''

Rosemarie blushed so furiously that Cassie could practically feel the temperature rising inside the car. "You know Boss and his rough language. But you're an adult now. That's why I'm telling you these things."

"Thank you for that." Cassie reached over and patted her aunt's hands to encourage her. "I don't remember any of this. I don't remember ever hearing my father yelling on the phone to the insurance company."

"I should hope not," Rosemarie said solemnly. "My goal was to keep you from hearing *any* of it."

"Then, why are you telling me now?"

"You must come to terms with Boss, Cassie. You don't have to approve of the choices he made, but it would be so much better, so much healthier if you did find it in your heart to at least understand those choices."

"Why are you telling me this?" Cassie repeated with the kind of flat, numb tone one would use to say, *Why are you ripping my heart out?*

"I thought if you understood…I thought if you saw that if Boss hadn't done what he did—not out of selfishness or greed, but out of desperation—Cassie, you might not be alive today—"

"You're saying that I should be *grateful* that he used his ill-gotten profits to buy me a bone-marrow transplant?"

"No! I'm only saying maybe it's time to forgive Boss for the mistakes he made. He has paid his debt. He will be eligible for parole in April."

Cassie had forgotten about that. Her mind whirled

with images of dealing with her father when he was on the outside. Selfishly, she didn't want to have to think about establishing some kind of relationship with a man who had been so carefully and conveniently contained by the state all these years. Especially not now, when she was, at long last, falling in love.

"But he never told me any of this," Cassie repeated woodenly.

"Of course he didn't, dear, and he made me swear not to—which I suppose makes me a bad person, for breaking my promise this way. But I thought this might be the right time to tell you, the right time to make peace with your father, because—"

Rosemarie stopped, and Cassie waited while the rain kept up a soft, steady rhythm on the car.

"Because I think, for you, things are changing. I think you, Cassie, are on the brink of falling in love."

CHAPTER TEN

THE MINUTE CASSIE UNLOCKED the door of her empty house she wanted Jake's warmth and solidity with her in the too quiet rooms while she mulled over her disturbed thoughts. She wanted to tell him everything she'd learned from her aunt on the trip back from Mayer, wanted him to help her process these sad and stunning truths.

Undoubtedly he was having a plate of Thanksgiving leftovers prepared by his competent cook, and watching a football game with his dad and daughter. Isn't that what normal families did on Thanksgiving? The total abnormality of her childhood, and even of her life as it was now, closed in on her again, and, steeling herself against self-pity, she went into her chrome-and-granite kitchen to fix herself a cup of herbal tea.

She resisted the temptation to turn on the TV for the noise, and sat at the counter on one of the sleek bar stools, sipping her tea and trying to think rationally. But her troubled emotions kept getting in the way.

Forgiveness. That's what Aunt Rosemarie had said was needed. She rolled the word around in her mind.

What, exactly, did her aunt want her to forgive Boss for? Bad judgment?

If she forgave Boss, and he got out of prison soon, did that mean she'd have to have a real relationship with the man? That idea had always bothered Cassie. How could she live down Boss's reputation without disassociating herself from him? She certainly didn't want him to get involved with Dream Builders after he got out on parole.

There didn't seem to be any answer. She thought about calling Stacey and pouring her heart out, but it was Thanksgiving, and Stacey and her husband would be tucking their two little ones into bed. She sipped the last of her tea and decided to go to bed early.

But she didn't fall asleep until almost one a.m., and then her slumber was short-lived. She awoke with a start, the touch lamp by her bed jolted on by a storm outside. Thunder boomed and another flash of lightning lit up the giant glass-block window above her sunken tub like a movie screen. She got up and closed the dressing room door, then wrapped herself in a yellow silk robe that offered little comfort or warmth.

During her brief sleep, the gentle rain that had followed them home from Mayer must have built into the wild thunderstorm that lashed at her windows now. A thunderclap cracked again, causing the touch lamp to flash off and on. She crossed the room and turned on the more reliable floor lamp beside her chaise longue. She pulled a woven jacquard throw over her shoulders and tried to ferret out the thoughts that were still nettling at her mind, at her heart.

Beyond Rosemarie's disclosures, there was something else bothering her. A worrisome thought crashed around at the back of her mind, as disturbing as this storm. Was it something Boss had said today or was it the way he had said it?

When Boss had mentioned his enemies, the fear in his eyes looked fresh, not about some old business he was dredging up. Was there something he wasn't telling her? Obviously, there was *a lot* he wasn't telling her. But if he'd loved her enough to do such desperate things to save her life, surely he wouldn't let her be in any danger now. She made a mental note to check her Day-Timer and see when she could return to Mayer and talk to him again. He might never come clean about his past, but Cassie had to know what was in his past that made him so uncomfortable about what had been happening out at The Heights recently.

She pulled the throw tighter and leaned her head back against the curved chaise, letting herself feel the full confusion and hurt of Rosemarie's revelations. She saw a vision of Boss—how his face lit up expectantly whenever she gave him an hour of her precious time at the prison. She saw herself—how she carefully withheld her love and warmth, how she had been so formal, so dutiful, to the very man who had ensured her survival by vanquishing his own future.

Guilt began to edge its way into her heart. How could her aunt do this to her? Revealing these sad truths now, when her life was on the verge of success? *Why* had her aunt done this to her? Just when she'd reached the place in life where she thought she could deal with Boss from a safe, healthy arm's length. Just when she thought she had him all tied up with a neat ribbon, relegated to brief visits on Sunday afternoons.

Outside the storm lashed on, the glow of lamps within her bedroom a weak talisman against its fury. Something heavy banged repeatedly against the side of the house downstairs, before it blew loose. She wondered if she should open the armoire and turn on the TV. In Oklahoma, the local stations would be broadcasting with full storm-watch crews. This level of vigilance was the only thing that had saved so many lives when an F-5 had scoured a massive path in the red earth only twenty miles north of Jordan a few years earlier. But Cassie didn't want to turn on her TV. She wanted to lie curled up, nursing her painful thoughts. When common sense won out, she turned on the set, leaving the volume low.

A young meteorologist pointed at computer images of the roiling storm, but the miniature map in the corner did not show a tornado warning. Still, she could hear the branches snap in the wild wind. Would the houses in The Heights be damaged? What else could possibly go wrong up there? Cassie felt like her dream was slipping through her fingers with each new revelation, each new disaster.

If she could only talk to Jake about her troubles. He would understand, she was certain. She imagined calling him up, waking him in his warm rumpled bed, hearing his voice, an octave lower from sleep.

Hi, she'd say, *the storm woke me and I'm scared, but it's not really the storm that's scaring me. It's my life. I think my business is in jeopardy, and my dad's keeping some kind of secret from me, and I found out today, on Thanksgiving Day, that he made a ghastly sacrifice to save me when I was little, and I've resented him all these years, and now I don't know how to stop. I don't know how to be a real daughter to him, but my aunt says I won't have a fulfilling relationship with you as long as I have this resentment about my dad in my heart and I worry—what if she's right about that? She usually is about these things. I mean, what if I've been so hard-nosed for so long, because of my dad, that I can't stop thinking that way. What if I end up treating you that way? Would you still come over and hold me?*

She pictured his eyes, gentle and brown, understanding and sympathetic, and she clutched the throw, inhaling its scent as if it were his. But the only thing she smelled was her own feminine fragrance, and that made her lonelier than ever. She wished he were here. Now. Not so she could pour her heart out about Boss, necessarily, although it seemed like if anybody would understand her conflict, Jake would. But more than she wanted to talk, she wanted him to *hold* her—lightning flashed at the windows again—to hold her against this storm.

She rolled to her side on the chaise. Maybe she would just sleep over here tonight. How she had come to loathe her lonely bed. Oh, how she wanted to hold Jake Coffey. Just hold him...and be held by him.

WHEN JAKE APPEARED in her doorway on Friday evening, she threw herself into his arms.

''Whoa, there!'' he cried, as if she were one of his romping mares.

"I'm sorry." She pressed her nose against his deliciously masculine-smelling neck. "It's just that it's been a shitty week."

He was bearing a single red rose, which he pressed into her back as he clutched her flush against him. "No more incidents of vandalism, I hope?"

She nodded. "The thunderstorm washed out the dirt work we'd just completed behind the Detloffs, and somebody stacked two-by-eights on their sides, creating a dam that diverted the muddy water into their newly carpeted basement."

"Good grief. Did you call the cops?"

"The Detloffs had already done it before I got there. They're both doctors and take Fridays off."

"And what did the cops do?"

"Plenty of paperwork, as usual. It was too wet to get any useful footprint castings, but let's face it, they don't have a clue as to who our vandal is, anyway. My case is not exactly high priority."

He frowned and eased his shoulders and torso back, which only pressed his hips more tightly against hers. "Sooner or later we'll catch him, Cassie, but right now methinks a nice romantic date is just what you need, milady." He swept the rose around between them. His face was as abashed as a little boy's when he saw that he'd broken it. "Sorry. I guess I bent it."

"I love it, anyway," she said. *And the man who brought it,* she added in her own mind. She took the broken rose, touched by his thoughtfulness.

He drove her to Legend's again. She was touched by that, too. He was, in so many ways, a simple guy. She found that endearing.

But he could also be very polished when he wanted to be. He held out her chair this time, ordered a fine wine.

"You look," he said as he held his wineglass toward her in a toast, "absolutely gorgeous tonight."

The light in his eyes raised her hopes that he wasn't saying that just to be nice. It was a thrill to realize that Jake actually thought she was beautiful, whether she was wearing overalls or evening black. Because for Cassie, dressing up was a formidable task.

She sighed and sipped her wine. "God knows I've tried." If Jake could only see the pile of discarded combinations that had landed on the floor of her walk-in closet before she'd settled on this black cashmere sweater and clingy floral skirt, he would realize she wasn't kidding. And these shoes. Black multistrap heels with a sinfully thin ankle wrap. Not at all appropriate for the chilly November weather. Was she trying *too* hard? Being too blatantly sexy? Cassie didn't have a clue. She studied Jake's face for a trace of approval.

He grinned and arched an eyebrow. "You don't enjoy dressing up?"

"I'm just not used to it, that's all. But I don't mind it as much…when I'm doing it for you."

Frank approval radiated from his eyes. "Well—" he reached across the table and grabbed her wrist, not her hand, and stroked the tender skin on the underside with his rough thumb "—the effect on me is certainly well worth the effort."

The effect of his touch on Cassie was certainly worth the effort, too. And it was instantaneous. A rush of feeling shot up her arm, across her breast, down to her belly. She couldn't have moved her wrist from his grasp for anything. She was surprised that she didn't feel the slightest bit of awkwardness, having him touch her so possessively in public.

She found she didn't mind, either, telling him the details of her visit with her father, describing what it felt like to visit a father in prison. Jake was a great listener. She didn't tell him everything, of course, like she had been tempted to do during the thunderstorm. That had been a fantasy arising from loneliness, she realized, studying her handsome date while the waiter removed their salad plates. She and Jake didn't know each other that well yet. She couldn't tell him about her dad, about her sad history. Not yet. Maybe—she bit her lip—not ever. But there *were* some things she wanted to get his opinion about.

"My dad said something that kind of creeped me out." She kept her voice low as she carefully cut her prime rib.

"Oh?" Jake frowned, stopping his horseradish-laden knife in midair.

"He thinks I need to worry about the enemies he made back when he was in the building business."

"Oh?" Jake repeated.

"Eat." Cassie waved her fork. "This isn't worth letting your prime rib get cold over."

She took a small bite of her own entrée, chewed thoughtfully, then swallowed and smiled. "You have to realize I don't put much stock in anything Dad says. He has too much time on his hands—I guess that's obvious. Anyway, he did ruin some people financially, according to my aunt. But that's ancient history. I think it's a little paranoid for him to assume that people are still out to get him—through me, no less—after all these years. But it got me to thinking that this vandal, or vandals, could be anybody. I've got to find out who's behind this nonsense.''

''It's a little more serious than nonsense, Cassie.'' Jake finally took a bite of his prime rib. After he swallowed he added, ''In fact, it seems to me this guy could be dangerous.''

WHEN THE EVENING WAS OVER, Jake walked her to her door.

''I'm sorry I got a little heavy this evening,'' Cassie apologized, while he used her key to open the lock. ''I've had a lot on my mind lately—a lot of problems, I guess.''

Jake handed her the key and stroked one finger lightly down her cheek. ''Don't apologize. I love being with you, problems or no problems. It makes me feel human again after a hellacious week of chasing down Jayden and worrying about Dad.''

''I'm glad. Well, unfortunately, Saturday or not, I have to work tomorrow—still trying to beat the first freeze, you know.''

''I know.'' He took one of her hands loosely in one of his and leaned down, tilting his face over hers, and feathered his lips across her mouth. It was the kind of light good-night kiss that was appropriate for a woman's front porch—innocent enough, but it made Cassie's breathing quicken.

He raised his head but did not release her hand.

"Good night," he whispered, but his gaze fell to her mouth again.

She would have lowered her eyelids modestly, the way she supposed most women did in this situation, but she was mesmerized by the little crease that was forming between his brows. She wanted to study his eyes while he studied her mouth.

"Aw, hell," he said gruffly as he lowered his mouth toward hers. "This is all I could think about yesterday."

Then his firm, mobile lips claimed hers again. This time not lightly and not innocently. She emitted a surprised mew and he pulled her more firmly against him. She wrapped her arms around his neck, flattening her breasts to his massive chest, clasping him, urging him to take more, to do more. *More.*

He tightened the seal of their mouths and deepened the kiss with his tongue. She answered him in kind. With their tongues mingling, with one's groans answering the other's, they communicated their passion without words. This kiss was as wet and hot as a kiss can get on a front porch, in plain view of the street.

Jake finally pulled back, glancing around him as if there were spies in the bushes. "I know you gotta work tomorrow, but can we do this again next week?"

They did it the next week, and the next. In the meantime, both of them struggled to keep their lives sane. Advancing peacefully toward one's dreams, Cassie joked on one of their dates, was apparently too much to ask of life.

Jake answered that with a wry grin that Cassie considered downright courageous. He had just told her that his ex-wife was taking him to court again, right after Christmas, to force joint custody of their daughter Jayden. Cassie supposed that might explain why the woman hadn't filed for any damages for the premature foal.

"She'll make Jayden live with her half the time."

"And where would that be?"

"On the Largeant horse farm."

"The Largeant farm? As in, Mayor Largeant?" Cassie remembered Jake telling the young cop who didn't want to take a plaster casting that he knew the mayor. She wondered if they were on friendly terms.

"Yeah. Lana's father. They live farther out on the Flats."

"Oh, so Jayden would still be close to home—not in another town or anything."

"But she wouldn't necessarily be safe. Lana's dad runs that household with an iron hand and a cold heart. I think he's the reason Lana's an alcoholic."

So Jake didn't like the mayor. "Your ex-wife is an alcoholic?"

"It happens."

"Has she had treatment?"

"Not that I know of. She claims she can stop anytime she wants to, claims she hasn't had a drink in years. But I don't buy it. I did what I could to help her, but I finally realized the whole co-dependent thing is real. If somebody wants to ruin their life drinking, you can't fix it for them. My concern now is Jayden. Lana is not getting custody at this late date if I have anything to say about it."

"No wonder you wanted to settle our little feud outside of court."

"There is no shortage of trouble in the world. I don't like to go looking for more."

Cassie agreed. There was certainly no shortage of trouble in her own world. The incidents of sabotage kept cropping up. And now, strangely, the vandalism was directed at both of them.

Someone had poked holes in the water tanks serving Jake's horses. Paint, a dark shade of decorator red that had obviously been stolen from the batch at the Detloff house, had been smeared like blood along an acre's worth of Jake's expensive white PVC fencing.

Cassie called the police, of course, as did Jake each time he was hit. Cassie reported that, yes, her guard dogs had been out all night, and, no, she couldn't imagine how an intruder had sneaked past them. Jake reported that, yes, the perimeters of his ranch were protected by guard dogs, as well. The whole pattern was puzzling...and disturbing.

Beyond the sabotage, there were the annoying shenanigans of the Spirit Tribe. Cassie might have thought these college kids were interesting, even idealistic, if they hadn't held up construction one Monday morning while they positioned their Native-costumed bodies across the road outside the gates of The Heights. They lay there, as still as railroad ties, staring at the sky, while their buddies put on a show with flutes, drums, and chanting dancers.

Unable to get to work, the construction guys had climbed out of their trucks and were standing around, smoking and looking disgruntled when Cassie arrived.

She slammed her truck's door and marched toward the protestors, determined to get this squared away. The Spirit Tribe had gotten into the act after the vandalism was reported in the campus newspaper. In Cassie's mind, this was probably a chicken-and-egg deal. Had they committed the vandalism to open the door to publicity?

Their apparent ringleader was an older, paunchy guy in an ill-fitting business suit. A scraggly graying braid trailed down his back. He was actually encouraging the protestors with a bullhorn!

"Who are you, and what are these people doing on my property?" Cassie confronted him with her hands planted on her hips.

He lowered the bullhorn and regarded Cassie with solemn black eyes. "I am Allen Pathkiller," he said, ignoring the intrusive beat of a nearby drum, "and this—" he swept an arm out over the recumbent protestors "—is the Spirit Tribe."

Great, Cassie thought, *he's pulling the wise old shaman act.* She shook her head. "I know who they are. What do you think you're doing, Mr. Pathkiller?" She said it as flatly as possible, to indicate that she didn't appreciate this nonsense on a Monday morning.

"We have been led to this place to protect our people, to protect our ancestors, to protect—" Pathkiller paused dramatically "—the dead."

"Are you referring to the little graveyard that was supposed to be located somewhere up on that ridge?" Cassie pointed in the direction of Brett Taylor's lot.

Pathkiller nodded, his black eyes glittering in the morning sun as they fixed eastward, where she pointed. "An ancient Pottawatomie burial ground. Our ancestors' bones are out there. No one must disturb the dead."

"I respect your ancestors as much as anybody, but this issue was thoroughly settled, *legally* settled, months ago when I bought this land." Cassie found herself shouting over the increasingly loud beat of the tom-tom.

"Dale!" Pathkiller swiveled his head toward the frenzied drummer. "Lay off!"

"In the Seminole Treaty of 1866," Pathkiller said, slipping back into his singsong shaman voice with a little part-time graduate-student historian mixed in, "it was implied that these lands were allocated for the use of Indians and freedmen only. Chief Pleasant Porter may have sold it cheap later, but the people buried here have a right to remain...undisturbed."

Cassie sighed. "The area behind Mr. Taylor's lot was the *possible* site of only *one* family's burial plot—ordinary folks who happened to be part Pottawatomie, not Seminole." She intended to show Pathkiller that she knew her facts, too. "And no one, Pottawatomie or otherwise, has been buried up in those blackjacks since the Sullivan family bought the land right after World War I."

"So you admit there are Native people buried up there." Pathkiller went on in his long-winded way to explain that the Spirit Tribe wanted the bodies excavated and moved—at Cassie's expense—before any grotesque houses were built on top of them.

"Now, you wait just a minute!" Cassie asserted. "My houses are *not* grotesque! And I didn't say there were bodies up there. When we checked, and when the Sullivan sisters checked, no one *ever* found any evidence of graves. So, I don't know where the bodies are, the family doesn't know where they are, and *you* don't know where they are! A large part of that lot is already covered in concrete. I suspect you know that already—"

"What?" The man looked confused.

Cassie decided this guy was an extremely good actor. This bold intrusion onto her property had convinced her that perhaps she had found her vandals, at last. Although a thought flitted through her mind, impossible to dismiss. *Why would they be attacking Jake, as well?*

"You know that someone has vandalized my freshly poured concrete, twice."

Pathkiller looked genuinely offended at the implication. "The Spirit Tribe does not engage in vandalism."

"Well, obviously, you engage in acts of *trespassing*. Now make those people get up and move, before I call the Law."

Pathkiller held up a palm. "I am sorry, but our nonviolent resistance is necessary. Our mission is to bring public awareness to Native issues, such as the desecration of these burial sites. We use whatever peaceful means are necessary to obtain justice for those who cannot obtain it for themselves."

Cassie sighed. "I *told* you, there is no way to find and move any burial sites. I am not digging up this entire ridge, no matter how long your people lie around in the road.''

"But you can pay," the man asserted, crossing his arms over his chest.

"*Pay?*" Cassie condensed all of her disbelief and anger over this ridiculous situation into that one word.

"Pay the Pottawatomie tribe for the damages, for the disrespect to their ancestors."

"I already paid the legal owners for the land." Cassie gritted her teeth. "And the Spirit Tribe had better—"

Pathkiller telegraphed a signal and the chanters started up again, their cadence rapid and loud, as if their aim were to drown Cassie out.

That's when Cassie called the cops and had the Spirit Tribe protestors forcibly removed. She knew enough about lawsuits by now to know that no judge was going to make her pay for something that had been put to rest—literally—almost a century ago.

Along with the cops, a campus reporter was there with a photographer in tow. *Great,* Cassie thought, *pictures with captions.* Before they got in their sensible Hondas and left, the dancers, the drummers and the guy with the ponytail all posed for the paper, pointing at a nearby Dream Builders sign.

Not long after the protest, the Detloff house was hit again. This time someone had slit sacks of drywall with a nail claw and then flung the powdery crap all over the interior. One of the sacks had a cheap souvenir tomahawk imbedded in it. Cassie immediately thought of Pathkiller and the Spirit Tribe, but then she realized maybe that was what she was *supposed* to think.

This whole situation was driving her crazy, and the more she and Jake looked at every angle, the more worried and confused she became. When Jake had become a target, too, they began to consider Lana as a suspect again. But how could Lana have known about the Spirit Tribe? She hadn't seen the protest.

"She reads the paper," Jake pointed out dryly.

Despite these disruptions, the pages on the day-at-a-glance calendar in the little trailer flipped by. The lots on the creek side of the hill remained quiet, as Cassie had promised Jake weeks ago, and Jake's mares grew rounder, putting on their winter coats.

The drywallers and cabinetmakers had finished under Cassie's watchful eye, and the Detloff house was at last ready for stain and paint.

Brett Taylor's house was being framed, though not nearly as fast as Cassie wanted. Redoing the concrete had cost her an entire week, and she'd barely gotten the second slab poured before the first hard freeze blew in from the north on December sixteenth.

That was a Friday.

Cassie hopped in her pickup, slammed the door against a biting wind and flipped on the heater. Her cell phone chirped, and she snatched it off the seat, thinking it was the paint contractor up at the Detloffs, calling to complain about the sloppy drywallers again. She pulled her glove off with her teeth and hit the send button. "Yeah?" she snapped.

"Tomorrow's our anniversary."

"Jake?" She smiled and relaxed against the truck's

door, so glad to hear his voice. "What are you talking about? Our anniversary?"

"We've been dating for a whole month."

She giggled. Man, this was fun, getting romantic calls from an exciting man in the middle of her workweek.

"I want to celebrate. I have something real special in mind."

Cassie had a little something special in mind herself. Had for quite some time. She found herself constantly thinking carnal thoughts about the man at odd moments, unable to deny or stem them.

But Jake was being sincerely romantic. "I'll pick you up at seven. Wear something pretty."

CHAPTER ELEVEN

THE "SOMETHING SPECIAL" Jake had in mind, bless his heart, was Legend's.

Cassie didn't care if he had a repetitious bent. It wasn't the creative romantic gestures that made the relationship, she had discovered. It was the *man*.

And Cassie hoped he felt the same way—that it was the *woman* that mattered, not how she dressed. With everything going haywire in her business, Cassie hadn't had time to buy herself a date wardrobe. Tonight she was wearing the same black cashmere sweater and clingy floral skirt that she'd worn the last time they'd gone to Legend's. She'd added some tiny silver snowflake earrings in honor of the coming holiday and opted for more sensible midheeled boots instead of the strappy heels.

"Do you think we're ever gonna get tired of this place?" He pulled out her chair at their "usual" corner table.

"Or of each other?" Cassie smiled up at him. They had already reached the point where they could admit such things to each other, and Cassie delighted in the freedom, the openness, of this relationship. How could she have lived without this sharing, this intimacy for so long? *Because she'd never before expe-*

rienced it. She'd never had someone like Jake in her life and she hadn't known what she was missing.

The restaurant was decorated for Christmas, with small white lights swirling around a cluster of gold wire trees on the grand piano near their table. Jake's eyes glittered with the reflected light as he looked into hers.

"Me? Get tired of you? That'll never happen."

"I feel so at ease with you," he said later when he lifted his wineglass to her. "These times we have together mean so much to me. You'll never know."

Cassie lifted her glass to him. "I feel the same way about you." She looked into his eyes as she sipped, realizing that she could come to this restaurant with this man, sit at this same table with him and look into his eyes this way for as long as she lived. She would never, ever get tired of it. Jake Coffey already seemed as familiar to her as her own skin.

BUT LATER, AT THE FRONT DOOR of her house, she wondered where that comfortable familiarity had flown to, because suddenly she felt as awkward as a teenager coming home from a first date…facing a first kiss. Only, they'd already had their first kiss—and quite a few others—right here on this porch. Tonight, Cassie sensed that Jake had more than a kiss in mind.

"Would you like to come in for a while?" The words came out of her mouth easily enough, but as soon as she said them, her immediate impulse was to stall and offer Jake a glass of wine. Since they'd polished off the bottle at the restaurant, however, she decided it might be unwise to lower her defenses any further. But wasn't that the point here? Not only to lower her defenses, but also to eradicate the stupid things entirely. To free herself so she could accept the love Jake so clearly wanted to give, the love she so desperately needed to receive.

"You want some coffee?" she said after she had unlocked the door.

"No." He pushed the door fully open with his fingertips. "I want *you.*"

She turned to him, holding her breath, suddenly unable to step across the threshold of her own house. "Me?" she said breathlessly.

"Yes," he said quietly. "And I think you want me."

He braced an arm above her against the doorjamb and leaned forward. The kiss he gave her, under the soft yellow glow of her porch light, was slow and deliberate, as if he were reminding her of something important. When it was over, he let his mouth hover over hers for an instant, allowing their breath to form a powerful, secret connection. A hunger grew in Cassie so that when he kissed her the next time it felt like a wholly new experience, like the first kiss that she'd ever truly let herself experience with her whole body. He kept his arm braced above her, creating space between their bodies, allowing only their mouths to meet. This had the effect of making her crave the feel of his hard body against hers.

When he drew a ragged breath, she thought he would break the bond of their mouths, but he only moved away long enough to twist his head for a better fit, to kiss her again. Deeper, hotter. Finally, he lowered his arm and circled her waist, pulling her tightly against his chest. The contact felt so magnificent that she sank into him. He reached up and braced her jaw with his other palm, the V of his thumb under her chin, and kissed her again, taking command of the angle of her head, urging her tongue to follow his, to taste him the way he was tasting her. He seemed determined to give, and take, the maximum amount of pleasure that any kiss could give.

Cassie emitted an aching moan—a new sound for her—and to her disappointment that is when he broke off the contact.

He leaned into her, breathing hard, and whispered next to her ear. "Are you sure about this?"

Cassie could only nod. She wasn't at all sure about taking this step, but she was sure about the man. That kiss had reminded her...he was the one she wanted. She would simply have to step over her own fears. She was not going to disappoint this man, and she was not going to disappoint herself. She loved him too much.

They went inside.

But now what? she thought as she stood in her lamp-lit foyer. *Now what?*

She turned, and Jake was studying her with that tender, brown-eyed gaze of his.

"Actually, I would like some coffee," he said lightly. "Have you got decaf?" He reached up and gently slid her jacket off her shoulders. "I'll hang up our coats."

Enormously relieved, Cassie led him to the coat closet, then into her vast, well-lit kitchen. While Jake eased himself up on one of the trendy bar stools, she whammed and whacked around in cabinets and drawers. Decaf, can opener, spoons, coffee dipper, cups, saucers, sugar bowl, creamer. Finally there was nothing to do but watch the rich brew drip down into the carafe. Self-consciously, she folded her arms over her middle.

"You're nervous," he stated from behind her.

The pot made a few gurgling sounds, then Cassie found her voice. "I haven't had sex in three years." She didn't take her eyes off the dripping coffee.

"That doesn't matter." But mentally, Jake whistled in disbelief. *Three years.* Right now he could be thinking she was one uptight chick, but he realized she was simply a very choosy one. He looked around the immaculate, un-lived-in, stylish kitchen and decided she was probably a perfectionist about most everything. Cassie McClean was not sexually frigid, he'd satisfied himself about that already. She showed all the signs of being as warm and sexy as they come. But she *was* awfully picky, especially about men. He hoped that was something in his favor, not something he would have to painstakingly overcome.

But *three years?* Bless her heart, she had to be awfully deprived and lonely underneath that perfectionistic veneer. How could a woman so attractive, so intelligent, so successful, be so bereft of love? Well, his track record in the race for love wasn't much better. He wasn't about to tell her it had been well over a year now for him.

He cleared his throat. He wanted their first time together to be special, memorable, beautiful. How to proceed without making this so awkward that she got turned off for good? Right now, she was acting more skittish than one of his mares. His gaze slid to the sugar bowl and he smiled. Instead of loose sugar it contained sugar cubes.

She decanted the coffee into a china coffeepot and put the cups and saucers and napkins and sugar and cream—the whole bit—onto a cutesy tray. "Let's go into the living room."

In her comfortable cocoon of a living room he found it easy to relax. Soft oldies music played on the CD player. She kept it on perpetually, she told him. The carpet was plush, the drapes were heavy chintz, the throw pillows were colorful and plump. She was a very sensuous woman, he was already certain of that.

"I had a nice time tonight," he said, while she poured the coffee. "I always do with you, Cassie."

"Me, too." She smiled and handed him his cup, complete with two lumps of sugar stirred in.

They sipped their coffee in companionable silence, enjoying the music. One thing he loved about Cassie—well, there were so many things—was the fact that she didn't feel compelled, as some women did, to keep up a steady stream of chatter during a date.

When their cups were almost empty, they leaned back against the soft couch cushions and smiled into each other's eyes.

"I like your house." He purposely steered the conversation to something that she could talk about with ease.

"I designed and decorated it myself after I made a

handsome profit off my first housing development. I
wanted to do a house from top to bottom, completely
to my liking.''

"It feels right." His gaze panned the room. "It
feels like you."

"I hate to see an overdecorated space that has nothing to do with the personality of the person living
there, don't you?"

Jake nodded, although he didn't know much about
decorating, overdone or not.

"My father's house was like that," Cassie continued. "A showplace, not a home. I was much happier
once I moved to my aunt's house, even though it was
cluttered and chaotic there."

"How'd you feel when you came to my house?"
Jake did care about that. He'd already been day-
dreaming a little about moving her to the ranch as his
wife. Which was just plain goofy. He looked at the
well-appointed room surrounding him, imagining the
woman who lived *here* setting up house in the spare,
rambling Coffey ranch house.

"Oh, I was instantly comfortable," Cassie said.
"Because it's an honest place—like you. In fact, everything about Cottonwood Ranch has that clean…
straight-arrow feeling—like you."

Jake wasn't sure he knew how to handle being ad-
mired this way, being appreciated for the things that
mattered to him. It certainly had never been that way
in his marriage. He put his cup on the tray and focused on Cassie.

"Feeling more relaxed now?" He took the coffee

cup from her hands and placed it on the tray beside his.

She nodded. "I'm sorry. My nervousness isn't about you. It's just that intimacy feels like such a big step."

"I know. Just relax. We don't have to do anything unless you want to." Reaching up, he stroked her hair back from her cheek. He studied her eyes, her mouth. "I think you are so very beautiful, and there's nothing to worry about. Once you find someone you're this attracted to, the intimacy is easy."

"I know." She angled her face closer to his. "It's just that...I feel so...I don't know...like this really *means* something."

"It does."

She looked down, suddenly shy. Then she puffed out her lips in a sigh of frustration and clasped her fists in her lap. "Why do relationships have to be so hard for me!"

"Whoa. How about first we actually *have* the relationship before we decide how hard it is?"

Cassie sighed again, willed herself to relax and smiled. This was Jake. He would never hurt her. He would never, she was convinced, hurt anybody. "I'm sorry. You're right. It's just that... Oh, Jake." For the first time ever—she couldn't help herself—her voice sounded whiny. "How do people ever, you know, get together and take this enormous step?"

Jake studied Cassie's profile, her cute nose and the full pout of her lips as she sat, looking uptight and conflicted, with her small hands folded together under her chin as if she didn't know what to do with them.

He frowned. Cassie McClean was a complicated one, all right, but he loved her, anyway. He loved her very much, and he wanted her in the worst way. Sex had never been anything but easy for Jake. Too easy sometimes. Every woman he'd ever been with had plastered her hands all over him from the first date. The fact that Cassie had shown restraint, that she thought of this as an enormous step, made him love her all the more.

But right now, she seemed truly unable to overcome her nervousness. No, this wasn't going to be easy. He was going to have to help her. Well, this was one woman who was worth a little trouble at the outset. She was everything he wanted, and more. Honest and hardworking and smart and funny and kind. And beautiful. And incredibly sexy, even if she didn't know it yet.

He cleared his throat. "Earlier, I was thinking about something." He leaned forward and lifted the lid off the sugar bowl. "When you're trying to convince a horse to do something for the first time, or when they get skittish, it helps to give them a little treat, like one of these sugar cubes." He plucked one out. "You know, to kind of bribe them to...you know, get a little closer." He leaned toward her, grinning. "Then you use your hands to settle them down and get them used to the idea of being touched, and before long that horse is tame as can be, ready to try whatever you want to teach them."

Cassie made a wry little face at the silliness of what he'd said. "Is that your plan, to slip me a sugar cube, and tame me with your hands like one of your horses, so you can...teach me things?''

"That's it exactly," he murmured as he leaned toward her. "Now open your mouth like a good girl." He touched the sugar cube to her lips. She smiled tightly and said, "Stop it" through clenched teeth.

"Okay." He popped the sugar cube into his own mouth. "Have it your way. No sugar. We'll just go straight to the hands-all-over part."

Cassie smiled, but before she could protest he had his hands on her, possessively, intimately. The one he'd slipped under her sweater, high up on her ribs, had an insistent thumb that made strong repetitive strokes upward toward the underswell of her breast. Immediately, Cassie ached for more. The man did have amazing hands. *Amazing.*

"Okay," she whispered, "I give. I do want to do things, learn things."

"That's good." He continued his warm investigation of her curves.

"I want to do things—eh!" She sucked in a sharp breath as his thumb grazed her nipple through the thin latex of her bra.

"Yes?"

"I want to do the...the things that..." His warm palm took possession of her breast, and Cassie found that she had trouble talking. "Whatever you want to do."

"That's good. Then we both want this." His other hand slid up her back, under her sweater, and deftly unhooked the clasp of her bra. Then he slid that palm around and over her other breast.

Instinctively, Cassie arched her back.

"You know what I want to do *right now?*"

She shook her head and closed her eyes, focusing on the sensation of his hands—so intimate, so surprisingly expert and intent, as if they knew exactly what they were doing to her.

"For openers, I want to kiss you," he whispered near her ear, "and kiss you and kiss you and kiss you. Until your lips are raw." He tilted his head and plundered her mouth, making a very good start at it.

All the while, as they tested and tasted each other with abandon, his hands caressed her breasts. The dissolved sugar cube got mingled between their mouths making the flavor of their whole uninhibited exploration even sweeter. Part of what felt so good, Cassie realized, was to finally kiss him with abandon in private, on her couch, with no chance of interruption; to let him touch her breasts this way, with no need to stop until they felt like it. Kissing him and kissing him, as he suggested, and having him touch her like this, she decided, would not be a bad way to spend the entire night.

He broke off the kiss and pushed her sweater and soft bra up toward her collar bones, and as his eyes took in the shape of her flesh, Cassie's cheeks flamed. She hadn't realized this would go so fast! Here she was, half-naked, and they were still in the living room.

"Don't you want to go into the bedroom?" She knew she sounded hoarse, and her heart was thudding so hard she thought surely he must be able to see the beats in the valley between her breasts.

"No." His voice was low, as always, but it held a reverence, Cassie had not heard before. "Not yet."

He slipped off the couch and bent on one knee, hovering over her. He framed her breasts gently between his palms, looking at them, then up into her eyes. "Oh, Cassie," he murmured. "You are so beautiful."

Cassie resisted the urge to squirm away, to cut this short because of her acute embarrassment. She lay perfectly still, looking down at his face, allowing him to gaze back down at her breasts, allowing him to have his fill, while her heart continued to pound wildly.

He pushed her breasts together and softly fanned his hot breath over the sensitive tips, back and forth.

"Oh, Jake." She sighed, afraid she couldn't stand much more.

But then his breathing arrested. A beat of sheer torment passed between them before he took one nipple firmly into his mouth.

"Ahh!" Cassie gasped. She pressed her head back into the couch cushions and thought she might lose control. Three years, she thought as the sensation of his warm mouth overwhelmed her, was an unmercifully long time for a healthy young woman to live without experiencing these powerful feelings. Why had she resisted lovemaking for so long? Because there had been no one she wanted to do these intimate things with. There had been no Jake in her life, that's why. But he was here now, kneeling before her, thrilling her as no man ever had. As his mouth seemed to tug at some core of feeling deep within her, her heart burst open in a cry of pure joy for this precious gift. At long last. *Jake*.

He stopped, and Cassie opened her eyes, meeting his smoldering brown ones.

"Cassie," he whispered. He brought his face up, level with hers. Framing her cheeks with his palms, he rested his elbows gently against the sides of her exposed, aching breasts. He paused, his breath shallow, before he said, "I love you."

"Oh, Jake." His admission took her breath away. "Say that again."

"I love you." He whispered it this time, with no hint of hesitation, while brushing his lips over hers. She closed her eyes and opened her mouth, and he answered her invitation with a bruising, lathing, consuming kiss.

As they kissed, Cassie felt herself opening to him, hot and damp, and she felt a certain awe, a kind of weak-in-the-knees gratitude, at how quickly and completely her body was responding to him. For his part, Jake was pressing ahead, hands everywhere, obviously determined to bring their bodies to fulfillment.

"Jake." She stopped him with a weak fist turned into his chest. "Wait."

He stopped his fondling immediately. "Okay," he said quietly, though he was breathing hard.

"I...this makes me feel...I think I'd rather go up to the bed for this. I'm going to be awkward enough as it is."

"You could never be awkward, but we'll do whatever you want." His gaze was tender and sincere as he brushed the hair back from her brow. He pushed away from the couch and stood wide-legged before her, offering her his hand.

She pulled her clothing down and let him pull her up.

JAKE FOLLOWED CASSIE UP her circular staircase with his pulse pounding. She was, by far, the most desirable woman he had ever known. It wasn't her body so much. Though her petite curves were certainly pleasing enough, enticing enough, to make any man hot, he knew it was something far beyond physical attraction that drew him so powerfully to Cassie McClean. Something far deeper than lust. But he couldn't articulate it, and he always ended up thinking it was just...*her*. The way she looked at him. The way she talked, moved. Everything about her, from her voice to her attitude to her smell, was womanly and soft and feminine...and uniquely Cassie. But mostly it was her face—her eyes, her mouth—that he saw in his dreams, both the day and the night ones. He wanted to fall asleep and wake up looking at that face for the rest of his life—he knew that already. Should he tell her so? No. Too soon. That level of commitment might spook her. It was enough that she was taking him to her bed so soon, despite her nervousness about it. But she wouldn't regret it, and she wouldn't be nervous for long, he'd see to that.

Though she was leading the way up, with each step Cassie felt her confidence weakening. What if he didn't like the way she made love? His ex-wife had looked incredibly sleek, incredibly beautiful, and surely he'd bedded other equally beautiful, and most likely skilled, women. She remembered how clumsy, how totally bumbling and strained, the sex had been with her college boyfriend. She'd consented to go all the way with him, even after she'd realized their relationship was immature. It was as if she'd been diving in, getting it over with, getting her virginity out of the way. After college there'd been that brief liaison with a young architect in the firm where she'd interned. He was sweet, decent and funny, but there had been no real passion between them. That's when she'd decided to forget about relationships and concentrate on work, channeling all her pent-up sexual energy into building her dream.

But then came Jake.

Jake.

Cassie braved a glance back at the top of his dark head, at his broad shoulders, as he climbed the stairs behind her. He looked up and smiled, and her heart skipped.

She wanted so badly to please him, to forge a deep physical bond between them that could never be broken. But she was so woefully inexperienced. She bit her lip, taking each step more slowly than the last and feeling vexed that her aunt Rosemarie had been so vague and uninformed about the womanly arts. But poor Aunt Rosemarie couldn't be blamed. She'd done her best, and she'd loved Cassie in her own sweet, bungling way. Thoughts of her aunt caused Cassie to recall that bittersweet conversation about Cassie's sterility. *Life,* her aunt had wisely said, *you have your life, Cassie, and you must live it to the full. Think of what you* have, *not of what you don't.*

And right now, by some miracle, what Cassie had was Jake Coffey, following her up the stairs of a beautiful house that she had designed herself. Jake Coffey, a man who had just told her he loved her and wanted to show her just how much. She wondered if she should tell him that she could never bear children. No. That sad news would surely spoil everything. No. If she told him she was sterile, he would want to know why, and it was too soon in their relationship for such sad revelations. She would tell him, and soon. Just not tonight. *Tonight.* Were they actually going to consummate this relationship *tonight?*

At the top of the stairs, at the very portal of the chamber where they would do the deed, she whirled around and threw up her palm like a traffic cop. "Wait!"

Jake froze on the step below her. "What now?" He poked his tongue into his cheek to gain control, immediately softening his tone. "I mean, what's wrong?" There was no denying that certain parts of him were getting mighty restless.

"I'm…I can't."

Jake wanted to smite his forehead. Hadn't they plowed this ground downstairs? But instead he gripped the stair railing and said, "Just tell me what's wrong." And this time he managed to make it more gentle.

"I'm scared."

That got him. He stepped up to her level. "Oh, sweetheart." He was swamped with genuine tenderness now. He stroked her hair back. It was thick in his hand, surprisingly soft. "It'll be okay. I promise.

I'll be real gentle." He ran his fingers down to touch her face.

But she turned away, leaning out over the baluster. "You don't understand. It's not about how you'll be. It's how *I'll* be. The last time I did this, it went—" she blushed "—badly."

"Maybe that was the guy's fault."

"No," she protested, "it was me. I think I felt like a hypocrite. I knew I didn't really love him, I knew that I wasn't ever going to marry him, even after we got physically involved. It was awful. I got so uptight every time we did it."

Jake was still stuck back on that word *marry*. Was this a good time to bring it up? Would getting that subject out in the open make her less nervous? Or more? He certainly wanted to broach it, but instinct warned him that it was way too soon for marriage talk.

"It'll be okay." He reached out and took her hand. "I love you. And I think," he bent forward to peer into her eyes, "that you feel the same about me."

She did. After all these years of wondering if she could even have these feelings for a man, she was almost overwhelmed by them now. The fact that they'd only been dating for a month seemed insignificant. "I do," she whispered. It felt so good to say it. "But what if..." She looked down. "What if I stiffen up on you?"

He arched an eyebrow. "That would be my job, wouldn't it?"

She barely relaxed and gave him a reluctant smile,

but it was enough to allow him to gather her into his arms. "Don't you feel safe with me, Cassie?"

"I do, but I'm afraid. And…" She sighed and put her palms on his chest, then pressed her forehead into the backs of her fingers. "There's something else I—" She stopped herself.

He raised her head and backed up a space, frowning down and thinking. He saw genuine fear in her eyes, and the beginning of tears. What had she been about to tell him? He could see that it was something serious, something deeper than first-time jitters, something that slow hands and sweet talk wouldn't necessarily fix.

But she pushed away from him and turned her head aside again, obviously not ready to tell him what it was.

He wondered how to get them off this landing and moving back toward the intimacy they both wanted, needed. "Okay." He sighed overdramatically. "I expect you are right. Since this is our first time, it's bound to go pretty badly. There's no help for it. We'll just have to march in there—" he jabbed a commanding finger at the bedroom "—and get this thing over with."

She grinned and slapped at his biceps.

He snatched her hand. "Come on." And he led her through the door.

CHAPTER TWELVE

JAKE THOUGHT HER BEDROOM was a perfect reflection of Cassie. Everything spotlessly clean, perfectly ordered, yet lush—a direct contrast to his spartan private quarters. Yet, despite their differences, he felt instantly at home here. As she went around switching on various lamps, he imagined her coming up here to indulge her creative moods, her reveries. The fabrics at the windows and on the bed were softly colored, but the atmosphere wasn't overly frilly or sentimental. For Jake, there was no sense of discomfort, no feeling of anything foreign or pretentious about this inner sanctum she had created. He supposed that was because everything about it—from the Frank Lloyd Wright prints on the wall to the well-worn teddy bear propped on the bed—broadcast a sense of ''Cassie.'' It was a room that begged him to enter, to touch, to explore, to stay with her, to luxuriate in her secrets.

He quickly assessed the physical layout—a huge four-poster bed with lots of pillows, matching chests, a floral chaise longue under a fringed lamp, casting shadows where he could almost see her body imprinted. He crossed the room to a door that opened into an enormous bathroom, and flipped on the recessed lighting.

"Whoa. Look at that tub." He stepped into an apricot-pink, granite-clad chamber.

Even though she had designed it herself, Cassie had to admit the tub was a work of art, with built-in steps, low seating and comfortable headrests. She had seldom had the luxury of looking at it through another person's eyes, and she enjoyed Jake's amazed reaction.

"This is pretty over-the-top."

"I figure it will boost the resale value of the house." She came up behind him, tiptoed and hooked her chin on his shoulder. "Twenty-six inches deep. Solid inlaid granite with ten pulsating water jets."

He smiled over his shoulder into her eyes. "Well, well. Who woulda thought you were such a little hedonist."

"Actually, I don't use it much." She nodded toward the glassed-in shower in the corner. "That's more my style—fast and efficient."

Jake bent and turned on the tap of the tub, then cupped his big hand under the flow. "Well, tonight we're not aiming for fast and efficient, are we."

He flipped the plug lever and the massive tub started to fill. He straightened and smiled at her. "Where are your bubbles?"

"Bubbles?" She had inched back toward the doorway, clutching her arms around the waist of her black sweater.

"Yeah, bubbles." His eyes narrowed and he pressed the tip of his tongue to his upper lip as if concentrating. "In here?" He opened a set of paneled double doors.

"Are we...are we really going to take a bubble bath?"

"Yeah." Jake had his hands braced high on the open closet doors, and was bending slightly at the knees while he peered in. "Ah-ha!" He produced a bottle of foaming milk bath that her aunt had given her last Christmas. He uncapped the lid, ran it under his nostrils, crossed the room to her. "This okay?" He waved it under her nose.

Cassie nodded stiffly. "Now, now," he chided as he stepped over to the tub and dribbled in the milk bath. "Don't act like I'm gonna drown you. This will help you relax. I promise."

"I'm relaxed!" Cassie gave a nervous laugh, making the words a lie.

Jake swished his hand around in the water. "I like it pretty hot, how about you?" He walked over and flipped on the heater fan, then faced her. "Ready?"

"Jake, don't you...don't you think we should do something else before we...before we get in a *bathtub* together?"

He put his hands on his hips. "Well, we could make love first, then take the bath. Although, I think you're gonna like the whole thing better the other way around. It usually helps to play a little first."

Play? Cassie thought she might faint right there on the granite floor, but Jake crossed the small room, anchored his hands on her shoulders and, steadying her, gently turned her around to face a bank of mirrors. Slowly, he raised her arms and slid the sweater up, up and over her head, revealing the only black bra she owned.

Cassie looked away from her reflection, running one hand through her hair and angling the other arm demurely over the front of the lacy bra.

"Tell you what." Jake's voice sounded strained. "I'll go out there—" he nodded toward the bedroom "—and you undress and get in the water. Let me know when you're ready." He left and closed the door with a soft *click*.

Cassie looked up at her reflection. Her eyes stared wildly back at her. Why was she acting so panicky if this was what she wanted? This *was* what she wanted, wasn't it?

Music drifted in from the bedroom. Apparently Jake had found the CD player beside the bed. Jackson Browne. One of her favorites. *Good choice, Jake.* Easygoing and masculine, sentimental and soulful. *Kind of like you.*

Oh, yes. This *was* what she wanted. *He* was what she wanted. With trembling fingers, she stripped off her boots, skirt, hose and panties. She twisted her hair up off of her neck and anchored it with a clip, then practically leaped into the water. It felt hot and heavenly and did calm her immediately, just as he had promised.

"I'm ready!" she called out.

He opened the door instantly, as if he'd been standing on the other side with his ear pressed to it. He was still fully dressed, and in one hand he held the pillar candle from her bedside table.

He didn't smile at her as if she looked cute amidst the bubbles, as she had hoped he would. Instead he regarded her seriously, intently, with eyes flashing, before he turned to the counter.

"Got a match?"

"In that drawer." Cassie nodded to the one at the end.

He took his time lighting the candle, while Cassie stayed low in the bubbles, her tension, her need to do this, building to a maddening crescendo. Holding the lit candle, he reached around and flicked off the light switch, and the softer lighting helped Cassie relax another notch.

"Now," he said, and set the candle on the granite shelf by the tub. "Let's take this real slow and easy."

He settled himself on the edge of the tub behind her and twisted his torso forward, looking into her eyes while he efficiently rolled up his sleeves. While his eyes traveled over her skin, shimmering softly in the candlelight, she looked and saw that he had already grown hard.

"Sit up," he said huskily.

She inched up and stopped when the water and bubbles grazed just above her nipples.

"Lean forward just a little bit," he urged.

He picked up a bar of scented soap, lathered his hands and started to massage her shoulders and back. Cassie released a small groan. "Jake, you really do have wondrous hands."

"Let's hope so." His deep voice had dropped to a hypnotic timbre.

As Jake slowly, tenderly, laid claim to Cassie's body with those hands, the sounds of Jackson Browne's "Our Lady of the Well" drifting in from the bedroom, Cassie closed her eyes and thought that, until now, their relationship had been like those lyrics: a long dance done in silence. They had both wanted this from the very start. Her earlier apprehension gave way to gratitude that at last their life as lovers was beginning.

"Kiss me again," she whispered.

"Whatever you say," he whispered back.

He braced an arm against the opposite side of the tub and leaned around and applied his lips to hers. As he did so, his other hand, tender, seeking, utterly perfect to Cassie, slid down over her breasts. When the kiss ended, he knelt on one knee on the step and leaned her backward in the water, exposing her front, supporting her back firmly with his other arm, his palm gripping her bottom. When he bent forward and trailed his mouth down her neck, toward her breast, Cassie felt herself quivering, giving over, completely, to him. She pushed up, higher out of the water, and he fastened his mouth on his target.

Cassie's breathing seemed to seize for one instant, and then she found enough breath to moan, "Oh, Jake."

He kept his mouth firmly working where it was, but slid his other hand down, seeking lower, lower. To her belly, pressing gently a moment and then lower still. His first deeply intimate touch of her was so exquisite, so perceptive, that Cassie gave another small cry of surprise.

"Trust me," he murmured as his fingers explored, finding her most sensitive bud. He took his time touching her, and raised his head, looking into her eyes, gauging the depth of her reaction. And though it wasn't long before Cassie wanted to close her eyes—for the pleasure he was giving her was that acute—she found she could not. Her eyes seemed locked to Jake's gaze. They looked steadily at each other in the flickering candlelight, while he encouraged her with shameless, skilled fingers and sweet murmurings about her softness, her femininity, her beauty.

The hunger in his eyes built and the movement of his hand got bolder, more demanding, and Cassie involuntarily rose to match his strokes. To match his hunger with her own.

She came that way, rising from the water, in his arms, with their eyes locked, until the very moment when, overwhelmed, she squeezed hers shut and turned her face against the wet fabric over his shoulder, crying out.

When her cries subsided and her breathing and body relaxed, he held her tightly against him in the water. "Cassie," he whispered as he pressed his cheek to the top of her head. But he seemed unable to find more words.

He lowered her back into the water gently, kissed her forehead. Then stood.

Cassie couldn't move. She found she could only float, watching him. Without speaking, he stripped off his soaked shirt. Then, with his hooded eyes still fixed on her languid ones, he removed his boots, socks, trousers, shorts. Still fully aroused, he climbed the steps and lowered his massive body into the water, facing her, with his arms open, and said, "Come here."

She raised her arms and floated into his.

"I want you inside of me," she admitted as she linked her arms tightly around his neck. "Now."

"Whatever you say." His reply sounded throaty, and he swallowed hard before he added, "Whatever you say, sweetheart."

He fastened his mouth on hers in another lusty kiss and kept it there as he guided her hips over his. But then he froze, lifting her back up with strong hands.

"Shouldn't we talk about birth control before we go any farther?"

She groaned and tilted her head back. Jake saw the anxious look in her eyes just before she closed them. "Did I say something wrong?" He searched her face.

She opened her eyes and looked down, then shook her head. But a moment later she nodded slowly. "Yes. I mean, no, you didn't say something wrong. It's just that there *is* something wrong…with me." She eased forward onto his chest, keeping her face turned toward his arm. "I wasn't going to tell you tonight, but I think I want to. I think I *ought* to, before we…before we do this."

"Okay." He slid his arms up around her back, settling her into a comfortable position against his side.

She sighed and rested her head on his shoulder. "This is so hard."

"There's nothing you can't tell me, okay?" Under the water, he stroked her back, her hip.

He felt her nod.

"So just tell me."

Cassie pressed her forehead to his jaw, ordering herself to be honest, to be brave. "I'm sterile." She hadn't meant to blurt out the word like that, but over the years, she'd found there was no other way to tell people this awful truth.

She felt his body tense for one instant, then he eased them down lower, covering them to their shoulders with the water and bubbles. He ran a hand low over her belly and rested it there, intimately. "You mean you can't have babies?"

She nodded again. "Right. I can never have children—at least, not my own." She drew a huge fortifying breath. "I think you need to know that before we get more involved."

"Cassie, let's face it. We are already involved."

She nodded. "Maybe I should have told you before now."

He wrapped his arms tightly around her and pulled her closer over his chest, entwining their legs. He planted a kiss on her temple. "Is that what you were trying to tell me on the stairs?"

Cassie nodded again.

"Cassie," he murmured tenderly. "Sweetheart. You know it doesn't matter, you know I've fallen in love with you, and you know I'll keep on loving you, don't you?"

She nodded. Somehow she did know. The attraction between them was stronger than anything she ever could have imagined. It had to do with the two of them and only with the two of them. Everything else was secondary.

"But I'd just like to know, because I care about

you—what happened? I mean, why? Why can't you have kids? You're so young. And your body is so healthy, so…perfect.''

She sighed again. ''I had leukemia when I was a girl. The chemotherapy and radiation destroyed my eggs.''

Jake felt the same way he had one time when Arrestado had landed a kick to his gut. ''Leukemia?'' was the only word he could get out as he fought to keep his breathing level.

''Yes. But I'm fine now,'' she reassured him. ''I've never had a single relapse. The sterility is a small price to pay for my life—that's what my aunt Rosemarie always said.''

''I agree with your aunt.'' Jake pressed another protective kiss to her temple. *My God, Cassie had almost died as a youngster.* He tried to imagine how he'd feel if anything like that ever happened to Jayden, and pushed the horrifying thought away.

''Let's not let this overshadow our time together,'' Cassie pleaded. ''It happened a long time ago. I just thought you should know before you make love to me. There won't be any pregnancies—not now, not ever.''

''I don't care,'' Jake said emphatically. He tilted her sideways in the water, facing her. ''Don't you understand that?'' He stroked her wet hair back and kissed her temple again. ''I'm just glad you're okay. I want *you.* I wanted you from the first time I saw you.'' He kissed her eyes, half-closed in a look of grateful relief.

''I didn't know how I was going to tell you.''

"It doesn't matter how we tell each other things. What's important is to get the cards on the table, and then try to understand each other. You hear me? I love *you*." He reverently touched his lips to her mouth. "I love you so much that—" he tilted her chin up and looked deep into her eyes "—I was even thinking about asking you to marry me tonight."

Cassie's eyes went wide.

Uh-oh. He had been right. It was way too soon to be saying these words.

"You mean it," she said, spreading her palm over his heart. And then he realized—she wasn't dismayed, she was awed.

He nodded solemnly, sliding his wet hand up over hers and thinking, *This is it, then—I am proposing to the woman of my dreams, here, in a bathtub.* Strange, he felt none of the predictable apprehension that such a moment might bring. He felt none of the old bugaboos about relationships that had haunted him since his divorce. Cassie seemed so completely different from other women, so trustworthy and kind and just plain good. And unlike the compromise marriage to his ex-wife, he wanted this woman with all his heart. Not because they were "a good fit" or because they shared horse-ranching interests. Or because she was a pretty little filly and he was a prime stud, as Lana's father had once crudely said. Or because a child was on the way. He wanted Cassie for herself. He wanted Cassie for *himself.*

He hoped he hadn't just scared the hell out of her. "So what would you say if I asked you?"

His heart thudded against their palms while her

pretty mouth worked, struggling to form words. "I'd say yes! Yes!" She threw herself over him, digging her fingers into his damp hair and showering tiny kisses over his face. "Yes-yes-yes!"

He finally subdued her mouth by consuming it with his own.

When they stopped the kiss, her eyes grew serious. "No one's ever asked me that before," she said.

"You're kidding!" Jake studied her face. He never grew tired of looking at her. To him, her face was perfect. His ideal. "I would think you'd have guys trying to lure you to the altar every day."

Cassie shook her head. "I don't think I ever let anybody get close enough to ask. I think I scare most men. It's a miracle you had the guts to do it."

"I didn't intend to..." He looked down and realized she might be taking his meaning wrong. "Don't get me wrong! I meant every word. I was just afraid you'd turn me down. This is so sudden."

"It is, isn't it?" Her thoughtful expression made Jake wish he hadn't reminded her. She untangled her arms from around him and sat forward in the water, putting as much distance between them as was possible in a shared bathtub. Jake studied her smooth, shapely back, hunched in thought—in withdrawal— and his heart sank.

"I mean, we don't really know each other." Cassie spoke quietly. "We don't know each other's habits or hobbies or hang-ups. We don't know how we like to eat or sleep or handle our finances. We haven't discussed our views on raising children—I don't even know your child yet! And what about religion? I don't even know your religion! We don't know if we have addictions or phobias or neuroses—''

"Phobias or neuroses! Have you got some phobias and neuroses you want to haul out?'' He was trying to tease her out of her sudden attack of nerves.

But she shot an apprehensive look over her shoulder that said he wasn't succeeding.

"Listen. There's plenty of time for neuroses and phobias and all that.'' Jake pulled her back to his chest, then hugged her tightly. "Right now, let's enjoy what we have. It's rare, believe me.'' If only he could tell her that he'd had enough relationships to be able to spot the genuine article. But talking about past relationships would probably only scare her more. "We know we are physically compatible, and that's a very big part of it, believe me. I know. And now we know we would at least *like* to marry each other. If you want to be old-fashioned about it, you could say we know our intentions.'' He felt her relax. "We can't take those words back, but it doesn't mean we can't take our time and do this in our own way.''

"In our own way?''

"That's what being a couple means—doing things together, in your own way.''

She rested her head completely on his shoulder and released a huge sigh. "Yes, in our own way.''

Relief and warmth spread through Jake. Maybe he hadn't scared her off, after all.

"For now—'' he swallowed ''—let's just consider the question asked and answered and then go one day at a time.''

"Asked and answered,'' she whispered.

He kissed her. It seemed like the best thing to do. And the passion rebuilt so fast it sent a tremor through him.

She broke the kiss and looked down, blatantly admiring him. Then she gazed back into his eyes, hers shining, as she closed a hand, at first tentatively then more firmly, around him.

He sucked in a breath and closed his eyes, his body involuntarily arched forward at her strokes. "Whoa," he whispered. "This is a surprise."

"Make love to me now," she insisted.

"I will," he said, "but I want to go slow." He'd gotten those words out by an act of sheer will. What he really wanted to do right now was drive so deeply into her that they might never be parted.

"You do?" she teased, with her hand making the prospect of going slow seem utterly impossible.

"I do." He put his hands on her, as well. "Because I don't want you to remember this moment as a painful one."

She flipped above him in the water and plastered herself around him, but he maintained his self-control.

"I don't care if it hurts!" She pushed herself up on his chest and beamed down at him. "I've been waiting for this all of my life."

And so, with her eagerness and Jake's forbearance enjoining them, the dance they'd done for so long in silence became, at last, fully embodied, fully real, as each to the other they were given and taken. At first, at Jake's insistence, slowly, carefully. And then, later, with fierce abandon. Given and taken. Taken and given again.

CHAPTER THIRTEEN

CASSIE COULDN'T BELIEVE how having a lover—a *fiancé!*—changed her life. Jake, once he'd gotten his hands on her, didn't seem to want to take them off. They stole time together every night—at her house, with the tub and the couch and the bed and the rug in front of the fireplace for their benefit—but he always seemed to want more. And Cassie did, too. Despite the increasingly dire distractions on the job, it seemed like she could think of little else but Jake. *Jake.* At long last, Jake!

He'd show up at one of the jobsites around noon. It got to where one of them would simply say, "Where?" and the other would give a one-word answer. As soon as the men broke for lunch, off Cassie and Jake would go to rendezvous. They made love far off, down by the river, hidden in the cottonwood trees, on a quilt that Jake had stashed behind his pickup seat. They made love in his truck with the tinted windows, down a secluded lane, parking like teenagers. They even made love in her little work trailer, after sundown, when all the crews had gone home, with the door locked and the blinds drawn and the taste of each other filling the close air like wine.

"You sure are creative," Jake told her once, after she'd attacked him wantonly.

"I'm an architect." Cassie tossed her hair. "Comes with the territory. Besides, I find you very... inspiring." She ran her tongue in a soft circle at the notch of his throat.

"Mmm." He groaned. "You'd better practice that move a little bit."

You'd better practice that had become their pet phrase.

"I want to get you a huge ring for Christmas," he said.

But Cassie made him wait. "I thought we agreed to work up to this slowly," she reasoned. "An engagement ring at Christmas would be awfully public. Other people need time to get used to the idea of us as a couple first."

"Why do you say that? It's nobody's business what we do. I want you to have my ring."

A couple of weeks of lovemaking had completely overturned his earlier temperate thinking about "going slow."

"Jake," Cassie urged, "think of Jayden. This is a bad time for her. What if Lana takes you to court? Your daughter's whole life will be upset. And you want to throw in the idea of a stepmom she hardly knows? And think of your dad. You've just now gotten him used to Donna and a healthy daily routine. Alzheimer's patients can't handle too many changes at once. It's enough that we know how we feel about each other right now. This is a huge decision, and even if we feel comfortable making it so quickly, we have to go gently with everybody else.''

So they agreed to keep their impulsive engagement a secret—at least until the custody suit with Lana was settled, at least until Jayden's future was more secure, at least until the vandal had been caught, at least until the mares had foaled, at least until... But Jake couldn't help an occasional bout of frustration. The whole point of being engaged, he figured, was to let the rest of the world know about it.

THE WHOLE WORLD might not have known about it, but Cassie's aunt Rosemarie quickly guessed the depth of Jake and Cassie's relationship. A week before Christmas she appeared at Cassie's house, uninvited, about suppertime, as was their old habit, just as Jake showed up, too, as was his new habit.

Maybe it was the poinsettia he carried in. Maybe it was the way he patted Cassie's bottom when he hadn't realized Rosemarie had stepped into the kitchen. Maybe it was the fact that he had showed up for supper at all, at Cassie's house, in the evening, uninvited.

In any case, it wouldn't take a genius to see what was going on. Especially when Jake excused himself right after supper. Cassie wondered if he went home to keep up appearances for Rosemarie's benefit. She wasn't surprised when her aunt waltzed up to the topic.

"What a lovely, lovely man." Rosemarie rinsed a plate languidly, as if dishwashing were the last thing on her mind.

"Yes, he is." Cassie stopped arranging the silverware basket and eyed her aunt.

"So...*manly.*"

"Uh-huh." Cassie went back to work.

"He is the one, of course, that you told me about before."

"Yes, he is."

"And?"

"And what?"

"Well...you know what I mean. Have you two become lovers?"

Cassie stopped loading the dishwasher and looked at Rosemarie, wide-eyed. "Aunt Rosemarie!"

"What?" Her aunt's answering expression was all innocence.

"You can't ask me *that!*"

Rosemarie's mouth made a little *O* and her cheeks colored furiously. "I didn't mean *that!* I meant, you know, is he your...oh, dear, let me rephrase it. Is he your boyfriend?"

Boyfriend. What a silly word for a grown woman to use to describe her...well, okay, her *lover.*

"Boyfriend?" Cassie's cheek's flamed and she resumed loading the dishes.

"Well? You know what I mean. Is it serious?" Aunt Rosemarie persisted.

Cassie glanced at her aunt. "I'm afraid it is."

"Afraid? Whatever is there to be afraid of?"

"Nothing." Cassie looked down, senselessly rearranging the glasses in the top tray.

The clanking of the glasses was the only sound in

the spacious kitchen for one moment, then Rosemarie said quietly, "So you've told him, then?"

Cassie looked up. She could see echoes of the old anxiety about the leukemia in the way her aunt held the dish towel. Clutched in both hands against her sternum in that pose she'd always had at Cassie's bedside, as if she were praying.

"You mean, have I told him that I can't have children?"

"Now, Cassie." Rosemarie fisted the towel down next to her thigh. "I thought you had that all straight in your mind. You *can* have children. You just can't get pregnant. So, have you told Jake...everything?"

"Yes."

"And how did he react?"

Cassie smiled. "He asked me to marry him."

Rosemarie looked stunned, then her face was graced with a smile that was as bright as the sun. She tossed her dish towel over her shoulder and swept Cassie into a fierce hug.

"Oh, my!" She released Cassie and flapped her hands beside her face. "And you said yes?"

Cassie, still smiling, nodded and got another bone-crushing hug.

Rosemarie pushed Cassie back, examining the bride-to-be. She pressed her delicate fingers to her crepey cheeks. "Good lands! A wedding! I'll have so much to do!"

Cassie held up a restraining palm. "Don't get carried away just yet. In fact, you must promise not to tell anybody. For now, Jake and I are keeping our engagement to ourselves."

Rosemarie looked crestfallen. "Forevermore why?"

"He has a vindictive ex-wife. She's trying to take their daughter out of Jake's home. Her history indicates that if she knew about me, she might get really hostile. We don't want anything to jeopardize Jayden's security."

"Jayden? That's his daughter's name? Goodness, Cassie! You will have a child in your life!"

The look on Rosemarie's face was so incredibly sweet that Cassie placed three fingers to her aunt's dear cheek. Aunt Rosemarie always knew how to react with perfect love.

"Yes, I will. And she's very cute. A young girl finding her way."

"How old is she?" Rosemarie asked with genuine interest.

"Twelve, going on twenty."

"How incredible! How *serendipitous!* That is the very age you were when you came to live with me."

"I know." Cassie smiled, remembering her rebellious disruption of her aunt's solitary, eccentric life. "I don't see how you did it. I was a bit of a pain, wasn't I?"

"No!" Aunt Rosemarie lied, as she always did when this subject came up. "You were an absolute darling! But twelve *is* a challenging age. No doubt this child will need lots of love from you."

"Well." Cassie patted her aunt's arm lightly. "I need to get to know her first. But I'm sure I'll get the hang of it. I learned how to love a child from the very best of teachers."

Rosemarie reached for Cassie's fingers, squeezed them. Rosemarie had always been able to show spontaneous affection this way. And now Cassie would pass that affection on to Jake, and eventually, she hoped, to Mack and to Jayden and perhaps even to more children. What would have become of her after Boss went to prison if she hadn't had the steadfast love of this dear, simple woman, this saving angel?

"Aunt Rosemarie, I thank God every day for you," Cassie said sincerely.

"Oh, Cassie, I'm the one who is thankful. You are the most precious gift God ever gave to me."

While they finished up the dishes they reminisced about all the fun they had when Cassie was a young girl, and talked about the beautiful wedding Cassie and Jake would eventually have. Cassie was feeling happy and relaxed, pleased that Rosemarie liked Jake. She was just finishing wiping down the counters when the phone rang.

"Hello?" Cassie said into the receiver. Then she said, "What?" The alarm in her voice caused Rosemarie to cross the kitchen to her, her aunt's face scrunched with concern. "Oh, no! How far has it spread?" She listened again. "I'll be right there."

CHAPTER FOURTEEN

CASSIE CALLED JAKE on her cell phone as she drove across town. She got his voice mail and left a frustrated message. "Hi. It's me. There's a grass fire at The Heights. The fire department called to notify me. Took my forwarding number off one of the signs. I just wanted to warn you and your family. And I...I was hoping you'd meet me up there."

She called the ranch house next.

"Hello!" said a chirpy preteen voice.

"Jayden?"

"Yes." Wariness.

"It's Cassie McClean. We met a couple of times, once when your pony died."

"*Pony?*" The child's voice sounded mocking. "A *pony* is a smaller breed of horse. You mean the *foal?*"

Cassie heard the giggling of another teenager in the background. "Yes. The foal. Listen, is your dad there?"

"No. He's not here." More giggling. Jostling.

"Jayden, listen. Is Donna Morales there?"

"No." An impatient sigh.

"Listen, then. Do you all know that there's a grass fire up on the ridge?"

"No—Emily stop it!" Jayden's voice moved away from the receiver. "There's a fire outside!"

"Is your grandfather there?"

"No. Just me and my friend Emily. Donna and Jose took Grandpa to the Alzheimer's support group. Buck and a couple of the hands are still out in the barns. Oh, gosh. Let me talk to my dad."

"He's not here, honey. Remember? That's why I'm calling—"

"But I thought my dad was with *you*," the child interrupted, making it sound like an accusation.

"He was, but he just left." Cassie felt like she wasn't getting through to the child. Now she understood why Jake had excused himself right after the meal was over. She'd thought maybe he was being considerate, giving her time to visit with Rosemarie, but he was making it an early night because Jayden, who looked mature but clearly wasn't, was home alone with a friend.

"I am coming over there, Jayden."

"Why? We don't need you—"

"Jayden, if Jose is with Donna and Mack, where are the other hands on the ranch?"

"How should I know?"

"I'll be there in a minute."

Cassie drove right past The Heights—time to deal with that threat later—and straight down the ranch road. She turned off through the gates and roared up the driveway to the house.

Cassie loaded Jayden and her friend Emily into her pickup and drove back the way she had come.

"I don't see why we have to go with you." Jayden

crossed her arms over her chest and sank against the passenger door. Poor little Emily, a sturdy brunette with more freckles than Cassie, sat ramrod straight between the two, obviously feeling the tension.

"Because you are children," Cassie explained kindly, "and until I know how far this fire has spread, I am not leaving you alone in a house in harm's way, with no adults in sight."

"My dad called. He's checking out the fire, then coming home. We'll probably pass right by him."

It turned out Jake was up on the hill, circling the fire on the back of Arrestado, trying to help the firefighters assess the parameters of the blaze out in the woods. Jake could ride the horse over paths where fire vehicles couldn't go. It turned out he'd given quick instructions to two hands when he stopped at the barn and told them that if the wind shifted they were to go get the girls out of the house.

The wind shifted several times, but the fire never got past The Heights. Some of the bare scrub oaks and winter-dry cedars went up like Roman candles, but none of the houses were damaged. When the smoke cleared, Cassie made a final drive through the addition.

What the hell? Donny Whitlow was standing at the curb of the cul-de-sac where the firefighters were loading up the trucks, petting her Dobermans, Brutus and Sugar.

She parked and walked over to where he stood, observing him closely. He was watching the firefighters with rapt attention.

"Whitlow, what are you doing here?"

The young man acted shy, uncomfortably diffident, the way he always did around Cassie. As he spoke, he kept his gaze fixed upon the area where the fire had so recently blazed.

"Uh, I don't live too far from here, actually. I heard the sirens. On the news, they said there were a lot of grass fires. I was worried about the dogs." He slid slender fingers into Brutus's coat. These guard dogs were not trained to be friendly, except with their handler. Their docility with this relative stranger disturbed Cassie.

"I'm real good with dogs." Whitlow turned to face her and gave her a twisted smile that disturbed her even more.

LANA HAD A FIT when she found out that Jayden and Emily had been alone in the house the night of the grass fire.

"They are twelve years old," Jake reasoned, "and it was nine o'clock in the evening. And Buck and Pepe were out in the barns."

"And where were you?"

"I stopped at a friend's house for dinner."

"A friend?"

"That is none of your business, Lana."

"Never mind. Jayden already told me about that woman, and how you're spending all your time with her."

"I have the right to a personal life."

"I just wish when you were having your *personal* life, you would let me know. I'd like to spend that time with Jayden, you know."

"We have your visitation worked out and I've always honored it."

Lana shook her head in frustration. "Jake! My visitation was set up for an unstable woman who couldn't be trusted with a young child. I've stopped drinking. I've got a real job. Are you ever going to forgive the past?"

Jake's gut clenched. Was he protecting Jayden or was he punishing Lana for past mistakes? He couldn't sort it all out.

"Jake, please try to see that I'm not that woman anymore," Lana went on, "and Jayden, in case you haven't noticed, is not that small child anymore. She's at an age when she needs her mother. I know Mack's getting sicker. I can see how he is. You must be overwhelmed. Let me help by taking up some of the slack with Jayden."

He couldn't decide if this was more of Lana's manipulation at work, or if she had a valid point. He squinted at her, struggling to read the real Lana of today without layering the flawed Lana of yesterday over her. He couldn't do it. Where it concerned Jayden, Jake worried that if he gave Lana an inch, she'd take a mile.

"I think it's better for us all if we stick to our legal agreement."

Lana sighed. "Fine. Then, we'll see what the judge has to say when I file my new custody suit."

"When are you going to do that, if you don't mind my asking?"

"Soon."

True to her word, Lana had her lawyer walk the

paperwork over to the courthouse the day before Christmas. It also happened that this was Lana's Christmas to have the child with her.

I hate divorce, Jake thought as he watched the Lincoln Navigator's taillights shrink down the long driveway late on Christmas Eve.

He picked up the phone to call Cassie. "Please," he begged.

She only needed to hear that one word for her heart to melt. They'd discussed it and discussed it over the past week. Jake did not want to spend this Christmas without her. He'd posed every alternative. He'd have Donna bake a ham in advance, and Cassie and Rosemarie could come to the ranch house with him and Mack. Or, he'd take them all out to dinner. He'd go to church with them. Whatever she wanted.

"I'm still going to the prison to visit my dad." Cassie wouldn't cancel that for the world now. Not after what her aunt Rosemarie had told her. It was a point of honor. No, she would never neglect her father again. No matter how misguided he had been, he had done the things he'd done because of her.

"Then, let me come with you. Don't you think I should meet him sometime? What better occasion than Christmas?"

"You're not on his visitors list."

"Isn't there a way to get me added?"

Cassie closed her eyes. Yes, there was a way. One could obtain a waiver through a prisoner's attorney. Which meant she'd have to call Miles Davies on Christmas Eve and ask a big favor of the man she'd

rejected and fired less than two months ago. But for
Jake, she would do it. For Jake, she would do almost
anything.

JAKE WONDERED how weird this was for Cassie—going to visit her father in prison on Christmas Day.

They were cleared at the gate easily enough. Cassie
had been wise to insist on taking her silver Avalon,
which was familiar to the guards. Jake's name was
on the list. The visiting room, plain and institutional
even with the scraggly fake Christmas tree in the corner lit up, was crowded to bursting. The low roar of
voices echoed off the cinder-block walls and linoleum
flooring.

"There he is." Cassie indicated a heavy-set man
seated at a corner table. He had a wary, hunted pose,
as if he were guarding the two empty plastic chairs
pushed up to the table.

His face looked as if it had been carved from shiny
pink granite. He had a full head of steel-gray hair,
eyebrows that canted like bushy black caterpillars
over small, haunted eyes and a tiny straight nose similar to Cassie's. When he spotted Cassie, his rugged
face split open in a smile. His mouth puckered back
to nothing when he stopped smiling and hugged her.

Jake stood behind Cassie, reading the emotion, the
tortured love, in the man's face, and instantly he knew
the guy wasn't all bad.

Cassie turned to Jake. "Dad," she said nervously,
"this is Jake Coffey."

"Glad to meet ya." Boss shook Jake's work-
toughened hand in the vise grip of his own rough one.

Cassie had told Jake the man did cabinetry work here at the prison. "Nice to meet you, Mr. McClean."

"Call me Boss. Sit down. Sit down." Boss indicated the chairs. "Takes a gun and bullwhip to save somebody a chair in this place."

Cassie shot Jake a wry grin. She had told him that all the prisoners here were nonviolent, mostly drug offenders in for possession.

"Cassie told me you all have been dating," Boss said.

Jake smiled. "Yes, sir."

"Well, that's nice."

A silence settled, as if the whole point of the visit had already been accomplished. Jake and Cassie smiled at each other.

"Whatcha got there?" Boss pointed at the foam carton Cassie had placed on the table.

"Aunt Rosemarie didn't send any food," Cassie explained. "Jake took us out to dinner. So we got you this." Cassie slid the carton forward.

Boss peeked in the carton and his bushy eyebrows shot up. "Did old Henry at the gate see this?"

Cassie smiled. Boss knew the carton had been checked.

"Surprised he didn't confiscate it."

"Go ahead and eat it, Dad. Jake and I are stuffed."

Boss plucked out the plastic fork and started in on the chocolate torte from Legend's.

"Where is Rosie?" he said around a huge bite.

"She's at Jake's house, taking care of his father. She'll see you next time."

At Boss's questioning look, Jake explained, "My

dad has Alzheimer's disease, and I don't like to leave him alone, but his caretaker needs Christmas Day with her family.''

Boss stopped eating and gave Jake a kindly look. ''I'm sorry about your dad.''

''We manage.''

Boss nodded his understanding and started in on the cake again.

When he finished, he said, ''Wish it weren't so danged cold outside. We'd go out there where it's quieter.''

Jake was wishing for more privacy, too. On the long drive up, Cassie had filled him in on some of her history, and Boss's. He wanted to question Boss about the enemies he'd made when he was in the building business. Cassie was of the same mind, Jake was sure. It seemed like a sorry way to pass Christmas, but the grass fire had made it impossible to ignore the threat of serious damage to both of their properties. And more importantly, to the people who worked there. They couldn't afford to leave any stone—especially a big one like Boss's shady history—unturned.

In her typical straightforward style, Cassie dived right in. ''Dad, I know it's Christmas, but we've gotta talk to you about something really important.''

Boss's face clouded slightly and he wiped his mouth on the paper napkin Cassie had tucked into the carton. ''What?''

''There's been more sabotage out at The Heights. At least, I think it's sabotage.''

"There was a fire, Mr. McClean," Jake chimed in. "Last week."

Boss frowned and looked around. "A fire?"

Jake's eyes skimmed over the faces of the people in the room, too. No one was paying them any mind. It was Christmas in prison, and no doubt everyone here had a sad story they were trying to forget.

Boss leaned forward and in a low voice said, "What kind of fire?"

"A grass fire," Jake answered. "But we have reason to believe someone set it intentionally—"

"You mean *arson?*"

"I've handled it, Dad," Cassie interrupted. "I hired a security guard."

"Arson," Boss repeated, as if Cassie hadn't spoken. "Cassie, honey." He glanced at her. "Have you told this fella why I went to prison?"

She glanced at Jake and nodded. "Manslaughter. A family died in a—" she finished so quietly that the word was hardly audible "—fire."

Boss nodded. "A fire."

"You think this sabotage could be connected to that?" Jake asked. He could tell by looking at Cassie's face that she was already dismissing her father as paranoid.

Boss's craggy face puckered and his pinched lips disappeared to absolutely nothing. Then he spoke. "They didn't all die."

Cassie's eyes went wide, she swallowed, and Jake closed his fingers around her wrist. He thought how similar this was to Jayden's relationship with Lana. How could you rely on a parent when you knew there

was always some fresh bad news, some further
shame, some complicated mess to deal with?

"Tell me, Dad. I need to know."

"There was a boy. He was badly scarred. Man!"
Boss clamped a hand to his forehead, drove fingers
into his squarish haircut. "I've been trying to think
of that kid's name ever since you told me about that
U Die 2 business in the concrete. I didn't suspect him
right off. I thought of his aunt. The guy's sister. She
hated me. She threatened me in open court. You don't
ever forget a thing like that." Boss laced his fingers
in front of him on the table, gripping them like a guilt-
ridden penitent. "But then, I remembered the boy. I
started figuring he'd be grown up now—" Boss
choked off his words.

A silence stretched, and the three of them absorbed
the implications. Jake thought maybe what Boss was
saying wasn't so far-fetched.

"Dad," Cassie urged, "don't think about it."

No, Jake thought, *do think about. Think about it
real hard.* "You don't remember the boy's name?"
he prodded.

Boss drew and released a huge breath, as if he had
to remember to breathe. "Billy? Danny? Timmy?
Something like that. Their last name was Nelson.
They were just working class—" Boss stopped, and
tears of remembrance jetted to his old eyes.

"It's okay, Dad," Cassie said. "It was a long time
ago."

Why, Jake wondered, was Cassie so determined to
absolve this man of his guilt? Why wouldn't she just
let him feel it, confess it?

"That doesn't make it right." Boss's face crumpled.

"No, but now…at least I understand why you did it."

Shock transformed Boss's features. "What do you mean?"

She glanced at Jake. "Aunt Rosemarie told me…everything."

Boss's eyes grew wide, then hardened. "She had no *right*," he hissed.

"What do you mean, she had no right?" Cassie leaned toward her father and spread a palm on her chest. "What about *my* rights? This is my life, my history we're talking about here. Don't you think I have a right to know what really happened when I was sick?"

Jake thought back to that moment with Cassie in the bathtub, when she had told him about her leukemia, and realized that's what they were talking about here. He felt a sudden rush of sympathy for Boss McClean. It must have been terrifying for him, coming so close to losing a daughter like Cassie. Had Cassie's illness taken place before or after Boss went to prison?

"I didn't even know how I got my own bone-marrow transplant!" Cassie cried.

"That was none of your business." Boss, so remorseful only seconds before, seemed defiant now.

Cassie looked around the room like she was suddenly aware of her surroundings. She stood. "I have to get some air." She turned and marched toward the door. Boss linked his hands on the table again and dropped his head.

Jake's eyes followed Cassie as she wove her way around the crowded tables. When she reached the door of the visitors' room, she retrieved her coat from the guard.

"Where is she going?" he asked Boss.

"Out there." Boss tilted his head toward a tall, narrow window set into the cinder blocks. "She'll sit on one of the swings, probably. That's what she usually does. She's walked out on me before. She'll cool down and come back in, acting like nothing happened. Then in a couple of minutes she'll say it's time to go. You wait and see."

Jake frowned, and the two men fell silent while waves of forced holiday hubbub in the crowded room crested around them.

Jake leaned back in his chair, craning his neck to see out the bare window. Just as Boss had predicted, Cassie was sitting in a swing. Hanging there in the sling, with her legs stretched out in front of her and her hands wrapped high on the chains. Her head was down so that Jake couldn't see her face, but he had the impression she was crying. He wanted to go to her.

"Don't," Boss said, startling him. "I can see that you're a good guy, Jake—" Boss was staring at his linked fingers "—and you mean well, but you can't fix this."

Jake eyed the man who would be his father-in-law someday, but who had no knowledge of that fact yet.

"I have a daughter, too," he explained. "She's twelve."

Boss looked up. "That so?"

"Her name's Jayden."

"You divorced? Widowed?" Boss said it in a tone that indicated Jake had better be one or the other.

"Divorced. Jayden lives with me."

"Take care of her while you can."

"What did Cassie mean, about her bone-marrow transplant?"

"How long have you guys been dating, if I may ask?"

"Long enough. She told me she had leukemia when she was a child."

"I see."

"What about the transplant?"

"I'm surprised Cassie doesn't remember much about the transplant. I guess children are really more in their own world than we realize."

"I think she meant something else. Was there something unusual about her transplant?" Jake was thinking it was the donor, maybe.

"The fact that she got the transplant at all—that's what was unusual," Boss said. "It was a fairly new procedure in those days. Damn insurance company didn't even want to pay for it. Didn't even want to look for a donor. Rosemarie started all this fundraising at her church. Don't suppose she told Cassie about *that*. That woman's a saint. And a damn dingbat blabbermouth."

Jake had to smile. Cassie had warned him that her father was blunt.

"What did Rosemarie tell Cassie that was so bad?"

Boss studied Jake, and Jake knew the older man was taking his measure.

"She told her what I did to get the money for that bone-marrow transplant."

"What you did?"

"I needed money. I needed money fast. I never dreamed one of those little cracker boxes I was throwing up would burn down. I thought they'd fall apart, maybe. You never saw such cheap construction. But people were buying them faster than I could build 'em."

"I see." Jake couldn't think of anything else to say.

"Cassie doesn't need to go around thinking I ended up in here because of her. I did it for *me,* so I wouldn't lose her, too. Do you understand?"

Jake did understand. He understood the desperation that might drive a man when he felt stripped of everything he had, except his child. But even though Boss McClean had made hard choices, Jake had to wonder if they were the only choices.

"Maybe there was another way—"

"You think I didn't ask myself that? You think I didn't try everything?"

Again, Jake wondered. But he hadn't been there. He hadn't lived through the hell that this man had.

"I did what I thought I had to do. And I wouldn't change any of it, except to bring that family back." Boss turned eyes on Jake that were again defiant, but full of sorrow, too.

"Have you ever told her that?"

"Hell, no."

"Maybe you should."

"What good would that do? I can't turn back the clock. I can't change anything. I can't bring those people back. I can't fix that little boy."

"Boss." Jake cocked an eyebrow at him, wondering again if Boss's suspicions about the boy had any merit. The kid was out there somewhere, badly damaged. Physically, at least. Probably psychologically. It made sense to Jake that this boy was someone from the past who might be motivated to seek revenge. "How can we find this boy?"

"I have no idea. The aunt fixed it so I could never contact him again, and moved across the country."

"And you can't remember his name?"

Boss shook his head.

Jake made a mental note to have Edward Hughes try to extract the name from court records. Then he reached for his hip pocket before he remembered that all visitors' purses and billfolds were left with the guard when they came in. "Listen, I want to give you one of my cards. Remind me when I get my billfold back from the guard."

"Okay."

"If you remember this guy's name, you give me a call. My cell phone number is on the card. I'll try to remember to keep it on all the time. Call me any time you remember anything. Cassie may think you are just being paranoid about this kid, but I don't."

Boss nodded again. "I can't call just anybody, Jake. You've got to be on a list."

"How do I get on the list?"

"You have to be approved. I'll try to get it done. Sometimes it takes a while."

"Then, how about if I call you?"

"You can try. But not in the evening. The guard then—Grunwold—he's a real Nazi. Just say you're Miles Davies. That's my lawyer."

"I've met him. Is it gonna cause trouble if I do that?"

"Nah." Boss waved his beefy paw. "Miles'll cover your ass."

"Okay. I'll remember that if I need to talk to you."

Boss looked out the window again. "I appreciate this, Jake. I can't take care of her, stuck away in here like I am."

"I'll take care of her, I promise you that."

"I hope you do a better job than I did." He turned his proud, sad eyes to Jake.

Just as Boss had predicted, Cassie came back in, red-eyed, red-nosed and red-cheeked, and cut short the remainder of the visit.

On the drive home, she said, "Well, now you've met my dear father."

"He's not what I expected."

"How so?"

"He's more...vulnerable. Sadder. I think he has a lot of guilt, a lot of regret."

"Boss? Regret?"

"You don't see it?"

"Not really." She sighed. "Seems to me, he keeps justifying what he did. Sometimes I feel sorry for him. Okay, *most of the time* I feel sorry for him. But sometimes I feel so angry at him, I'd like to punch him.

The decisions he made killed a mother and a father, and nearly destroyed my life.''

''But those decisions also saved your life.''

''He *told* you that?''

''Not in so many words. But that's the upshot, isn't it?''

''That's debatable. I was a child, so I'll never know. Am I supposed to be grateful?''

''No. I don't think he wants that. I think he's accepted it all. He is where he is because of what he did. You're the one who can't accept your father the way he is, where he is.''

''Easier said than done.''

A silence fell while the tires hummed on the pavement. The sky grew steely with cold clouds.

After a long time Cassie said, ''Jake, do you think accepting and forgiving are the same thing?''

''No. But they're close. The past is done, Cassie. Boss can't change it. You can't change it. All you can do is accept reality.''

''I had accepted it all, until my aunt laid this business about my bone-marrow transplant on me.''

''You had no idea that's why he did it?''

She shook her head dejectedly. ''Can you imagine how that makes me feel?'' Her mouth grew tight.

''Cassie, it's not your fault that family died.''

''I know. It's just…I wish I could at least help the little boy.'' A tear trembled on her lashes, then spilled over.

Jake reached over and massaged her neck. ''Do you want me to drive?''

She shook her head, swiped at her cheek.

"Sweetheart," he said. His love was the only consolation Jake could think to give. "I love you so much."

Cassie angled her head into his hand, welcoming his touch and his love. "I'm sorry my family's so screwed up. I'm sorry you have to be visiting a *prison* with me on Christmas Day."

Seeing the sad set of her mouth, Jake saw how wrenching this was for her. He wondered—no, he pretty much knew—that this was the reason Cassie had kept herself unattached until now.

"No family is perfect," he said quietly. "Look at mine. You'll be shouldering the burden of my father's illness with me when we marry. And you'll be getting a stepdaughter in the deal."

"I love Mack already, and in my mind, Jayden's a good thing. You think I want to live the rest of my life childless?"

"I have no idea. We haven't discussed it. I figured you were gonna have to accept Jayden regardless of how you feel about kids. Just like I'll have to accept your dad. I think that's the way it works in families. You accept everybody the way they are, and do your best to be a loving person."

"Jake?"

"Yeah?"

"I love you."

Moments later, like a cleansing benediction, snow started to fall. It came straight down in great, gentle, fat flakes, unusual in Oklahoma where the first snow of the year usually appeared in little flurries that blew sideways.

"We need the moisture," Jake commented like the agricultural man he was.

"Yes." Cassie smiled. "Maybe we won't have to worry about grass fires for a while."

By the time they reached Jordan, the snow was thick, sticking to the windshield and coating the ground like a layer of soft sawdust.

Cassie pulled off on Highway 86—they'd already agreed to go directly to the ranch house and spend the remainder of Christmas there with Mack, and with Rosemarie if she wanted to stay.

As she turned onto the ranch road and drove parallel to the acres of fence, Jake pointed out in the field.

There in the dusky evening light were the horses, all running in the same direction, their hooves raising puffs of snow, their manes and tails flying high like dark trailing ribbons. The screen of snowflakes gave the scene an impressionistic feel, like a blurry oil painting in motion.

"They're after the hay," Jake said, pointing to the red pickup in the distance where one of his hands stood in the bed, breaking thick chunks off of a bale.

"How beautiful!" Cassie exclaimed, and brought the car to a stop.

They sat there in silence, enjoying the familiar landscape bathed in unfamiliar white. The black, snow-draped trees lining the river beyond, the charcoal sky creating a closed globe above, the Flats with fences and fields stretching silently to The Heights in the distance, where all was quiet on Christmas Day.

And across this stillness, the horses moving in tandem—running, running, running.

"I think," Cassie said as if in a trance, "I'm gonna love sharing my life with you."

CHAPTER FIFTEEN

JAYDEN CAME BACK from Christmas at Lana's and announced that she wanted to stay at her mother's for the remainder of Christmas break. Jake stood in her bedroom door while she packed, feeling like he was losing his little girl.

"You like it over there?" He couldn't see how that was possible—not after his years of listening to Lana complain about her father's tyranny.

"They're nice, Daddy. Especially Grandma. You know how sweet she can be."

He did know. He'd always liked Phoebe, truth be told. Phoebe Largeant was as kind and gentle as Stu Largeant was rude and overbearing.

"Mom has a job now, you know." Jayden stuffed a plastic baggie full of preteen makeup into a backpack.

Jake's eyebrows shot up. He didn't know. But come to think of it, Lana had said something about a real job. "She's doing something besides training Grandpa's horses?"

"Yeah. She's a receptionist at a law firm. She loves it. She's saving her money because she wants us to get our own house soon."

The words *us* and *our* sent a wave of warning through Jake's gut.

"Really?"

"Yeah. I get to go to the law office with her on Monday. We're gonna have a long lunch because she has her meeting right after work."

"Her meeting?"

"Yeah. Her AA meeting. You know about that."

Again, Jake didn't. The waves in his gut turned into a vortex of disequalibrium. Lana was going to AA? Why should that unsettle him? It didn't, he told himself. But it did, somehow. As if Lana getting whole would interfere with all that he had done to make Jayden's life stable. That was ridiculous. Did he need Lana to be a loser so he could feel strong, so he could feel like the Good Parent? Was he truly so base?

"What about your play?" He wanted to change the subject.

Jayden had a small role in the town's New Year's Eve production of *Grease*. The annual event was a way to give local teens something to look forward to on New Year's Eve besides drinking and driving. The middle schoolers participated in the play, which was held at the historic Sooner Theater downtown, and then tagged along with the high school crowd for pizza at the high school gym. A fifties-style dance followed, during which the younger kids usually watched awkwardly from the sidelines.

"Mom will take me, and I'll see you there." Jayden turned from her bed and crossed the room to him. "Daddy. Chill. You'll still see plenty of me over the break. And Mom is different now. She really is."

Jake remained unconvinced. He knew how manipulative Lana could be. Maybe she was courting her daughter the same way she had once courted him. When Lana was on her best behavior, no one was more charming.

THE NIGHT OF THE MUSICAL, the lobby of the Sooner Theater was crowded with excited teenagers and their families. The low roar of conversation kept Jake from hearing Jayden and Lana calling his name until they'd come up right next to Jake and Cassie.

"Hi, Daddy." Jayden stood up on her tiptoes and kissed Jake's cheek. "Hi, Ms. McClean."

"Hi, Jayden."

The two women glanced at each other. Both blond. One tall. One petite. One dressed in velvet and leopard skin. One dressed in soft cotton and wool.

"I'm Cassie McClean." This time Cassie offered her hand to Lana. They shook.

"Yes, I remember you." Lana's greeting to Cassie was carefully neutral.

Jayden spotted her friends and dashed off, squealing.

"Well, I guess we should go to our seats." Jake pressed a palm to Cassie's back.

"Enjoy the play," Lana said. Cassie felt sorry for the woman as she watched her go to a seat alone.

After the play, Jayden ran up to them in the lobby, still in her poodle-skirt costume, flushed with excitement.

"You were great, Jayden!" Cassie gushed.

"Thanks."

"What do you say we all head out for a giant banana split?" Jake clapped his hands and rubbed them together.

"Daddy! The *dance!*"

"Oh, yeah. Well, I guess we'll drive you over to the gym."

"Mom's taking me." Jayden turned. "She signed up to be a chaperone."

They followed Jayden's gaze to the spot where Lana stood, by the glass doors. She was smiling patiently, with a giant leather purse hitched over her shoulder.

"Oh." Jake blinked as if he'd had cold water dashed in his face.

Cassie intervened sensibly. "You have fun, Jayden. I think your mom's ready to go."

"'Bye." Jayden gave her father a quick peck.

"'Bye, Ms.—"

"Cassie." She smiled.

"'Bye, Cassie."

The child bounced off to her mother, ponytail swinging.

Out in the chill wind, on the nearly deserted downtown sidewalk, Jake seemed disconsolate.

"You have to share her," Cassie offered quietly as they walked to Jake's truck.

Jake cocked an eyebrow at her. "With Lana? That's like saying I have to share my baby with a dragon."

"The woman doesn't seem all that bad to me. And Jayden is her baby, too. Are you sure you're not misjudging this situation?"

"What do you mean?"

"I mean, Jayden seems happy to be with her."

"Lana can be tricky. She's lied to me. She's let Jayden down. You don't know how it was."

"You're right. I don't know about all that. But sometimes people change. They grow. Relationships change. They heal. Look at me and my father. I never dreamed I'd be able to get over what he did. But I'm trying. I still don't like it, but I'm trying to stop being angry about it. I've stopped hating him. And I do know how much a girl Jayden's age needs her mother. I was a girl that age once, remember?"

Jake grinned at her. "And I'll bet you were a real cutie, too." He looked up the street, at the pale blue neon light of a jewelry store. His expression brightened. "Hey. It's New Year's Eve. You deserve a little romance. Let's go window shopping."

FOR THE NEXT TWO WEEKS, the pages on the calendar flipped away faster than leaves in the wind. Lana filed her lawsuit, asking for joint custody of Jayden, and, at Cassie's urging, Jake tried not to be suspicious of her motives. He wondered what evidence Lana would have to produce for the judge to alter the original decree. Would she try to show that his involvement with Cassie was causing him to neglect Jayden? Or that Dad's illness had changed their situation at Cottonwood Ranch?

Jake talked to Cassie about these worries, late at night when they were alone, and she always applied her sensible outlook. The child support Lana paid him every month did not even come close to what it was going to cost her to keep up with her half of Jayden's expenses.

For a young woman, Cassie could be incredibly insightful. Her childhood trials had made her wise beyond her years. With each passing week, Jake had become more convinced that she was the only woman for him.

With a glad heart, in mid-January he called her and made arrangements for their second "anniversary" date.

The evening at Legend's went well, as always. He brought her a rose, as always. "Are you sick of roses?" he said as he handed it to her.

"Absolutely not." She smiled. "I'm making a collection of dried rose petals."

Later they made love, as always. This time, they hurried straight to her bed, undressing each other in a frenzy beside the chaise longue. This time, when the first wave of passion had been satisfied, Cassie seemed suddenly shy again, as if it had all been too intense for her. She came out of her dressing room wearing a creamy, flowing, long-sleeved, high-necked flannel nightgown with tiny satin ribbons trailing from the gathered neck. The sight of her wearing something so utterly feminine, looking so... vulnerable, made him hard all over again.

"It's so cold outside," she explained as she slid under the covers.

This time, he tried to be tender as he brought her demure gown up over her arms, but at the feel of her hot skin under his palms, he felt himself losing it, going wild, shaken to his core with unspeakable desire. This woman was in his blood, all right, so much so that he couldn't remember what his life had been before her. Joyless, maybe. Automatic. He didn't know. He didn't want to know.

When it was over, Jake had just gotten himself comfortable, all wrapped around Cassie—as soft and sweet and delicate as a doll—and was drifting into a warm postcoital sleep, when the phone rang.

Cassie cleaved her moist skin from his, a most unpleasant sensation because of the sudden cold front that had sent temperatures into the teens that night. Damn unpredictable Oklahoma weather. He hoped none of the mares foaled in this sudden, bitter cold. He eyed the green digits on the bedside clock—two a.m.—and reached down to his jacket for his own cell phone to make sure it was still charged, while Cassie groped for her bedside phone on the other side.

Jose would stay in the little sleeping room in the foaling barn tonight, despite the weather…or rather, because of it. He would call Jake if any of the mares started to deliver. With a full moon and the mammas at ten-and-a-half months gestation, that was a real possibility.

"Did *what?*" Cassie sat bolt upright, gripping the phone, not even bothering to grab the sheet in her usual modest pose. "When? How bad is it? But…but…" She listened, her back as rigid as if someone were flailing it with a whip. "I'll be right there."

She hung up the phone and leaped from the bed, hysterically pawing at the dressy clothing they'd discarded earlier on the chaise longue. "Oh, God," she railed, "where—" she threw her skirt off the chaise "—are—" then Jake's slacks "—my jeans?" Her voice rose to a panic pitch. "I need my friggin' jeans!"

"Cassie!" Jake had jumped from the bed. "Calm down. What happened?"

She stopped thrashing in the clothes, looking at him wild-eyed with a sweatshirt clutched to her naked front. "He struck again."

"The vandal?"

"The *arsonist,* Jake. The psycho's a damn arsonist and now he's torched one of my houses! That was the f-fire department." Frustrated tears burned up. "The D-Detloffs'." She buried her face in the sweatshirt, muffling a sob.

Jake crossed to her and pulled her against him. While she fought her tears, he wrapped her in his arms and pressed her head to his chest. He kissed her hair. "It'll be okay" was all he could say.

His cell phone bleated.

He guided Cassie to the bed and sat her down on the edge, then retrieved the phone. Mechanically, she pulled the sweatshirt she'd found over her head, while he answered.

"Yeah?"

"Jake? It's Jose."

"Yeah."

"Another fire up on the hill."

"I just heard."

"This one looks pretty big, man."

"We're on our way." He punched End.

Cassie was on her feet pulling on her panties and jeans. "You don't have to go, Jake."

"I'm going with you." He started gathering his clothes.

While she went to the dresser and pulled out some thick socks she argued, "You need some sleep. What if one of the mares starts to foal later? You could be up all night. This is my problem."

"Everything that affects you, affects me. I thought we'd settled that."

As it turned out, they were both up for most of the night.

While Jake drove her truck, Cassie called and woke the Detloffs and told them the horrible news. Jake heard her promise that she would call back with a report as soon as she saw the house.

But when they got to The Heights, there was nothing left to see. Unless you counted three fire engines, a bank of floodlights, miles of snaking gray hose, a dozen or so exhausted firefighters in yellow turnouts and the fire marshal's red Suburban with its strobe lights flicking repeatedly over the whole scene. The blue and white lights seemed to be quietly blinking, *It's over, it's over,* against the scorched limestone ruins.

The visible flames were out. The skeleton of the house looked eerie, with a cold moon and the white-hot lights illuminating its face. Black-and-tan stone, charred two-by-fours, collapsed roof, shattered glass. It was as if it had imploded back to its semiconstructed state of a few weeks before. The whole mess was dripping in water that was rapidly turning into a thin layer of ice.

At least the firefighters had been swift and thorough, Cassie thought. At least the whole addition, the surrounding dry woods, the nearby horse farms with their enormous hay barns, hadn't gone up in flames.

A man in a helmet and a turnout coat snapped over civilian clothes came around the corner of the house into the lights. Cassie figured this was the fire marshal. He stopped and talked to another man, then spotted Jake and Cassie and walked out to the curb. He was built like a refrigerator, with a thick red mustache and alert eyes rimmed by pale lashes.

"I'm Dick Mather," he said, "the fire marshal. Are you the owner?"

"No. I'm C. J. McClean, the builder." Cassie shuddered against the biting wind, and Jake came up beside her and wrapped an arm around her shoulders. "I've just called the owners. They live up in Oklahoma City, but they'll probably come on down."

"I'm Jake Coffey," Jake said, and shook the man's hand. "I own the horse farm down the hill."

"Right. Bet you're glad this thing didn't spread." Mather eyed the burned structure. "We're still working on hot spots in the wreckage, but we've got it under control. It's a good thing somebody called it in early. We were mighty close to having another grass fire to battle in addition to this."

"Who did call this in?" Cassie's eyes, alert now and fiercely angry, snapped up to the big man.

"Not sure."

"But you can find out?"

"Probably. 9-1-1 data will at least show us a number."

"Any idea how it started?" Jake asked the question that he was certain Cassie was mulling as she squinted up at the destruction.

"Well, it was a pretty powerful accelerant. The place practically exploded at flash point, right after the first unit arrived. Paint thinner, most likely." Mather turned to Cassie. "When was the staining and so forth done?"

She sighed heavily. "It was finished today."

Mather nodded as if that confirmed something. "My best guess is, a light was left on above those stairs. We've already located a switch left in the 'on' position in a standing wall. Do you normally leave lights on in the houses at this stage of construction?"

"No—" Cassie's head snapped around with a sudden thought. "Where are my guard dogs?"

"The boys have 'em over there. They came running out of the woods. Didn't bother us, though. Funny how dogs can sense when you're there to help."

"Why would a lightbulb left burning cause this?" Satisfied that Brutus and Sugar were safe, Cassie steered the talk back to the cause of the fire.

"My guess—and it's only a guess at this point—is your painters stuffed paper around the eyeball lights before they sprayed the ceilings, right?"

Cassie nodded.

"There was one spotlight above the stairs?"

"Several," Cassie said.

"But was there one on a separate switch? To light the landing only?"

"I think so. I'll have to double-check the plans. I usually put one light on the stairs that works off two switches, one at the bottom and one at the top."

"Right. So people can turn on the light at the bottom, then go up to bed and turn it off at the top."

"Right."

"Well, that might blow my theory, then."

"Which is?"

"The switch left in the 'on' position. If the house was wired the way you think, the switch at the top could have been used to turn it off and the switch in the wall at the bottom—the one we found—would still be on. Even so, I'm pretty sure somebody forgot to take the paper out of that one eyeball light. The light—with the paper covering it, no one could see that it was left on, of course—finally got hot enough to ignite the paper. The burning wad fell to the stair landing—" Mather made a downward stroke with two fingers toward what was left of the stairs "—and the fresh stain and polyurethane—you use polyurethane?"

Again Cassie nodded.

"The polyurethane on the stairs ignited, the stairs burned through, the burning oak splintered down around those cans of mineral spirits inside the front door—and the house went up."

"You're saying it was an accident?" Cassie asked incredulously.

"You think it wasn't?" Mather frowned.

"Don't you guys ever talk to the cops?" Jake interjected.

"Actually, I did." Mather glanced at him. "Right after that grass fire a month ago."

"Then, they told you what's been going on out here."

"Yes." Mather turned to Cassie. "I promise, Ms. McClean, there will be a thorough investigation."

"And you'll let me know what you find?"

He nodded. "I hope you have builder's risk insurance."

"Of course." Cassie sighed deeply.

Walking back to her truck, Cassie looked up at the full moon, high overhead now, and thought how she was beginning to dread the sight of it. It seemed like every time—

"Wait!" She grabbed Jake's jacket. "Look at that moon."

"Yeah?" Jake frowned up at it. The black winter sky, cold and clear, made the moon stand out like a big hole cut in the firmament, with pinpricks of starlight all around it. Jake had to admit that it looked kind of romantic, but he couldn't imagine that Cassie was feeling so right now.

"It's *full,*" she said meaningfully.

"Yeah?"

"It was full the night of the grass fire."

Jake pushed his hat back, studying the night sky again. "You sure?"

"Positive. And the night I found the U Die 2 message, it was full then, too."

Jake studied her face in the cold lunar glow. "So

you're thinking he always strikes around the time of the full moon?''

"He...or them."

"Them?"

"The Spirit Tribe. Don't Native Americans have some kind of thing about the full moon?"

"Doesn't everybody?" Jake argued sensibly. "Somebody could be trying to throw you off the scent with this full moon stuff. Or, it could just be a coincidence."

"What about that tomahawk in the drywall sack?"

"Cassie, they're fanatics, but they're college-educated fanatics. They wouldn't do something that hokey."

She signed heavily. "You're right, of course."

"Let's see what the fire marshal comes up with. He seems pretty competent."

Cassie sighed. "He does. But it's just like the grass fire—what's he gonna find? What's he gonna prove?"

Jake gave her a warm hug. "Want me to take you home?"

She sighed again. "No. I guess I'd better wait and talk to the Detloffs."

ENCANTADORA FOALED THAT NIGHT. At ten-and-a-half months, the baby looked sound, stood immediately and nursed. Even after the relatively uneventful, normal birth, Jake was exhausted, but on the way back to his house he called Cassie's cell phone, anyway.

"How's it going?"

"The firefighters have got all the hot spots put out now. It was hell seeing the Detloffs' faces. She started crying. I don't blame her. I wouldn't mind having a good cry myself right now. How's the foal?"

"Cute. Frisky. Want me to drive up there?"

"Why? So you can watch the sun come up over the ashes?"

"So I can hold you."

Those words, in his low, resonant voice, washed over her tired body like a drug. She loved him when he said things like that. Well, she loved him all the time. More and more, all the time.

"That would be wonderful, but I'm afraid I can't afford to indulge myself right now. The fire marshal is meeting me at the trailer to go over the plans. I'm so tired I can't think. And guess what?"

"What?" Jake was so tired he could hardly speak himself, much less play guessing games.

"Tomorrow, or rather *today,* the blasting on the red rock is scheduled to resume."

"Oh, no," Jake groaned. "Well, I hope it's fast. At least my foals all made it this far."

"You're sure they would all survive now?"

"I'm pretty sure. I can't thank you enough, Cassie, for holding off like this. You've had so much stress. Is there anything I can do for you right now? How about some doughnuts for the firefighters?"

"No. The construction guys will show up soon. I'll send one of them. You go get some sleep. You could have foals arriving every night for the next two weeks.''

"Let's hope not. I love you.''

"I love you, too.''

MACK WAS AWAKE, prowling around the kitchen in his faded flannel robe, when Jake let himself in the back door. Donna usually arrived early, by five or five-thirty, but sometimes she didn't beat Mack to the draw.

"We had a baby last night,'' Jake told his dad as he took over making the coffee.

"Healthy?'' Mack reached into a cabinet for a box of Cheerios.

"Very.'' Jake went to the fridge for milk.

"That's good. Any idea what all those si-reens were about last night?''

"A fire up in The Heights.''

"Really?'' Mack stopped with two cereal bowls in his hands, studying Jake with clear, alert eyes. Apparently he was having one of his good days.

"Yeah. The great big limestone house at the bottom of the cul-de-sac?''

"The one with the real tall chimney?''

"Yeah. Burned to the ground.''

"You don't say. How so?''

"The fire marshal will determine that later. Cassie thinks it's arson.''

"Arson!'' Mack took two forks out of the silverware drawer.

Jake stepped over and reached in for spoons, instead. "It's complicated, Dad. I'll explain it later.''

Donna came sailing in just as the men were digging

into their cereal. "A little prebreakfast snack?" she teased.

"Where have you been?" Mack demanded irritably.

Donna and Jake exchanged tolerant glances. "I've been to the barn, actually, looking at the new filly. What a cutie!" She removed her coat and hung it up on a peg. "You can already see Arrestado's stamp upon her. She should bring a good price."

"Yes." Jake was too tired to enthuse about the foal.

"You look beat," Donna observed as she opened the fridge.

"Up all night. Long story."

"One of Cassie's houses burned down," Mack informed her.

Donna looked shocked. "No! Another grass fire?" She slapped bacon into a frying pan.

"Arson!" Mack exclaimed.

"Now, Dad, we don't know that yet." Jake stood and stretched. "Listen, you two, try to hold it down out here. I'm going to go try to get a little shut-eye before another foal comes."

But Jake's head had barely hit the pillow when the first blast rocked the valley.

Ah, the dynamite, he thought with an exhausted, sardonic smile. *No rest for the wicked today.*

AND NO REST FOR THE WICKED for the next four weeks, it turned out. Cassie was preoccupied with the aftereffects of the fire, and getting the houses on the red rock lots back on schedule. She felt like her work was supplanting her relationships, and the new Cassie hated that. She missed seeing Rosemarie, talking to her good friend Stacey, and most of all, she missed her time with Jake.

The blasting had not gone as planned. Extra dynamite had to be brought in. Obviously, somebody had lost count of the supply of explosives because the BlastCat guys asked her if they could lock the dynamite in her trailer one night, then tried to claim they were short a box the next day.

"No one has a key to this trailer but me," Cassie told them.

Jake was preoccupied with getting thirteen foals up and running. His days were spent running between the foaling barn and the small freestanding building that was his field office.

After each foal was born, he had to spray iodine on the cord, then give the foal a tetanus antitoxin shot and an enema. He or Buck would lay out the placenta and make sure it was intact, and then dispose of it. The vet usually arrived in time to check the mamas.

Then there was the endless paperwork. The small steel building that was his field office became saturated with the smell of apple cores and day-old coffee. Jake got thoroughly sick of looking at the brown wood paneling, the bare linoleum floor, the dusty picture window and the two cluttered desks.

Jake hadn't seen much of Cassie at all until the second week of February. He called her late one night after each of them had finished a grueling day. Cassie was soaking her sore muscles in a hot bathtub brimming with bubbles, and thinking of how Jake had initiated her to this particular luxury...and a few others.

"Tomorrow's Valentine's Day," he said as soon as she picked up and croaked hello. "Will you be my valentine?"

"Sure," she deadpanned. "Who are you?"

Jake chuckled. "I am the man you've been practicing on lately, young lady."

"Lately? *Lately,* mister, I'm afraid I haven't been *practicing* on anybody. Now, are you gonna tell me your name or not?"

"Name's Jake. Jake Coffey."

"Jake Coffey?" Cassie said thoughtfully. "Sounds familiar. Are you the fella that hauled me into court back in November?"

"No. That wasn't me. I'm the fella from the—" he lowered his voice a notch "—bathtub."

Cassie smiled and slid farther in the water, bringing her chin down into the bubbles. "The bathtub, huh? I *do* remember you, come to think of it. Short guy? Balding? A few missing teeth?"

"Is that water I hear splashing?"

"Mmm-hmm."

"Tell you what. Why don't I come over and be *your* valentine?"

"Will you have to leave in the middle of everything to deliver a foal?"

"Does it matter?"

"Not if you bring chocolate."

He brought her a Hershey bar from the 7-Eleven.

THE NEXT DAY, Cassie whistled along with the oldies tunes on her favorite station. Jake had slipped out after she fell asleep and left her a note. *Legend's? Tomorrow?* He'd signed it with a heart. She smiled. Of course they'd go to Legend's for Valentine's Day. Which meant she wanted to get out of The Heights early, for once, and run to the Hallmark store and buy Jake a special card.

She didn't dare skip her evening rounds, though. Immediately after the grass fire, she'd hired a security guard, an older man named Collins, with a silly little flashing light atop his silly blue GeoTracker. But the old guy was the only security guard she could find on short notice, and he did pack a pistol on the gun belt that swagged below his paunch, and he had been a deputy in the sheriff's department before he retired.

She had installed security cameras, with the tapes constantly running. And she made a loud business of telling the painters to store their mineral spirits and supplies way out in Brett Taylor's unfinished pool house. After the police had come up empty-handed on the footprints, after the fire marshal's report showed the 9-1-1 call came from a pay phone, after hearing, "Sorry ma'am—nothing yet," one time too many, Cassie had decided to set her own trap. She would sacrifice Brett's pool house if she had to, but she *would* catch this guy.

Boss didn't like the idea of the trap when she told him about it on one of her visits. But Boss didn't care for any of the risks Cassie took in her life. She had the feeling Boss would probably be happier if she decided to take over as the church secretary when Rosemarie retired.

An enormous tissue-paper moon hung in a sandal-wood sky as she slowly drove around the deserted streets, looking at the half-built houses, their un-adorned windows like the blank eyes of skulls. The sun was sinking fast in the late-winter sky.

She rounded a bend and glanced down the hill at the burned-out Detloff house. Two trucks were parked there. No one was supposed to go near the place until the insurance adjuster's investigation was complete.

She pulled into the cul-de-sac and saw Mel Daugh-erty and his skinny shadow, the Whitlow boy, staring up at the structure. They turned and watched her drive up.

She got out of her truck and slammed the door, peeved that these two were down here, against her orders.

Donny Whitlow darted a look at her as she walked up. Then he spoke to Mel and jogged to his pickup.

"Mel? What're you doing here?"

"We didn't cross the tape," he said calmly. "I was just trying to see if any of my tools made it. I had a nail gun, a compressor and a table saw in there."

"Yes, I know." Once the house had been secured with solid doors and windows, many of the subs had left their tools locked inside. "But almost nothing inside the house made it. I'm sorry. The insurance will cover your losses."

Donny had backed his truck around, and as he headed up the incline, a thought came to Cassie. "Do you know where that guy lives, by the way?"

"Somewhere out there." Mel jerked his head in

the direction of the Flats. "Rents a room from some hay farmer and his wife, I think."

This should have reassured Cassie—it jibed with Whitlow's story on the night of the grass fire. But for some reason, it didn't suppress the niggling worry that wormed into her mind now.

DONNY WHITLOW PULLED his battered truck to a stop on a rutted weedy road that led to an oil rig. He was good at finding these places. Places where he could wolf down a hamburger, make his plans and nurse his grudges. This particular road was not far from the dump where he'd taken a room. He hated that fat old couple. The woman was always talking about Jesus like he was her best friend. And the man was always trying to get Donny interested in the hay farming business. He'd often imagined how those twenty-foot-high barns stuffed with dry hay would go up. *Man,* that would be awesome. He'd burn them to the ground if he hadn't already laid his plans for tonight.

That McClean woman. He'd heard her yelling at Mel, right before he'd climbed in his pickup. She was rich and thought she was smart, and she really enjoyed bossing the hell out of the men.

But tonight, at last, she was going to die.

He took out the second hamburger and broke it in half. He ate one half in two gulps and rewrapped the other. He'd need it later for the dogs.

When he'd glugged down the last of his Coke, he reached into the glove compartment and took out a box of large kitchen matches. He struck one and watched the flame as it ate its way down the stick.

He sat, hypnotized, holding it until he felt the heat lick at his thumb, then he snuffed out the flame between the thumb and forefinger of his other hand.

Immediately he wanted to strike another. He wanted to toss one out on this oil rig and see what happened. He'd often experimented like that when he was younger, but now he'd learned to control himself, to control the fire.

From the start, he'd learned that control was the real trick. His first fire had been in the small, sterile kitchen at the locked psych unit where he'd spent a year when he was thirteen. Four of them were in there with one of the aides, supposedly learning to cook dinner. Three disturbed adolescents. That's what the workers and doctors called the boys—*disturbed adolescents*—with one dumb aide…and Donny.

He had hated that psych aide. Just like that witch McClean, she was way too bossy. *Do it this way, not that way. Set it here, not there. Wash your hands. Don't lick the spoon.* The other guys were making fun of her behind her back, pointing at her enormous rear when she bent to the oven and stuff like that, but Donny was gonna really fix her. It had been so easy.

The burners on the stove were electric. He reached up—*pip!*—and depressed the button that said *Hi* on a front one. When the burner was hot enough, but before it had started to glow orange-red, he'd grabbed a towel and started horsing around, popping one of the other guys in the leg with it. He made sure to pick on the fat kid that nobody liked. The other two guys would have pounded his head in the ward room that night.

"Donny, stop it!" the aide ordered.

He swung the towel again.

"Put that towel down!"

He did. On the hot burner.

Donny struck another match now, remembering the power he'd felt at that moment. He'd done some other good stuff lately—cutting that fence, the concrete, even stealing the witch's "urgent" fax off her bulletin board—but none of it did the trick like fire. *Fire.* Cleansing. Exciting. Satisfying fire. Donny thought it was cool that he wasn't afraid of fire at all. He'd shown them. They said he was scarred. He wasn't scarred. He'd just been through the fire and won.

The aide had freaked when the towel burst into flame. "Get back!" she screamed at the hollering boys. But Donny didn't get back. He rushed forward and grabbed it, like he was a hero or something.

He'd tried to swing it so it would hit her hair—she wore it hippie long—but she'd ducked out of the way.

"You idiot!" she shrieked as she grabbed the burning towel from him. She tossed it in the sink and turned on the water, then looked up at him, her eyes wild. She was afraid of him, he could tell.

The charge nurse came running in—because of the yelling and the smoke, Donny supposed. He thought he did a pretty good job of acting freaked out and innocent, like the other boys.

The staff had one of their secret meetings about it, around the table behind the big window, like they always did. They started taking Donny off into the little room with the lamp and the couch more often. Dr. Shafer wanted to talk about "anger" and "fire" all the time. Donny lost it with the other kids more often after that.

But in the end, he'd fooled them. He'd told Dr. Shafer he was dreaming about clouds and dogs instead of fire and death. He'd made them think he was all better, and then they'd let him out. And he hadn't gone back to his aunt's house, either, not after what he told the good doctor about *her.* The foster homes weren't too great, but at least the people there didn't tell him that his scars made them sick. He moved a lot, which ended up being a good thing. Nobody ever figured out that he caused the fires.

Donny permitted himself to strike one more match. *A match,* he thought while it flared. Like Miss Fancy-Ass Witch and her macho cowboy. A match that would soon *burn.* He smiled crookedly at his misplaced pun, then stared, letting the flame soothe him and make him feel powerful at the same time.

Still, as it neared the end of the stick, the flame shook because his hand shook. But who wouldn't be nervous? Dynamite. What a deal. He wondered if there'd been a stink about the missing box.

CASSIE SPOTTED THE SECURITY GUARD'S blue Geo in front of lot number six. Tall piles of sand had been hauled in late in the day, ready for filling the stem wall tomorrow, and when Cassie climbed out of her pickup, the dry wind blew it around her in stinging miniature cyclones.

"Mr. Collins?" she called into the wind, shielding her eyes.

"Up here!" He answered from back in the trees.

"Is everything okay?" Cassie put her head down and walked toward the man, who was ambling from the woods, swinging a police flashlight and grinning.

"Everything's fine except for this wind. You know what they say, 'In Oklahoma, you'll eat your words, 'cause the wind'll blow 'em right back in your mouth.'"

Mr. Collins was full of witticisms like that. Cassie wondered if security guards had a lot of time to think up folksy sayings while they made their boring, lonely rounds.

Cassie eyed the moon over Mr. Collins's rounded shoulder. She half wanted to stay out here herself to-night, warding off the trouble that was sure to strike again. But Valentine's Day beckoned—her first Valentine's ever when she actually had someone to share it with.

"You have my home number and my cell phone number if anything goes wrong?"

Collins nodded and slid a small paper from his neatly creased shirt pocket. Some dear little wife ironed his shirts, perhaps. Cassie wondered if they still observed Valentine's Day together.

"Right here."

"Call me if anything looks at all suspicious."

"I will, ma'am."

"Okay. You stay warm."

"Got my hot coffee in the Tracker. Wife made me some banana-nut bread, too." He winked.

Cassie smiled. "Sounds nice." She wondered if the day would come when she would fix Jake a sweet to take with him out to his office or the barns or what-have-you. She headed to her truck, leaning into the wind. ''My cell phone's on,'' she called before climbing in.

Mr. Collins smiled and waved a two-fingered salute.

IT WAS THE SAME OLD LEGEND'S, but nothing could ever be ''the same old'' when she was with Jake Coffey.

He asked for the corner table. He pulled out her chair. After he sat down he kissed her hand and ordered a nice wine. Everything the same.

But an hour later, when they'd finished off a sumptuous meal—prime rib for him again, lamb chops for her—and topped it with dessert—four-layer lemon cream cake for him, chocolate-raspberry cheesecake for her—Jake slowly drew a small black velvet box from the pocket of his blazer.

''What is that?'' Cassie said, feeling as if her eyes were going to pop out of her head.

''Is the answer still yes?''

''Jake,'' she whispered. ''What have you done?''

''You said we should wait a few weeks. It's been a few weeks. Jayden likes the new arrangement with her mother. Everything's working out fine. At least—'' he popped the box open with shaky hands and held it out to her ''—try it on for size.''

First Cassie looked into his eyes. Oh, those eyes! The man's pure heart, his honesty, his intentions, his hopes and dreams for their future—all of it shone through his eyes.

Then she looked down at the ring. "Jake," she said.

It was the ring Jake had teased her about when they were strolling downtown after Jayden's play. The small script sign below it had said the four-carat diamond was "semibezel set in 18K gold." They had assumed semibezel referred to the small parentheses of gold at the sides, which allowed the light to pass through the round brilliant-cut solitaire. Jake had slipped a hand around her waist, snuggling her close as they gazed through the shop window. "Do you like that one?"

"I love it! But, Jake, we have to be realistic. Four carats! Can you imagine what that rock costs?"

Now Cassie looked up into Jake's eyes again—he was waiting—then back at the diamond. It captured the light of the flickering hurricane candle on the table and radiated it back to Cassie like a brilliant star.

"Oh, Jake. It's so…beautiful. But can we afford this?"

Her use of the pronoun *we* told him everything he wanted to know. Her common sense, her practical concern for his situation touched his heart. It was her down-to-earth nature that he loved most, and she would always be this way, he supposed. A true helpmate at his side. But her sensible attitude only made him want to spoil her all the more.

"We can, sweetheart. Every single Andalusian, save one, was born healthy and sound."

Cassie touched the side of the box, but not the ring.

Jake captured the fingers on her left hand. "Let's see how it fits."

Cassie pressed her thumb to the backs of his fingers. "If I put it on, I will wear it forever," she said solemnly.

Jake smiled. She meant it, he could tell. Having been divorced, naturally he had his residual fears about "forever," although Cassie's strength of character did much to abate those fears. "I hope so," he said.

He removed the ring from its velvet slit. When Jake slid the diamond on Cassie's finger, the rounded gold band felt cool and perfectly fitted, as if it had been made especially for her.

He looked in her eyes. "I love you," he said simply.

"I love you, too," she replied.

The grip of his fingers told Cassie that, had they not been in an elegant restaurant, he would have kissed the breath right out of her. As it was, he simply lifted the newly ringed finger and kissed the first knuckle. Feeling the warmth of his lips and looking at the top of his chocolate-brown hair as he bent his head, Cassie experienced a surreal, dreamlike sensation.

She was going to marry this man—this handsome, sexy, tender, honest, decent man. She actually felt light-headed with the realization. All these years she had never dreamed, never, of having and holding a man as amazing as Jake. And yet, he had just roared up the hill into her life one crisp fall day, disrupting what she had thought was her real dream...and now *he* had become the dream that she would cherish for the rest of her life.

When he raised his head he said, "Let's go to your house. I have a surprise for you."

The surprise was *him*. More passionate than he had ever been. Much later, Jake curled around her from behind, with his arm draped over her middle, one hand cupping her breast.

"Happy Valentine's Day," he murmured.

Neither of them had had sufficient sleep lately, and when Cassie heard his breathing deepen, the sound worked like a soporific on her. She went to sleep with her arms crossed over her naked front, the fingers of her right hand lightly touching the ring on her left.

But within an hour, another unwanted call in the night disturbed the lovers' blissful sleep.

CHAPTER SIXTEEN

"Ms. McClean?" The crackly voice on the line was the security guard, Collins.

"Yes?" Cassie sat up, clutching the bedside phone, instantly awake. While she listened, she focused her gaze on a cool, blue line of light beaming through a gap in the drapes. *There was a full moon.*

Jake groaned to wakefulness beside her, rolled over and propped himself on one elbow, frowning and listening to her side of the conversation.

"I see... Yes, that is odd... You're sure it's out now?... Okay. You stay up there and keep your eyes open. I'll find you."

Cassie slammed down the phone, flipped the covers back and bounded from the bed. This time she had warm clothes stacked at the ready on the chaise. In her pickup she'd stashed a high-beam halogen light, mace, bottled water, a camera with high-speed film...anything that might help her catch a vandal.

"What's up?" Jake sat up.

"The cameras inside the house won't do much good when the creep is out setting fire to the woods."

"So, he didn't bite at the setup in the pool house?"

"Not the way I wanted him to. Collins was down at the trailer—I suspect he spends quite a bit of his

time in there stretching his legs out on the bunk—and
he looked out the window and thought he saw flames
among the trees up the hill. When he drove up there
to investigate, he found a stack of smoking lumber,
out in the woods behind Brett Taylor's house. The
fire was out. Still smoking, but out.''

"So he left us another calling card.'' Jake stood
and started yanking on his jeans.

"What are you doing?''

"Going out there with you. The guy could still be
hiding—in the house, in the woods, anywhere. Remember how the fire marshal said arsonists like to
see the effects of their handiwork?''

"Yeah. If he's still out there, I'm gonna catch him.
My pickup's all packed—''

"Wait. I don't think we should go charging into
The Heights in your white pick-up,'' Jake interrupted.
"I have an idea. We'll take the ranch road up and
stop at the barns. We'll ride Arrestado across the
meadow, up the back way, tether him, and go in
through the woods to meet Collins.''

She nodded. "That way the creep won't see us
coming. Hey, why can't I ride my own horse?'' she
said after a moment.

Jake stopped buttoning his shirt, regarding her seriously. "I guess I should have asked before now.
You know how to ride?''

"Uh, no.'' Cassie blushed at her own stupidity.

"Then, you're better off on Arrestado with me.''

"I'll call Collins and tell him we're coming in the
back way.''

While they quickly finished dressing, Cassie said,

"Collins said he called the fire department. They told him they'd send a water truck over and make sure the lumber was put out. I don't get it. If the creep gets off on seeing his destruction, why would he put the fire out?"

"Doesn't make sense, does it?"

"Nope. Let's hurry."

WHEN THEY GOT INSIDE THE Cottonwood Ranch barn, Cassie wasn't too sure about getting up on the back of the wild-eyed Arrestado, but she was amazed at how easily Jake controlled the huge stallion.

"You can wedge your bag of stuff between us," Jake said as he led the horse out of the stall.

"No saddle?" Cassie asked, as Jake hoisted himself onto the horse.

"Nope. If I have to leave him tethered all night, he'll be calmer barebacked."

Once Jake had pulled her up onto the horse behind him, Cassie wrapped her arms around his waist, clutching the bag to her belly, and off they went, galloping along the meadow fence line in the moonlight, then up the steep wooded slope toward The Heights.

At the V-mesh fence, Cassie took a moment to scan the valley below, while Jake tethered Arrestado. In the moonlight, she could clearly make out the small white trailer inside the main gates, the skeleton of the burned-out Detloff house, the roofs of the two newest houses being framed, and Jake's white horse barns in the distance. They switched on the halogen light, aiming it low, entered the woods and hurried toward Brett Taylor's lot.

Collins, waiting near the pile of lumber, waved his flashlight when he saw them emerging from the trees. "This is it." He shined his high-beam flashlight on the wood, which was stacked helter-skelter like a small high school bonfire. Wisps of smoke still danced sideways in the wind.

"Mr. Collins, this is Jake Coffey, my *fiancé*." Using the word out loud for the first time gave Cassie's heart a small skip of joy, even under these circumstances.

"Mack Coffey's son?" Collins asked.

"Yes." The two men shook hands. "You know my father?"

"Knew him when I was in the sheriff's department. Good man."

"I think so."

Cassie hated to interrupt the friendly exchange, but the situation made her tense. "Any sign of anybody?" she wanted to know.

"Nope," said Collins. "Didn't hear any vehicles, didn't see any headlights, nothin'."

"Tell me again. You were in the trailer..."

"Making coffee."

"Yes. And you looked out the window and saw flames up here in the trees."

"Yes."

"But when you got up here, there was only smoke, no fire."

"It was burning pretty high when I drove up the hill. Then—*poof*—it was suddenly out."

"So he had to still be in the vicinity when you

pulled up.'' Cassie couldn't suppress an involuntary shudder.

"I looked for footprints. There's a few in the sand—over there.'' Collins pointed with his flashlight. "But they could be anybody's. I did a search of this whole area. Couldn't find anything out of order.''

Cassie thought that was dumb, implying that anything was ever *in* order at a construction site, for crying out loud. "How'd he put the fire out so fast?'' Her voice was frustrated, she knew.

"Sand.'' Jake indicated the big mounds of sand at the curb of the next lot. He squatted on his haunches, examining the edge of the woodpile with the flashlight. "He used gasoline, smells like, to start a high, hot fire, then threw shovels of sand on it before Collins got here.''

"That's what I figure,'' Collins agreed.

The yellow water truck pulled into the cul-de-sac then. Two firefighters muscled the hose down, scattered the smoking wood with their axes, and sprayed the area, while Collins, Cassie and Jake watched from the curb.

One of the firefighters walked over when they were done. "The fire marshal can't look at this until morning,'' he explained. "He's working an apartment fire across town. Has a victim. A death takes priority.''

"This is clearly arson. And I want this guy stopped. Didn't you just destroy all the evidence?'' Cassie asked him.

"With this wind, we can't leave anything smoldering.''

Cassie released a frustrated hiss. "Would you ask the fire marshal to call Dream Builders in the morning?"

"I sure will, ma'am."

When the lights of the water truck disappeared around the bend, the cul-de-sac seemed twice as dark.

Cassie dug the cell phone out of her bag to call the cops, though she couldn't decide what it was, exactly, she wanted them to do. They said they'd send a detective out in the morning to try to find a match to plaster casts they had taken earlier.

"What now?" she said when she'd punched off.

"I think I'll patrol the addition," Collins offered. "Is your cell phone turned on?"

"Yes."

They double-checked their numbers.

With Collins pulling away, Jake switched off the flashlight. "We can't just sit here, right where he wants us, waiting for him to make a move. We need a hiding place where we can see out, but not be seen."

"I know the spot." Cassie looked up at Brett Taylor's mansion, towering in the moonlight. "Unless the creep's already up there."

They picked their way around through the trees. The moonlight provided adequate, if ghostly, illumination as they edged past things that fluttered in the cold wind, making the deserted lot seem full of sudden movement. Bright red plastic ribbons tied to smaller trees marked for removal, yellow caution tape roped around a hole ready for the septic tank, tiny red and orange flags marking buried cable and gas lines.

Cassie led Jake to Brett Taylor's back entrance. Inside the dark unfinished structure she took his hand. "Careful," she said. "There are tools and debris everywhere."

They moved along quietly, speaking in low murmurs near each other's ears.

"You sure you know where you're going?"

"I designed this joint, remember?"

She led him up unfinished, narrow, winding stairs. Jake got the feeling they were ascending to a tower. At the top, there was a small room where one entire wall was still a gaping hole, partially covered by a thick sheet of plastic flapping in the night wind. Cassie led him to the opening and peeled the plastic back like a drape. Far below, the addition with its partially constructed houses, the valley beyond, the horse farms, the river—all was spread out in the moonlight like a toy village.

"Wow," Jake said softly as he looked out over her shoulder. "What an incredible view."

"I knew it would be. Brett calls this the valley view room. He plans to come up here to compose his songs. This will eventually be a twelve-foot-high palladian window."

"Wow," Jake murmured.

She anchored the corner of the plastic sheeting out of the way with a board, and they settled themselves on the bare wood subflooring, facing the view. Jake was cross-legged and Cassie was in his lap, nestling her back against him.

"I know he's out there," Cassie whispered. "It's like waiting for the other shoe to drop."

Jake hugged her tightly to him. "Are you scared?" he whispered.

"No. I'm with you."

"I wish I could make this all okay. I want to catch this guy in the act and put him away, before he causes you more trouble, before he hurts somebody."

"I know. It'll work out. It's funny—" She smiled up at him, and for one second the sight of his strong face, touched with moonlight, made her feel safe and happy. "It suddenly seems like everything will work out, now that I'm with you."

"I feel that way, too. Jayden, Dad—lately I feel like there's enough love and energy to take care of everybody."

"At dinner, when you gave me this ring—" she flared her fingers out, making the diamond glint in the moonlight "—I was thinking how it used to be so important to me to succeed, to prove myself. My whole life revolved around my business, this addition—"

"Dream Builders," he added. "Have I ever told you I like your style, Cassie?"

"No."

"I do. It's about excellence. Even the names you choose—Dream Builders, The Heights—reflect your ideals."

"I've spent my whole life striving for excellence. Excellence has been my dream. That's why all these setbacks, all this sabotage—it's all been so frustrating. But now—this is what I was thinking earlier—*you're* my dream. *We're* my dream."

He kissed her ear. "It's funny about dreams, isn't

it, how they change when you meet the right person?'' He dropped his head and pressed his rough cheek to hers, and she cupped her hand around his stubbled jaw. They'd both lost so much sleep lately. How long could they go on like this?

But Cassie thought it would surely be another long night, a dreamless night. Jake snuggled her tighter. She wasn't exhausted. She wasn't afraid. Cassie would never be afraid again, as long as she could stay like this, close by Jake, in his arms, forever.

Hidden in the dark shadows, facing out over the peaceful view, as still as statues in the moonlight, they held each other...and waited.

CASSIE DID BRIEFLY DOZE, leaning against Jake's solid chest, but she awoke with a start when he hissed, ''Cassie!''

He gave her an urgent shake and she straightened. ''What?'' She instinctually held her voice to a whisper.

He stretched his long arm out at her eye level and pointed. ''There.''

She squinted toward where his finger aimed and saw it—an orange flicker, in the vicinity of the trailer.

She unfolded her legs, jumped up and stepped to the edge of the bare two-by-six wall where the gaping hole was. ''It's another fire!''

They ran down the stairs side by side, using the flashlight to guide them.

BOSS WOULD HAVE A HELL OF A TIME convincing Grunwold to let him make this call. But he felt some sense of urgency to let Cassie know that name. He had finally remembered the kid's foster family's name. Ten to one, the boy used that name now. It all added up. The strange message in the concrete, similar to the one the kid had scrawled into the still-wet concrete of the patio at the house Boss had built so long ago. At the time it had reminded Boss of the silly coded messages people made up for license plates. *U R 2*. He'd forgotten that, but it came back to him in a dream, or rather, a nightmare.

Arson.

The child had been so badly burned. The doctors had told Boss the scars were all on Donny's trunk, that they would never be visible as long as he wore a shirt, but that didn't stop Boss from having nightmares. Nightmares where he was tangled in the faulty electrical wiring that had caused the fire. That's what the fire marshal had ruled at the time. The boy's aunt, bitter toward Boss and the electrical contractor, had gotten a court order preventing Boss from ever making inquiries about the child. The last time he'd seen her, she had railed at Boss right there in the courtroom, swearing vengeance for the death of her sister and brother-in-law.

"This is not one of the numbers on your list." Grunwold had finished running his puffy finger down the clipboard. Each prisoner was allotted twenty approved numbers he could call.

"No. It's her...her boyfriend's cell phone."

"And I can't let you make another call, anyway, not for at least an hour. Them's the rules."

"Grunwold, you dadblamed hayseed! This is an

emergency! Now you know good and well my daughter didn't answer at home. You stood right over there—'' Boss pointed toward the vending machines "—and listened in—''

"Yep.'' Grunwold tightened his fat lips. "Heard you leave her a message. And that counts as a call.''

Boss rubbed his brow. This was no time to lose his famous temper. "Look. That message took less than a minute. What I have to say to Cassie's boyfriend will take less than a minute. Can't we bend the rules and pretend it's all one and the same call? Huh?''

"Why can't it wait one hour?'' Grunwold argued. "Then, I don't have to bend no rules.''

"Because.'' Boss took an enormous breath, collecting his thoughts. "There is a dangerous man—at least, I think there might be—stalking my daughter. His parents died in the fire that helped land me in this joint. The boy—he's grown now—was burned, pretty badly. And I think he's found my girl. He may have already committed arson. You hear me, Grunwold? This guy is sick! And my bullheaded daughter thinks she's gonna lay a trap and catch him tonight because it's a full moon. *Now* do you understand?''

"And she's with her boyfriend?'' Grunwold, usually as dense as a post, seemed to be getting the picture. "That's why you gotta call him?''

Boss's hopes rose. "Yes! So let me call him! Let me stop them!''

Grunwold nodded, and relief swept through Boss like a slug of bad liquor.

As Grunwold punched the number with his stubby finger, Boss knew he was taking a chance, calling

Jake. Grunwold would not let himself be talked into another call. But when Jake had given Boss the number, he had assured Boss he always left his cell phone on. Jake struck Boss as one upstanding guy. Jake understood, at least, how a man worried about a daughter all alone in the world.

If he told Jake to find Cassie and protect her from her own foolish schemes, Jake, by God, would.

COLLINS WAS LYING FACEDOWN near the little blue Geo pickup at the entrance to the cul-de-sac where the trailer was parked. Cassie stifled a cry and ran to him. "My God," she whispered, as Jake turned the portly guard face up. "We were talking to him not thirty minutes ago."

In the oblique halogen light, Cassie could see that the poor man's gaze was fixed. Jake was feeling his neck for a pulse. "Pulse is strong. Looks like a blow to the head," he said quietly. He ran the beam of the flashlight over Collins's body, checking for other damage.

Cassie looked over her shoulder while she fished her cell phone out of her jacket. She could no longer see any sign of fire.

"The cops'll *have to* come now, won't they?" She called 9-1-1.

They roused Collins and propped him in his Tracker. He had seen the fire, too. He kept rubbing his head, but insisted he was okay. Jake said he and Cassie would be right back, as soon as they made sure the fire was out.

When they got to the bottom of the hill, all they

found was a pile of smoking leaves where a fire had recently been doused with water. Jake shone the flashlight on them and kicked them around with his boot.

"It's another trap," he said, scanning the ridgeline, the woods around them.

But before he could stop her, Cassie took off running toward the trailer. That's when Jake saw the flames flickering at the small bathroom window.

Jake jumped up into the door of the trailer right behind her. "Cassie, no!" He tried to grab for her, but she was already at the little desk.

"My plans." She coughed at the smoke spewing from under the door of the little bathroom. "My laptop. My records."

"Where's the fire extinguisher?" Jake yelled, panning with the flashlight.

"It's gone!" Cassie slapped at the metal bands that had held it to the wall.

Jake started to grab things with her.

Suddenly, the small metal door of the trailer slammed shut behind them. "I've got the extinguisher." A rail-thin man, the young carpenter Whitlow, emerged from the dark shadows into the rays of the flashlight.

In one hand he held a red fire extinguisher. In the other, a gun.

He kept the gun trained on them while he kicked the bathroom door open and calmly sprayed at the fire, filling the small six-foot-wide space of the trailer with smoke and noxious chemicals. The fire flared in the doorway of the bathroom for an instant, and then was gone. The young man tossed the extinguisher to the floor with a clatter. Cassie coughed at the sulfates and phosphates in the talc. Jake clutched her to him, positioning himself between her and the carpenter, shielding her face against his chest.

The young man waved the gun. "Put the flashlight, beam pointing up, on the desk."

Without releasing Cassie, Jake did so. The cone of light created an eerie coziness, casting the dark interior and their faces in upside-down shadow.

Another flick of the gun barrel. "Over here." He indicated the small built-in seat. "Not you." He grabbed Cassie as they went by, wrenching her from Jake's grasp and practically yanking her arm out of the socket.

"How the hell did you get in here?" Cassie demanded, as he hauled her against him on the opposite side of the small space.

"Didn't lose it." He nodded at something lying in the clutter on the desk. The spare trailer key.

He gripped her chin with viselike fingers and twisted her face to his. His eyes were strange, glittering with dark hostility in the slanting light. "Ah, now. Don't look so vexed. You didn't know. Hell, I didn't know. Not until the key was laying in my palm. That's what arson's all about. It's a game, finding the opportunities. Outsmarting the stupid firefighters and cops and people who all think they're smarter than you do."

"You think it's *smart* to destroy people's lives?"

"Shut up." He pressed the gun to her temple.

Cassie gasped, and Jake froze, palms in the air.

"What do you want?" Jake said.

"Just do what I say. Sit down." He indicated the small bench seat behind the table.

Jake did so, and that's when he noticed the cardboard box with the *Dyno* label, on the floor, ripped open. His eyes trailed to the setup near it—the yellow and red sticks laid out in a neat row, with blasting caps affixed. The radio transmitter next to them on the floor, switch at the ready.

Cassie yelped as if the guy had hurt her.

Jake's eyes snapped up to them. "Don't hurt her." Jake's voice had never been lower or more chilling. And his eyes had never been more piercing.

"Oh, I'm gonna hurt her, all right. I'm gonna blow *her* and *you,* and this whole freakin' place to kingdom come."

"Who the hell are you?" Jake's voice was threatening.

"People call me Donny Whitlow now."

"Oh my God, he was Donny Nelson!" Cassie cried out. Her eyes, brimming with comprehension and fear, radiated a dire warning to Jake.

Jake's heart rocketed in his chest. Boss had thought the guy's name was Billy or Danny.

"That's right, and Boss McClean killed my parents." Donny's voice was filled with hate.

"No, Donny, he didn't." Despite the fact that Donny's arm clutched her like an iron band, Cassie managed to keep her voice even, sympathetic. "An accident killed your parents."

"Apparently a jury thought otherwise."

"A jury called it manslaughter. That's different than murder. And because of that jury, he's paid for his negligence. Fifteen years in prison. Harming his daughter, and this innocent man—'' she flipped restricted fingers toward Jake ''—isn't going to bring your parents back.''

Jake's cell phone trilled and three pairs of eyes locked in alarm. ''Don't answer it,'' Donny said.

The phone bleated again.

''If I don't, my boys'll just come up the hill looking for me with shotguns,'' Jake lied. ''You don't think I'd come up here without leaving instructions to check in?''

The phone rang again. ''Answer it.'' Sweating profusely, Donny clutched Cassie tighter. ''And get rid of them quick.''

Jake fished his phone out carefully and answered in the middle of the fourth ring. ''Hello.''

''JAKE!'' BOSS SHOUTED, sending Grunwold a grateful glance. ''Listen. Has Cassie got a guy named Danny Whitlow hanging around her construction sites?''

''Thanks for calling,'' Jake said calmly. ''That horse is trouble, for sure.''

''Horse? I'm talking about a *man,* a *young* man. About twenty now.''

''Me, too.'' Jake sounded hostile. ''And he's dangerous.''

''Wait, uh, wait.'' Boss rubbed his brow, adding two and two. ''So, you know who I'm talking about?''

''Sure do. Like I said, that animal is dangerous.''

''He's there? Cassie caught him?''

''More like the other way around.''

''Oh, *shit*.'' Boss finally understood the dire reason for Jake's coded ''horse'' talk. He felt his chest tighten, but now, he told himself sternly, was not the moment for a heart attack.

''He's pulled the same stunt he pulled a couple of weeks ago, and we have to get him corralled—'' Jake's controlled voice made Boss's palms sweat ''—but you'll have to take care of it, I'm stuck up here in The Heights.''

''Gotcha.'' Boss felt like he was breathing underwater. ''I'll call the cops.'' He'd said it low, in case that little sicko was standing close to Jake.

''You do that. I'd like to help, but I'm stuck in this little construction trail—'' The line went dead.

Boss put the wall phone in its cradle and, for the first time in his entire sixty years, he prayed. Hard. ''Grunwold,'' he called to the guard, who was fishing a package of potato chips out of a vending machine. ''I can either make this next call or you can—'' he gripped the phone ''—but one of us is dialing 9-1-1.''

DONNY HAD WRENCHED THE PHONE from Jake's hand and disconnected. Then he tossed it into an open can of paint thinner that Jake hadn't noticed before. That must have been the accelerant Donny used to torch the bathroom.

''Now nobody else can call. It'll explode—'' Donny seemed to be talking to himself ''—right along with everything else.''

Donny's free hand snapped up to Cassie's throat

and the barrel of the gun pressed harder into her temple.

"Donny." Cassie could hardly breathe past his gripping fingers. "Please. Let me explain something to you."

She felt the spiny fingers loosen, but his arm still held her fast, pressing into her front, as rigid as a two-by-four.

"I know we can never bring your parents back, but you have to understand, Boss never intended to hurt anybody. He was cutting construction costs out of desperation. You see, he needed the money for me. I was dying."

"Dying?" Donny's voice was flat, dry, near her ear.

Cassie felt little hope of reaching him, but still she tried. "Yes. I was very young. I had leukemia. Our insurance had run out. I was in the hospital for so long. So you see, I know how that feels. I had a lot of pain when I was a child, too. I even had to have a bone-marrow transplant. Do you know what that is?"

Cassie felt him nod, heard his dry throat contract in a swallow. "I was like you with those skin grafts. I was in sterile isolation for so long. Couldn't go to school. Needle sticks every day. Nausea all the time. Radiation treatments are terrible, Donny. It was like having my whole body burned, a little at a time."

Jake stared up at Cassie, and the horror and pity in his gaze pierced her before he quickly snapped his eyes away. She had never wanted him to hear the real story of her illness, certainly not like this, but it might be the only way to reach Donny.

"I lost a lot of weight. I had to take a lot of pills. I was afraid and alone a lot of the time. Is that how it was for you, Donny?"

Again the nodding. Another swallow.

"See? We've both suffered. But destroying things—your job, my houses—what good will that do? You need some help, that's all."

"No! I'm not gonna be locked up again." Donny dragged Cassie with him to stand over the dynamite switch. "I'm gonna do what I promised my momma and daddy. I can't get to your daddy and kill him, but he'll know what happened to you, and why, when he gets the letter."

"The let—ter?" Donny was squeezing her throat so hard that Cassie had barely eeked out the word.

"Sent today. You think I'm just a dumb carpenter, Ms. McClean? Boss will get that letter, and, oh, he will suffer." Donny hissed the last word in her ear.

When Cassie felt him angle his head, felt him groping with his foot for the switch, she jerked her face around and sank her teeth into the hand that held the gun.

Jake lunged forward in the same instant that Donny cursed and the gun hit the floor. Jake's fist sent Donny's body crashing into the counter opposite and his head ricocheting off the cabinet above.

Jake yanked Cassie out the door and ran with her toward the dark woods. There, his powerful legs churned over the composted ground toward the place where Arrestado was lightly tethered. With one hand he dragged Cassie along, with the other he sent up a shrill two-fingered whistle for the horse.

Arrestado came bounding through the moonlit trees like an apparition. Jake steadied the horse and flung himself on its back. Cassie stretched her arms, and Jake pulled her up hard as she swung her leg over the huge animal. The horse dodged through the trees toward the V-mesh wire fence at the meadow where Jake kicked again and yelled "Yhah!" Arrestado, like the champion he was, sailed over. They hit the ground at a gallop, churning up the earth as they flew hard and straight, through the meadow in the moonlight, away from the coming explosion.

Halfway across the field, they spotted the flashing lights of a police cruiser sailing up the ranch road.

"Gotta stop 'em," Jake yelled to Cassie. "Hang on!"

They rode harder in the moonlight, Arrestado's pounding hooves nearly jarring Cassie's teeth out of her head.

Then a *boom* split the air; a flash lit the ground in front of them.

The hillside rocked with the blast, throwing Arrestado off his stride, hooves skittering sideways on meadow grass. Cassie screamed and crushed herself into Jake's back.

The shock waves continued as Jake twisted with the screaming, bucking horse. Arrestado's hooves tore high in the air as Cassie held on to Jake for dear life and Jake's fists hauled hard on the reins.

Finally the rumblings stopped, Arrestado's hooves settled on the ground and Cassie raised her head.

Breathing hard, Jake turned the animal to see what could be seen. The sight of the massive black cloud of destruction rising in the cold moonlight made him shudder, and he felt Cassie do the same. Then she clutched his neck.

"Oh, dear God!" she sobbed. It was a plea of invocation and gratitude and lamentation, all rolled into one.

Shaking, Jake closed his eyes and clasped a hand over hers. Then, looking up, he sent out an appeal and a relief and a thanks of his own.

CHAPTER SEVENTEEN

One year and one month later

AUNT ROSEMARIE WAS ALL ATWITTER. She ran into the ranch house, long arms churning like a windmill, yelling, "Boys!" and practically knocked Donna Morales flat.

"Where are your boys?" she demanded with uncharacteristic bluntness. "There are cars coming up from Highway 86. The guests are arriving!"

"Everything's okay," Donna soothed. "We have it covered. Joe is already down at the gates of The Heights, directing traffic. Manny, Julio and Nick are helping to get the cars parked on the cul-de-sacs and they will escort the guests to their chairs in the common garden. One of them will come back down here to the house to get Mack—" Donna nodded her head toward the old man napping in his chair "—in plenty of time. My boys can read their watches."

"Oh, I didn't mean to insult—of course, your boys are such darlings. So responsible and so...*manly* in their tuxedos." She sighed and pressed a bony hand to her bony chest. "So, Jayden and Emily and you and I will go in the limo with Cassie and Stacey?"

"Yes."

"Who is taking Jake up? Jose?"

"Jake is riding Arrestado, and leading Placidora by her reins. Jose and Buck are coming in the Jeep after they get the horses decorated."

"Oh, yes. Of course." Rosemarie sighed again. "I just wish Boss hadn't spent so much money on this wedding. I think he's spent every dime he's earned since he got out of prison."

"I don't blame Cassie's father." Donna glanced over her shoulder as she finished stacking small net bags of birdseed into a box. "He doesn't want everybody in this town to think Cassie is supporting him. I guess that's why he moved to Tulsa."

Rosemarie nodded. "Working as a handyman. But he seems to have some peace at last…and his pride."

Donna smiled. "Men and their pride. What about this barbecue or brunch or whatever it is afterward? Mack can't really afford this shindig, either, believe me."

"They both should have let Jake and Cassie pay for this wedding."

"At least Jake and Cassie made them keep the guest list small."

"If you call a hundred small." Donna winced. "I'm just glad I'm not doing the cooking."

"You've certainly had plenty of other things to do. I'm sorry I yelled at you," Rosemarie apologized. "This has been stressful for both of us."

"Cassie and Jake are worth it," Donna said.

The two women, one so short and round, the other so tall and gangly, stepped forward and gave each other the awkward, accommodating hug they had perfected the first time they'd met at the engagement party, one year ago.

A gust of wind rattled the ranch-house windows.

"Oh!" Rosemarie straightened and clasped her hands in prayer under her chin. "I do wish we weren't having this wedding outside."

"It's what Cassie wants," Donna reminded her.

"Oh, yes. And as we've seen all year, Jake always lets Cassie have exactly what she wants."

"Thank goodness, because they sure didn't start out that way."

"Oh, I know." Rosemarie started to help Donna stack the little send-off packets. "Cassie told me how they met."

"Jake was a little grumpy back then."

"Well, so was Cassie," said Rosemarie.

"Thank goodness that's over." The two women exchanged a knowing smile. Then, simultaneously, they grew pensive.

"Thank goodness," Donna repeated, "that a lot of things are over now."

"Do you really think Boss is okay?" Rosemarie was worried. "I mean, after the way that boy died and all."

"He's bound to have some guilt, but he seems happy to me. Seeing Cassie happy makes him happy."

"Cassie really does seem happy at last. Though I suppose she'll always have some lingering regret about that poor boy…"

"We all will," Donna added. "We are all hurt in some way when a poor soul like that is lost."

"Yes," Rosemarie agreed, "but at least Cassie found the strength to forgive her father for his mistakes. Boss was amazed that Cassie came to his parole hearing."

"Yes, I heard him talking to Jake about it."

Rosemarie looked off in the distance again, and Donna wondered if it was simply the old sorrow about Cassie's father that was bothering her. "I just hope this weather holds out," she said quietly.

Clouds had been scudding across the vast blue Oklahoma sky for two days, but so far they hadn't managed to stick together and rise into the kind of monster thunderstorm that could annihilate an outdoor wedding.

"I told Cassie, a wedding up on The Heights? In this Oklahoma wind in late March? Why, her guest book will be blown all to pieces—the ribbons, the flowers, all of it will simply be blown away!" Rosemarie gave a flutter of her long hands to demonstrate. "Oh, dear. I shouldn't say it that way. Sometimes I forget all about that awful explosion."

"At least it won't be hot." Donna turned to give Rosemarie an encouraging smile, but the woman was still staring out the large picture window with a pensive frown.

Donna doubted the wind would be that much of a problem. The area of the common gardens Cassie had chosen was sheltered by a rock wall on one side, and by the hillside and a thicket of sizable blackjacks on the others. When Cassie emerged around that rock wall, now banked by masses of newly sprouted daffodils, tulips and phlox, riding sidesaddle in a pure white dress on the pure white mare Jake had given her as a wedding gift, Donna was certain the guests would gasp in delight.

But Donna didn't remind Rosemarie of all of this. She merely completed her task. She'd only known Rosemarie this past year, but she had never seen the kindly older woman looking so distressed, or acting so distracted. It simply seemed impossible for this lady to be cross and carping, but yet she had been exactly that for the past three days. Nervous as a cat and making Donna that way herself. Donna knew Rosemarie was a spinster. Surely this irritability wasn't an indication that she was jealous of her own niece's wedding. Donna sent up a little prayer. *Show me what to do.*

"Is something bothering you, Rosemarie?"

"Huh?" Rosemarie snapped her eyes back to Donna, and Donna spotted the glint of tears in them.

"I said, are you okay?" Donna asked sympathetically.

"No," Rosemarie squeaked. She covered her mouth, breathing hard until she could speak again. "I'm not okay! I've done an awful thing," she confessed before pressing thin fingers back to thin lips.

"What do you mean, you've done an awful thing?"

Rosemarie drew and released a dejected breath, as

if fortifying herself for a confession. "It's so hard to explain."

Donna crossed the room to her, keeping her expression carefully neutral.

"My sister Amelia, Cassie's mother, was so like Cassie. So organized. So...perfect. She had amazing decorating instincts, like Cassie. When I moved Cassie into my house...well, you've seen the place."

Donna had. She and Cassie had gone there to dig the Cowan family's crystal champagne flutes out of the crammed, dusty attic. The place...well, gently decaying might describe it best. Filthy and chaotic, but delightfully brimming with life. Flowers and windchimes, a gummy-keyed piano, a parakeet, a goldfish, cats, unfinished sewing and artwork and magazines and books.

"When I moved Cassie in with me I was so insecure—let's be honest—so jealous."

"Jealous?" Donna didn't understand. At that point, after Boss McClean had gone to prison, Rosemarie and Cassie were completely alone in the world. What, or who, was there left to be jealous of?

"Yes, jealous. Of my sister. Amelia had always been the perfect one, and I had always been the...ugly duckling. Boss and my sister had lived a very...upscale lifestyle. I was afraid Cassie wouldn't accept me, afraid she would hate living in my house, hate the way I lived. And at first she did. But then she settled in, met the neighborhood kids out on her bicycle, discovered her artistic gifts—"

"Because of you, I imagine." Donna wanted to

soften the guilt this poor woman was suffering. Unnecessary guilt, in her opinion. Cassie adored her aunt. It was obvious.

"You don't understand!" Rosemarie's face twisted with regret. "I...I hid the pictures!"

"The pictures?" Donna repeated.

But Rosemarie went on as if in a trance. "I told myself it was for Cassie's sake, that it was best if the child were not confronted by painful reminders, that it was best not to remind her of her former life, of her mother. But the truth was, it was I who did not want to be compared to Amelia. I wanted Cassie to myself! I wanted her to identify with *me!*"

"You mean you didn't show Cassie any pictures of her mother?" Donna was taken aback to hear this. She felt suddenly out of her depth. She couldn't imagine this gentle lady doing such an awful thing. "I can't imagine a bright girl like Cassie not asking to see images of her mother."

"Oh, I made an album of carefully chosen ones. Formal poses and special occasions and the like. And I constantly told Cassie about her mother's beauty, her accomplishments, her efficiency, how much she adored Cassie. But I put the other pictures away—the ones that told the true story of their family before Amelia died, before Boss became so hard and bitter. I never let Cassie see the *fun* they had together. You see, I wanted her to associate the *fun* with her aunt Rosemarie."

"Now, now." Donna tried to sound soothing. She walked to a box of tissues on the nearby coffee table and plucked up two. "Don't cry. It's not too late to fix this. You can give Cassie all the photos when she and Jake move into their new house."

"I can't live with this guilt another day! Cassie won't start their house until she's back on schedule in The Heights. And even then, that house won't be finished for months, the way Cassie obsesses over every detail."

Donna nodded. She herself wondered how long it would take to finish the new Coffey house. The lot looked out over Cottonwood Ranch from up on the westernmost slope in The Heights. Cassie had been a delight to have around the ranch house and never tried to interfere with their normal routine. But even so, Donna was going to be glad when Jake and Cassie and Jayden moved up to the hill, and she and Jose could move in here and take care of Mack and his old house in peace.

"Well, the point is, there must be a way to give the pictures to her without disclosing all your old insecurities and jealousies. Telling Cassie what you did, and why, would only disrupt her newfound happiness. I can see that you regret what you did, but it's in the past. And now, what matters is righting the wrong, don't you think?"

Rosemarie nodded, dabbing at her eyes and sighing hugely. "You are such a wise person, Donna—such a comfort."

But Donna, ever practical, remained focused on the problem. "How about giving Cassie the pictures as a wedding gift?"

Rosemarie sniffed. "That's what I was thinking, so I brought one—the one that I thought would mean the most today." She pulled an envelope—quality cardstock stationery—from the pocket of her suit jacket. "I thought I'd start with this and give her the others later. But..." Rosemarie seemed truly tortured. "Do you think giving this to her today, of all days, is a bad idea? Will it make her sad?"

Donna took the envelope, slid out the picture, got misty-eyed at the image and then carefully slid the snapshot back into the envelope. "I think it's a perfect wedding gift." She smiled.

"You're sure?"

"Yes. Now, we'd better get back to Jayden's bedroom and see if Cassie and Jayden need our help."

CASSIE AND JAYDEN DID NEED their help. Cassie, organized to the nth degree, as always, had thought of everything, except her own white panty hose. And Jayden had started her first period. Her best friend Emily stood off to the side, embarrassed yet wonder struck.

Cassie asked Jayden if she wanted to call her "mother." She was trying to support the child's blossoming relationship with Lana, now that Jayden lived at Lana's farm half the time under the new custody agreement. But Jayden said no.

Donna started to whisk Jayden off into the master bath, but Jayden wanted Cassie to help her, so Cassie went with her instead.

Aunt Rosemarie checked her watch, quickly assessed the timing, sent Stacey off with directions to the new drugstore two miles away, and said if they all helped Cassie by holding the full skirt aloft, she could go ahead and dress now and wiggle into the panty hose at the last minute.

Stacey took off, and when Jayden and Cassie returned, Rosemarie dropped the dress over Cassie's head and started pinching the twenty-seven buttons down the back through their almost invisible holes. Cassie had designed her own wedding dress, and a friend of Rosemarie's made it.

"This dress," Rosemarie said as she worked, "looks like something from a fairy tale." The simple long-sleeved, off-the-shoulder bodice of oyster silk topped a Degas-like ballerina skirt made from over a hundred yards of the finest white tulle.

"Auntie, this *is* my fairy tale," Cassie said, her face glowing.

Next, they touched up Cassie's hair—tamed into a shiny long pageboy—and her makeup.

Rosemarie helped Cassie arrange the yards-long tulle scarf that would function as her veil. They draped it like a belled hood, wrapped it loosely across her bare neck and trailed it down behind her shoulders. This left a triangle of tan flesh showing between the wrapped scarf and the low neckline of the dress. The final effect was stunning.

Then came the tense wait for Stacey to return with the hose. They all laughed, even Jayden, as Cassie clowned around, struggling into them under her voluminous skirt.

Then it was time to gather the flowers, pile in the limo and roll up the hill.

On the way, they passed Jake on horseback. He glanced over his shoulder and gave the long white car a wave.

"Look at that man!" Cassie cried.

All the women leaned around to stare out the limo windows.

Jake looked like a prairie knight, headed at a gallop across the meadow to claim his ladylove. His tuxedo and cowboy boots formed one long, black, muscled line from shoulder to stirrup. His dark hair glistened in the sun. The stallion and the mare, with flowing white tails and manes, matching sleek bodies, matching white satin saddle blankets, and matching wreaths of pieris wildflowers circling their necks, looked like something from a fairy tale, as well.

"Dad!" Jayden cried and waved. Then her friend took up the game, waving and giggling as Jake galloped parallel to the limo. They started to roll down the window, but Rosemarie exclaimed, "No, child! You'll ruin our hair!"

Then all the women waved and giggled, but through the limo's tinted glass, Jake couldn't see them. He rode steadily on, finally veering away at an angle to ride straight up to the ridge.

High on the hill, the ten o'clock sun lit the backs of rows of white chairs full of chattering guests. They waited in a clearing at the bottom of a winding stone path flanked by spring blossoms. Ground cover, encouraged by landscape architects for over a year, gave off the fragrance of new life to mingle with the earthy smell of last fall's leaves in the nearby woods. Birds flitted across the contained little space, connecting treetop to treetop, singing and chirping the arrival of a glorious spring day.

Finally the wedding party appeared on the path, all except Jake and Cassie. The minister and Jake's brother Aaron took their positions, and a lone Spanish guitarist strummed a sweet and simple rendition of "Dance of the Blessed Spirits," as first Jayden, then Emily, then Stacey marched down the stone path and up the aisle created between the chairs.

On a signal from Buck, Brett Taylor, along with his band, stepped up to the outdoor sound system and sang his hit song, "I Promise You."

From the east, out of the trees, Jake rode Arrestado forward, slowly, majestically. Cassie appeared from the other side, riding Placidora sidesaddle. She rode the length of the rock wall that defined the area before the ridge dropped to the valley below. They met in an area at the front, bordered by large pots of pink geraniums that would be kept alive and later moved to Cassie and Jake's new home. Above and behind, the tall trees formed a semicircle, like a silent reward for Cassie's faithful preservation of them.

Jake dismounted and walked toward Cassie, their eyes on each other the whole time. He stood beside Placidora, his trim middle disappearing in the folds of Cassie's dress, and looked into his bride's eyes for a moment before raising his strong arms. She leaned into him, bracing her hands on his shoulders while he

fitted his hands around her waist. The wind caught
the ends of her hooded veil, raising them like wings
of tulle above her. He swung her out of the saddle in
one graceful sweep, lowering her to touch down like
an angel coming to earth.

Buck and Jose led the horses away, and Jake and
Cassie walked up to face the preacher hand in hand.

The preacher, Rosemarie's lifelong minister, was a
dear, white-haired man who had baptized Cassie after
she moved in with her aunt. Cassie thought he had
seemed a bit frail when they met to discuss the wedding at his quaint home office, but he had insisted
that he wanted to perform the ceremony. He waited
until the music ended, then gave a short homily on
the sanctity of marriage in his reedy voice. He talked
about the fireworks love of youth and the warm-
embered love of maturity, and encouraged Jake and
Cassie to strive to incorporate both into their lives.

By the time he went on to the vows, his aging voice
was difficult to hear, but no one in the assembly
seemed to mind. They knew what he was asking of
Jake and Cassie. Will you love and honor? Will you
cherish? Will you value your spouse more than
money, looks, success? Will you keep only to each
other? Will you never allow anything but death to
come between you? Both said yes to it all.

When it was done, Jake kissed Cassie reverently,
they turned, and he took her hand and raised their
joined arms high. The little crowd of well-wishers
rose and broke into spontaneous murmurs and ap-
plause.

Brett Taylor and his bunch started up the couple's chosen recessional song, "True Dreams."

Jake and Cassie, still holding hands, went to their dear ones in the front row, while the other guests edged forward, drawn by the magnetic force of happiness.

Cassie bent to Mack and kissed his weathered cheek.

"You're my daughter, now," Mack said.

"You bet I am." Cassie smiled.

Jake took both of Rosemarie's hands in his and said, "I promise to take good care of her."

"I know you will." Rosemarie dabbed at her eyes.

Then Cassie and Jake turned to Boss. The gruff man looked like he just might cry, too.

"Thank you for giving me Cassie," Jake said in his simple way.

The meaning of that, so complex and so deep, made Cassie bite her lip and sent quiet tears brimming onto Boss's broad, rugged cheeks.

Cassie took his hand, and while she held it, Boss could only manage three wordless thumps on Jake's shoulder before he swiped at his face. The couple blocked the older man from view while he composed himself.

"Sorry," he finally choked out, "to be b-blubbering like an old lady, but no one knows how I feel."

"I do, Daddy." Cassie laid a light hand on Boss's arm, and they looked into each other's eyes. "Because I feel the same way. Grateful.'' *Thank you,* she mouthed with tears in her own eyes, *for everything.*

Jayden and her friend came up from behind, and Jake and Cassie hugged the girls, then Donna, then Stacey, then Jose, and even Buck.

Once this hugging got started, it seemed impossible to stop. There in the open air, beneath the radiant Oklahoma sky, people stepped forward in clusters. Jake and Cassie were surrounded, turning this way and that, hugging and handshaking until everyone had been touched.

''Dad.'' Jake leaned down and spoke quietly near his father's ear. ''Don't you want to remind everybody of something?''

Mack snapped to attention. He stood bracing his unsteady legs wide. ''Barbecue at the Coffey ranch house!'' he announced at the top of his lungs.

''And a huge wedding cake!'' Jake added.

The assembly trouped down the hill to eat and drink and laugh and dance and share the stories and the warm feelings that always come out at weddings.

It was not until late in the day, when the sun was making its farewell dip over the South Canadian River, that Rosemarie found a way to see Cassie alone again. She worked up her courage and followed Cassie and Stacey back to the bedroom. Out in the long, low ranch house living room, the remainder of the inner circle toasted and congratulated themselves on a fine celebration.

''Could I do that?'' Rosemarie said at the door,

when Stacey already had her fingers on Cassie's buttons.

"Sure." Stacey seemed to sense that Rosemarie wanted a private moment with her niece. She closed the door on her way out.

"I know I didn't give you an expensive wedding gift..." Rosemarie started as she worked at the buttons.

"Aunt Rosemarie! You worked your fingers to the bone on this wedding. What greater gift can you give than your time?" Cassie turned and gave her aunt a little kiss on the cheek. "You've already given me the best gift—yourself."

"Oh, I know. I hear that. Time with your loved ones—that is the best gift. But I do have a little...memento."

"You're so sweet!" Cassie turned and wiggled her arms out of the fitted sleeves. "What is it?"

"A photograph. It was taken the year before your mother died," Rosemarie said. "I should have given it to you before now. I've always told myself that I didn't want to stir up memories of that awful time. But I don't know...well, never mind all that. Today was your wedding day, and I must say, it was the most beautiful wedding I have ever seen." Rosemarie smiled. "Cassie, dear, you were such a tomboy, so independent. I was afraid you'd end up like me and never get married. But here we are. So..." she held out an envelope "...happy wedding day."

Cassie stepped out of her dress, and Aunt Rosemarie immediately scooped it up. While Rosemarie busied herself shaking out the dress and putting it on its hanger on the front of Jayden's closet, Cassie opened the envelope.

Inside was a faded snapshot of Amelia, Cassie and Boss. Five-year-old Cassie grinned directly at the camera, as secure as if she were the Princess of the Universe, high in her laughing father's arms. Her mother smiled up, one palm pressed tenderly to Cassie's cheek. It was a picture Cassie had never seen.

Tears stung at Cassie's eyes as memories of the day when the picture was taken came flooding back. She was wearing her favorite Halloween costume. The one she had called the "most perfectest." Her mother had made it. Cassie remembered the feel of it, how real and elegant the cheap polyester and nylon netting had seemed to her young mind. Her mother had let her wear the thing as soon as she'd come home from morning kindergarten.

Cassie had tripped on the bottom stair while dancing around madly, and had torn the lace at the hem. Her mother had rushed over and scooped Cassie up, concerned only for her child's safety, trying to find an injury, some cause for her hysterical crying. Cassie, however, was crying less about her bumped shin than about the torn lace.

The sharp memory of Boss—that came unexpectedly. He had come in from his long day supervising construction jobs for Cassie's grandfather and, teasing, asked Cassie what in the heck she was supposed to be. In the snapshot he was trim, muscular, darkly handsome. Cassie remembered how he had smelled.

Like clean sweat and fresh sawdust and rich cigars and loving daddy.

"Let's see—" he had winked at her mother "—are you a tiger?"

"No!" Cassie had yelled, twitching with Halloween excitement.

"A cowboy?"

"Dad-dee!"

"Emory McClean, would you stop teasing that child and get upstairs and get cleaned up. It's late." Only her mother, Cassie remembered, had been permitted to call Boss "Emory."

Boss had feigned ignorance. "Are we going somewhere?"

Cassie remembered launching herself into her father's thigh. "We're goin' trick-or-treat! It's Halloween!" He had scooped her up, laughing.

This was the familiar game her parents played, but Cassie had long ago forgotten it, had forgotten how she had just been learning to join in the fun when her mother died. Her dad would tease and pretend he didn't want to bother with the family or social outings that her mother constantly arranged. Her mother would tease him back, order him around, tell him what to wear, make him behave—and the tough man would end up thoroughly enjoying himself.

But when her mother died, the teasing stopped and only the toughness remained.

The strongest memory of that Halloween evening, however, was of being surrounded by love. A love so freely given, so consistently present that it seemed limitless, immeasurable. She closed her eyes, remembering the feeling of that love. Remembering how she had been the center of her parents' attention, their joy.

It was a feeling a lot like the one she had had today when all this love and attention had been poured out on her behalf, on Jake's behalf, on *their* behalf.

"Who took this picture?" Cassie said to Rosemarie's back.

Her aunt's hands stilled on the soft white fabric of the wedding dress. And then she turned with a look of utter surprise, a look of awe, and Cassie thought, strangely, something akin to relief.

"Why, *I* took it."

Cassie smiled down at the picture again. Immeasurable love. She studied her own five-year-old face. Just like today, back then she had felt utterly beautiful. And what five-year-old wouldn't, dressed in the "most perfectest" white bridal gown and veil…made for her by her very own mother.

Princes...Princesses...
London Castles...New York Mansions...
To live the life of a royal!

**In 2002, Harlequin Books lets you escape to a
world of royalty with these royally themed titles:**

Temptation:
January 2002—*A Prince of a Guy* (#861)
February 2002—*A Noble Pursuit* (#865)

American Romance:
The Carradignes: American Royalty (Editorially linked series)
March 2002—*The Improperly Pregnant Princess* (#913)
April 2002—*The Unlawfully Wedded Princess* (#917)
May 2002—*The Simply Scandalous Princess* (#921)
November 2002—*The Inconveniently Engaged Prince* (#945)

Intrigue:
The Carradignes: A Royal Mystery (Editorially linked series)
June 2002—*The Duke's Covert Mission* (#666)

Chicago Confidential
September 2002—*Prince Under Cover* (#678)

The Crown Affair
October 2002—*Royal Target* (#682)
November 2002—*Royal Ransom* (#686)
December 2002—*Royal Pursuit* (#690)

Harlequin Romance:
June 2002—*His Majesty's Marriage* (#3703)
July 2002—*The Prince's Proposal* (#3709)

Harlequin Presents:
August 2002—*Society Weddings* (#2268)
September 2002—*The Prince's Pleasure* (#2274)

Duets:
September 2002—*Once Upon a Tiara/Henry Ever After* (#83)
October 2002—*Natalia's Story/Andrea's Story* (#85)

**Celebrate a year of royalty with
Harlequin Books!**

Available at your favorite retail outlet.

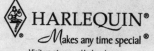

HARLEQUIN®
Makes any time special ®

Visit us at www.eHarlequin.com

HSROY02

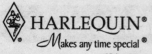

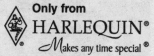